The Sodality

A Jack Connolly Novel

By
M. Charles McBee

Based on the award winning Screenplay
"The Messenger"
Written by M. Charles McBee

ISBN – 13: 978-1530949434
ISBN – 10: 1530949432

Inquiries regarding the use and/or purchase of the contents of this work for use in,
but not necessarily limited to, books, television in any form, film, magazine, both trade and
public, or any other currently available media, both printed or electronic, or media to be
available in the future, may contact the author and his representatives at:

www.mcharlesmcbee.com.

Thank you for your support of the author's rights.

On Twitter: @MCharlesMcBee

Published by:

MCM Productions, Inc.
Advance Mills, Virginia 22968

First Printing, Spring, 2016

Jack Connolly Novels

Counterpoint
Succession
The Sodality

**Novels, Screenplay Treatments,
and Cable Television Spec Treatments
by
M. Charles McBee
in production at this writing:**

Sign of the Cross
The Monticello Protocol
Negative Action
Absolution
The Winemaker

Visit our web site for more information:

www.mcharlesmcbee.com

And on Twitter: @MCharlesMcBee

Cast of Significant Characters

Jack Connolly, Assistant Director, United States Secret Service; retired Navy Captain and nuclear submariner;

Commander Bonnie Biersack, U.S. Navy; DIA Intel Officer, assigned to the Department of State; former White House aid to the President;

His Excellency, Joseph Mendoza, Archbishop of the Roman Catholic Church in Washington, DC, and American leader of the international Christian movement "*Opus Dei;*"

Gilbert "Gilly" Gonzmart, (R-FL), President of the United States;

Franklin Hennessy (R-CT), United States Senator, and Senate Majority Leader;

Howard Hall, special assistant to the President;

Doctor J. Butler Shannon, Headmaster, The Abbey Prep School, New Milford, Connecticut;

Monsignor Roger Schneider, special assistant to Archbishop Mendoza;

Sister Mary Anunciata, S.M., elderly nun; personal assistant to Archbishop Mendoza;

Brother Malcolm Lamb, Benedictine Monk;

Tommy Trumble, government computer tech, a/k/a IT contractor; nerd;

Henning & Pellicane, "twiddle dumb and twiddle dee," White House wannabe security personnel assigned to Howard Hall;

Noah David, longtime acquaintance of the President, and candidate for Prime Minister of Israel;

Lieutenant j.g. Corey Fanning, Jack Connolly's attorney, working undercover for DIA Flag Officers;

Various Scene Locations

Washington, DC; The White House, Department of State, The Pentagon, United States Senate, Union Station;

Alexandria, Virginia; current residence of Bonnie Biersack; 5 miles from the Pentagon, 6.5 miles from the White House;

Avondale Campus; residence of the Archbishop of Washington, DC, and director of Catholic University, Joseph Mendoza; located on the Washington, DC, NE, line in Prince Georges County, Maryland; 0.75 miles from Catholic University; 4.5 miles from the U.S. Capital Building;

United States Senate; located in the U. S. Capital building;

The Abbey Prep School; located in New Milford, Connecticut;

Gulf of Aqaba; a large body of water at the southern tip of Israel; the port of Eilat is near the Eilat Mountains where Moses and the Jews settled for 400 years after fleeing Egypt;

Opus Dei Headquarters; Calle Ramon, Rincon de Espana neighborhood, Madrid, Spain;

Jerusalem, Israel; Office of the Prime Minister;

A Benedictine Monastery; 91 miles west south west of Washington, DC, hidden in the Blue Ridge Mountains of Virginia;

Marymount University; Arlington, Virginia;

Union Station; the Amtrak Railroad Center for Washington, DC, located 0.5 miles from the U. S. Capital Building;

Dedication

To the Marist Brothers at Mount St. Michael Academy in the Bronx, New York City, who accepted an immature thirteen year old boy, and four years later graduated a renewed, young Christian man ready to take on life at its best.

"Always lead, never follow."

Preface

In November, 2008, Americans elected the 44th President of the United States. And thus began the rhetoric that is best summed up as "us versus them...the have and have not's...the 1% who need to pay their fair share in order for the 99% to have...and, of course, screw the Supreme Court."

On January 21, 2010 the United States Supreme Court issued their decision on a case known as:

Citizens United v. Federal Election Commission.

In this landmark case the Court held that the First Amendment to the Constitution prohibited the government from restricting independent political expenditures by an assortment of groups, and not limited to just non-profits. Such restrictions were previously viewed as an apparent violation to the 2002 Bipartisan Campaign Reform Act, known inside the beltway as the McCain-Feingold Act, a law created by a former Republican Presidential candidate and Senator from Arizona, and a defeated Democratic Senator from Wisconsin.

Since that decision a wide variety of both public and secret Super PAC's have been created, raising hundreds of millions of dollars in an effort to influence the lives of ordinary American citizens.

But, in an effort to thwart their influence, the Obama administration (and perhaps Obama's re-election campaign officials in the White House and in Chicago) blocked most conservative Republican groups from raising money prior to the 2010 and 2012 election cycles, utilizing senior officials at the IRS to delay approvals for these Super PAC's to claim tax exempt status.

However unknown to, or at least known but left alone by officials in Washington, there exists an underworld of "secret" PAC's largely funded from sources overseas, and perhaps influenced by a wide range of American citizens masking their progressive liberal tendencies.

And these groups are influencing the course of certain personal freedoms. But more importantly they are influencing religious dogmas in places like Jerusalem, the foundation of most Christian and non-Christian religions.

President Woodrow Wilson, the father of liberal progressive thinking in America, is spinning in his grave.

Notes:

Some of the events, places and organizations detailed in this novel are true and factual. The author has merely taken liberties at expanding on these in a fictional sense, in order to dramatize the plot.

The following may be of interest to the reader:

Cardinals of the Roman Catholic Church:

These men are appointed personally by the Pope. They serve as "electors" of future Popes and are themselves eligible for that high office provided they are under the age of 80 prior to a "conclave" or the secret assembly of all Cardinals in the Sistine Chapel who gather there to elect a new Pontiff.

They are known as "Princes" of the Church, and wear red to symbolize their willingness to sacrifice their own blood in the name of Jesus the Christ.

Opus Dei

Formally known as **The Prelature of the Holy Cross and Opus Dei, founded in Spain in 1928.**

It is an institution of the Roman Catholic Church, and it teaches that everyone is called to holiness, and that ordinary life is a path to sanctity. The majority of its membership are lay people, with secular priests under the governance of a prelate (bishop) elected by specific members and appointed by the Pope.

Opus Dei is Latin for *Work of God*; hence the organization is often referred to by members and supporters as *the Work*.

Sodality

A **sodality**, also known as a "union of prayer" or "confraternity," is an older designation for a lay organization in the Roman Catholic Church. Most private Catholic secondary schools and universities organize Sodalities made up of particularly devout religious students.

<u>Chapter 1</u>

A Monastery
Hidden in the Blue Ridge Mountains of Virginia
Near Mid-night

The room is completely dark.

Except for the glow off an LED computer screen that highlights the keyboard.

And a pair of hands. Hands that show some age. A man. Perhaps mid to late fifties. And in need of a serious manicure. Hands that have seen years of manual labor in the dirt.

His fingers rest in the "hunt and peck" method on the keyboard, frozen. Not knowing how to proceed. Heavy, yet evenly spaced breathing accompanies a faint rasping sound from his lungs.

His right hand, its yellow stained index and middle fingers prominent, now moves slowly to the right, lifting a smoke from an ash tray.

A long, deep pull, followed by a silent exhale fills the keyboard and screen with the putrid odor of spent tobacco. He replaces the smoke back into the ash tray. With his left hand he re-positions a 5 x 7 silver picture frame. He holds its edge for a moment or two as if contemplating its significance to him.

The photo illustrates five young men. Perhaps teenagers. And on closer examination, the dress code of these young men suggests a photo taken in the early 1970's. They stand, posing in front of a small, yet well-appointed altar. The trappings in the background easily identify this worship space as Roman Catholic.

On the computer screen, an e-mail template is visible. And in the "To:" space it reads Bonnie Biersack. There's no subject nor any indication of the senders' name or e-mail address. The man mumbles to himself. He reads pieces of the e-mail he has composed.

"Bonnie…look to the Lord…the Holy Spirit…for guidance. The Gulf of Aqaba Framework is a sham. A hidden agenda. If implemented after the current elections this weekend, religious terror will rain down on the entire middle east…"

Another long pull on his smoke, the man taps his desk top with a finger rapidly contemplating what he should say. But not losing sight of an intuitive feeling in his gut. Less is more. In the distance he can hear the dull muted sound of a bell. The sound is more like a gong.

He types a close to the e-mail.

"I cannot be known. But please pray. Pray the Prince will be guided by the Holy Spirit. And your efforts at aiding the development of this framework. Exposing its secret outcome will result in the spiritual riches you merit."

A long heartbeat.

He moves the mouse to "send."

Click.

Chapter 2

Alexandria, Virginia
Morning

Old Town Alexandria sits several miles south of Reagan National Airport, along the Potomac River. And no more than a twenty minute ride into the District. The seat of power on planet Earth.

Cherry blossoms brighten the new spring day amid commuters choosing to casually walk to the Metro for the commute into Washington, DC.

Visibility couldn't be better. A view across the Potomac to the east north east one can clearly make out the Capitol dome. To its left, the Washington Monument.

Traffic into and out of Reagan National is at its peak as aircraft roar down the north-south runway.

In a quiet piece of this old village, not far from a sign that reads "Old Town Alexandria," the early morning traffic sounds are muffled. Traffic noise near the River is replaced with kids chatting loudly as they run for the school bus stop.

Doors slam. Dogs bark on the usually quiet suburban street lined with 200 year old homes.

Homes with doors in bright colonial colors. Iron fences and Charleston gates accentuate the comfortable and cozy feel to this neighborhood. It's home to decent, hardworking Federal employees, alongside those employees tagged as "short timers."

Those who move in with a new administration. Then leave when the "big guy" has to leave the White House. Like the recent wave of new comers several years back. Those taunting the long term residents calling them wimps during heavy snow falls. Not at all like the hearty souls from Chicago.

Up and down the street hanging perilously over a multitude of cars parked head to toe old elm and oak trees burst with the first signs of spring.

On the second floor of one house in particular with a private entrance to the rear, a light flickers on. It's comes from a window that faces the street. A blonde woman in the window steals a quick glance up and down the street.

She vanishes.

Inside this second floor apartment one instantly notices a simple feel. The feel of a young woman. Simple, yes. But tasteful. In her bedroom, lots of stuffed animals. "Porky Pig" stands out, almost out of place. Watercolors of easily identifiable scenes from Dayton, Ohio, at least for those in the know, surround the room.

Coffee cup in hand, a slender, youthful thirty - something blonde woman strolls into the bedroom. She's followed by a needy black and white cat.

BONNIE BIERSACK moved to Alexandria after graduation from the U.S. Naval Academy at Annapolis. After the required "sea duty" she took a position as a staff assistant for Naval affairs in the OEOB. That's the ugly looking structure once the War Department that houses the "permanent" White House staff.

Those 2500 plus Federal employees, some with party affiliation. But who keep it a secret doing the hard work.

Unlike the 150 or so who occupy offices in the West Wing. Those pretending to be experts at their excessively high paying "politically" appointed jobs. But in reality make an eleven year old sixth grader look over-qualified. Most take on the persona of being in charge confidently setting strategy and mission goals regardless of who is in the Oval Office.

Of late, it's been called the "Valerie Jarrett syndrome."

This environment prompted Bonnie to seek a more challenging opportunity. Promoted to Lieutenant Commander because of her extraordinary intel abilities, she was re-assigned to the submarine warfare center at Camp Peary in Williamsburg, Virginia. That one year tour propelled her career once again.

She was re-assigned to the Pentagon.

Bonnie now sits in front of her lap top computer scanning her e-mail screen.

The usual junk and spam gets quickly moved to the trash folder. She makes a mental note to empty the trash folder this coming weekend.

Her slender well-manicured fingers work the keyboard quickly.

In the background sounds are coming from a television tuned to MSNBC.

"In the latest development, super PAC administrators connected with the Obama administration, namely Bill Burton and numerous others, have come under intense scrutiny by the FEC." As one commissioner said just yesterday morning "unregulated PAC money reaches our borders secretly, from God knows where, with a spirited vengeance. It's the bond that commits special interests and elected office to an unbreakable alliance two directional in flow."

Bonnie's head shifts slightly to her right in the direction of the television. Her expression turns quizzical.

Another voice is heard responding to the commentator.

"Well, Joe, let me ask this. How in the Lord's name do we enforce good moral behavior. I mean not lying to the electorate despite advice that comes from, say, the AG and campaign staffers - in a town that so artfully skirts it?"

Bonnie shakes her head in disgust. A woman with a true moral compass. Solid mid-west Christian values. She's continually astonished about sordid events in this town.

Bonnie focuses on her e-mail screen pondering a message with no subject nor senders' ID. Yet it got past her firewall despite the bells and whistles placed there by her buddies that manage IT at the Pentagon. And her current assignment with the Defense Intelligence Agency, a/k/a, DIA.

Odd, she thinks. And no attachment to open. The red flag that would signal a possible virus.

Then the message.

It refers to her by name. It's not threatening. But makes a clear point. A point that makes specific mention of an agreement she has worked tirelessly on for the past six months. An assignment that resulted in her transfer to the DIA. A transfer she was told had the President's personal approval.

With these facts in the front of her brain, she takes the e-mail seriously. She believes its message and instructions are significant.

But rather strange to say the least. And why now just days before the Israeli elections?

Skippy, her self-absorbed black and white cat, and constant companion while at home, leaps onto her lap. Caressing his soft fur she mumbles to herself.

"You're the messenger. Guided by a higher spiritual authority. You must expose its hidden agenda."

Bonnie thinks hard about this statement. In all the conversations she has been part of including those with the President, his friend Noah David, Israel's current rock star politician, and members of Congress and the White House staff and the experts in Middle East policy, the Gulf of Aqaba framework never strayed from the core principal.

That principal was developed with a concise and lasting mission: to formerly recognize Jerusalem as the true and only capital of Israel. With that recognition as the center for all Christian and non-Christian religions of the world.

And a philosophy that needed the right person at the DIA to judge any and all potential problems.

Bonnie thinks back over the past six months about her involvement in helping the President craft a peaceful agreement. As well as abiding the President's wishes that she be "given the opportunity to learn the ropes of as a potential senior administration official."

Proving herself as a competent analyst and negotiator given several Executive Branch projects connecting negotiations with Congress, she caught the attention of the President. She was quickly brought into high level staff meetings in the West Wing involving more than just Naval affairs.

Bonnie's personal life took a small hit after leaving Camp Peary. At least with regard to the dating scene. Her responsibilities had put her romantic life on the back burner.

Until she hooked back up with a guy about ten years her senior who now has a lofty position at Homeland Security. The President feared the potential for foul play. Conducting talks with Israeli diplomats, particularly Noah David, he thought the assignment of a senior Secret Service Agent was needed to quietly shadow Bonnie's life. He used the excuse that it was routine for security officers to accompany certain personnel who are involved with classified information.

Bonnie still is not clear why this Agent spends a lot of his time at the Pentagon. The DIA has its own security force. But the relationship has moved back to the personal level. Something Bonnie has been secretly longing for since they went their separate ways after Camp Peary.

But it's not like Bonnie to question the motives of the President. Although at times she has her doubts. She brushes off those concerns. She was told by a White House confidant several years ago most high level administration officials have parallel agendas.

It's keeps the playing field level in this crazy town.

Assistant Director Jack Connolly accompanied Bonnie and the President and his Joint Chiefs' staff for the final talks aboard a 95 foot yacht, the *Sabra*. A ship owned by Noah David's father Seth David, Israel's wealthiest citizen.

Those talks took place in the Gulf of Aqaba. At the very southern tip of Israel. Talks that struck Bonnie as "odd" to say the least. The relationship between the President and Mr. David was cool at best. It was those few days that Bonnie and Jack spent time together connecting. The result being Bonnie developing an interest in Jack all over again. Especially his experiences in the Navy as a submariner and his recent tour as a Secret Service Agent. Who has directly served four different Presidents.

One of whom was assassinated in Dallas, Texas.

Still thinking about the message that stares back at her Bonnie re-reads the final point.

"The Abbey is key to his past. A repugnant past where the Prince hatched his plan."

Huh?

She's stumped.

"Bonnie you cannot let religious freedoms be compromised. You hold the key as the messenger."

Messenger?

"God bless you, Bonnie."

Chapter 3

Avondale, Residence of the Archbishop
Washington, DC
Morning

The hands that move swiftly across the computer keyboard are grandfather old.

Despite the obvious advanced age of this gentleman, the manicure is clearly professional. Black sleeves cover all but an inch of starched French cuffs. And held together by a pair of large 14 caret gold cuff links in the shape of a family crest. A crest that just happens to match the crest of a small gold pinky ring on his left hand.

On his right hand, a ring with a different crest. This one the seal of a high office. And a Latin inscription barely visible to the naked eye. Roughly translated reads the wearer will "sacrifice his blood in the name of Jesus, the Christ."

The black sleeves reveal a thin line of blood-red fabric piping. The color indicative of his willingness to sacrifice his own blood.

Without knowing much more, it's clear this is a cleric of the Roman Catholic Church. Someone very important.

ARCHBISHOP JOSEPH MENDOZA is the most important resident here at AVONDALE. He leans back in his comfortable executive chair and contemplates the Excel spread sheet.

Columns of numbers by year in dollars. The amounts reaching into the seven and eight figure category. The time frame spans almost twenty five years. A time frame not all that alarming to Mendoza. But highly significant in its purpose.

He develops a thin smile. He looks upon the completion of a long and arduous task.

On the left side of the spread sheet are three names. Names that are not only well-known to the prelate. But to the nation and perhaps the world at large.

Gonzalez-Martinez, a/k/a, Gonzmart, Hennessy, David.

The names of men he knows and has known, intimately for decades.

His boys.

Young boys he nurtured and developed. Bringing them into manhood with the ethical and intellectual character to be leaders, not followers.

Guiding their every move with precision and purpose. And doing so with the necessary funding required in today's world where money means power.

And it's power that sets the agenda.

Men whose mission was and is always to serve the epitomes and ideology of one.

The Prince.

Chapter 4

Old Town Alexandria
Starbucks Coffee Shop
Morning

I glance at my watch wondering where the esteemed Monsignor Roger Schneider could be. Perhaps the infamous Washington, DC traffic has delayed his rendezvous with me. Or better yet his rather controlling, overbearing boss, Archbishop Joseph Mendoza, has sent him on some meaningless errand. He knows full well the Monsignor was to meet with me this morning.

I'm concerned because I need to catch up with my current charge Commander Bonnie Biersack at the State Department this morning. Although my former, and I can't stress former enough, main squeeze is currently assigned to the DIA at the Pentagon.

Former by the way is not my choice.

It's hers. And I'm working overtime to fix that little wrinkle in my love life.

Anyway my meeting with Monsignor Schneider likely concerns the relationship Mendoza has with my family.

Specifically my Mom's side of the clan. I've tried to keep my distance as the good Bishop is somewhat of an enigma. But I'm certain Mendoza is likely after a favor from me of some sort.

My status with the Secret Service makes much of everything out of bounds for him. But a man as financially powerful as Mendoza puts me in a tough spot. Because of the fact that he and my Great Grandfather Don Pedro Segui, and my Grandfather Don Mateo Segui, have been connected on many levels for decades.

My remembrances of him from my youth are sketchy at best. Moving documents by hand between Don Pedro and Mendoza always created an aura of suspicion. This while I was an altar boy in Mendoza's parish.

As I dig deeper into my little brain, I see Monsignor Schneider has arrived. He's looking around Starbucks for me.

Time for yours truly, Jack Connolly, to hear his fate.

A Quiet Residential Street

The Suzuki 650 Savage motorcycle roars from the driveway behind the two family, two story home.

Birds flap away in panic. The noise startles a young mother strapping her three-year son into a car seat. Lifting her head quickly to see the source of the loud noise, she whacks her head on the door frame.

"Shit!"

The three-year old checks out his Mom. Then adds his own take on the noise.

"Shit."

He gets a scolding look from his Mom.

On the bike is a lean figure clad in black leather and gripping the controls. On the bikers head is a helmet with the tinted black sun visor pulled down. A long shock of blonde hair is visible.

The biker makes several quick turns. She finds her way onto the George Washington Parkway. Zipping through traffic as if in a race against time, the biker flies past Reagan National Airport. Then weaves around stalled traffic along the Potomac River.

Now the biker has momentarily vanished under the Memorial Bridge.

The biker is seen crossing the 14th street bridge quickly. Perhaps above the speed limit. She bears down on the gently blossoming cherry trees that frame the Jefferson Memorial Park.

Appearing almost oblivious to pedestrians and other foot and moving traffic, the biker winds her way up 14th street. She turns onto Constitution.

A few lefts. A few rights.

At the State Department the biker stops at the guard booth outside an underground parking garage. The guard looks with skepticism for a long moment as the biker fishes for some ID. Now showing her ID, the guard relaxes, waving the biker through.

In the hollow confines of the underground garage the biker roars around sharp corners. She tactfully weaves around cars pulling into reserved spaces.

Then just like that the biker pulls into a spot reserved for a full sized car.

On the wall, painted…

"Guest."

The biker dismounts.

Removes the large black helmet.

And shakes her head covered with lush, blonde hair.

The woman is shapely and sexy. She's confident in her looks and stance. Attractive in that all-American mid-western way. She grabs a small leather case from the bike's rear pouch.

Standing near-by I take a deep breath, wanting to savour her looks and knock-out shape leaning on my Beemer.

I haven't been waiting that long. That earlier meeting with Archbishop Mendoza's bag man, Monsignor Roger Schneider, went longer than expected. But now one look at her and you know it's worth the wait.

I'm not sure why the President picked me for this assignment. He had several hundred other Secret Service Agents to choose from over at Homeland Security. But I need to make a note to profusely thank him.

Although, I don't know what he meant when he asked me to keep an eye on this woman about six months ago. He said, "I think she might be your type, Jack."

He of course knew we once had a "thing." There may be a conspiracy at work here trying to get me to settle down.

Maybe my experience with the former President, Melissa Callen and now that super star Naval Officer, Commander Bonnie Biersack, both gorgeous blondes, made this assignment more appealing.

In any event I've got a job to do. To make sure Commander Biersack stays out of danger given her involvement in a rather touchy agreement with Israel. There have been threats largely from ISIL, and a splinter group of religious fanatics who have some issues with the agreement.

And Bonnie being a woman makes for some interesting possibilities. But still I think there's something missing. A connection that has not yet come to the surface. And if the President doesn't know for sure what it is then he must at least suspect something fishy.

In the meantime I have to grin and bear it.

But she is pretty.

I stroll in her direction approaching from behind.

"Whatever happened to that Wall Street image diplomats aspire to, Bonnie?"

Without stopping she looks over her shoulder, giving me a small smile.

"Hey, Jack Connolly! My one true shadow once again sneaking up behind me."

"Duty calls. So visiting the State Department again huh? You keep showing up here someone's gonna think you work here and not at the Pentagon. You need to wear your uniform. And the view from here? Well…"

"I've been asked to brief the Secretary at some point today. I told you that last night, Jack. I guess you were shall we say otherwise preoccupied?"

Preoccupied? That's a novel way to explain sex.

Still walking and focused on the elevator. She stops.

"And by the way, well what, Jack? You know us Ohio girls. God fearing decent folks. Honest values? Tell it like it is. You didn't get that dating hockey girl from Michigan what's her name? That Naval officer out in the Pacific somewhere?"

She's still clearly bummed about my former lawyer the very sexy and cute Lieutenant j.g. Corey Fanning.

Like I've said before I need to train my brain not to get all true and forthcoming during sex. Someday it's gonna catch up with me. Like now. Fortunately I've learned not to talk too much about my family. Which explains why I never brought Corey, the subject of Bonnie's current comments, home to meet the folks.

Although I've heard through the grape vine that Lieutenant Fanning has been recently re-assigned to the JAG office at the Pentagon. That's what happens to very pretty, immensely talented young women in the Navy…who look fetching in an Officer's uniform.

Something about her intellect as well…you think?

As a former Naval officer familiar with the mind set of certain Admirals, I could be over-stating the obvious.

Actually my time with Corey in Hawaii usually at my place or hers late at night playing strip scrabble away from that pesky hearing before the Disciplinary Board was time I definitely will not let those Admirals know about.

Bonnie may find out. She is an Intel officer, you know.

Now the bigger issue is what if I bump into the sexy Lieutenant Fanning at the Pentagon? I'm there on assignment keeping one roving eye on Bonnie.

I can't catch a break. But maybe I don't want to.

Keeping a safe distance seems to have worked as Corey is still talking to me. Through e-mail of course and the occasional text.

Somehow I think fate is gonna take a turn.

Anyway as we wait for the elevator I should say that I did bring Bonnie up to Martha's Vineyard this past weekend. Just to get her out of Washington. Since the season has not yet kicked-off, I thought a preview of where the Connolly family sometimes visits when we're all talking to each other could serve to break the ice if this relationship develops.

My silence must be having an effect of her.

"Thanks for the cool weekend in Martha's Vineyard, Jack."

"We're thinking about building the Connolly family compound. My Dad wants to compete with the Kennedy compound over in Hyannis Port. It's on the Cape."

"Huh?"

"They're Democrats. Did you know that?"

She sighs as she hits the elevator button.

"Do you think your parents will like me?"

Okay. She's slipping into dangerous territory.

"Hey! How about we fly out to Dayton to meet my parents. Memorial Day weekend could work."

I need to think fast. Meet the Biersack family? Sounds like a challenge. Cousins alone count for at least sixty. Not counting the ones who she said to me "may be elsewhere."

I wonder if she means federal prison.

While I carefully consider my options i.e. potential excuses, she yanks out a thumb drive from her leather jacket.

"Got a weird e-mail early this morning. Anonymous sender…no subject. All the things my Pentagon firewall should have kicked out."

Now that got my attention. I personally had her home computer scrubbed and sealed tight.

Routine protocol for certain OEOB personnel.

"Let me take a look."

"I could have Tommy Trumble play with it. I understand he's a cracker-jack IT security guy here at State. Whatdaya think?"

Before I can answer a beat-up Volvo chugs on by. It looks like something you'd find in a trailer park up on cinder blocks.

And I know it belongs to the aforementioned Mister Trumble.

"I think Tommy would like to play with *you*."

She gives me that look.

"Well. I think he's smart as a tack with this IT stuff. Anyway. I think he likes me. He'd give it his full attention today if I asked. And would make a special trip to the Pentagon just for me."

"Do you know that deep throat drove a beat-up Volvo?"

"Are you jealous, Jack?"

"Hey. If Tommy Trumble's your type, good night, and good luck. I'm outta here."

She sighs watching the elevator call button light.

And I focus on that cool biker outfit she's modeling this morning. Things are getting…shall we say…frisky down below the equator.

I need to control myself.

It's still early in the day. And with these Ohio girls you gotta take it slow and careful.

And that Michigan girl? Well it's game on. Fasten your seat belt and watch that blue line.

Control, Jack. Control. You're breaking out into a sweat.

"So, Bonnie. Talking about deep throat. Cool outfit."

There's that look again.

Like I said I had better play it safe. It's still early in the day.

"What did it say?"

"Huh?"

"The e-mail. What's got you on edge?"

The elevator arrives and I follow her into the small space. And now I get a whiff of that body wash she wears.

I back up against the rear wall and hit my hit head against it several times.

Facing forward I know she's smiling. She does that, you know. Guys call it something not appropriate to mention here. But at least I can still fantasize.

A long moment passes as she hasn't given me a clue about that e-mail. I'm about to ask again when she speaks softly.

"Having pleasant dreams, Connolly?"

I sigh.

She says "I still don't know why the President has you follow me around."

From this view I'm not complaining.

Chapter 5

Residence of the Archbishop
Washington, DC
Late Morning

The poorly lit hallway is deathly quiet except for the shuffling of fabric and soft foot-falls on the tile floor. Shoes prescribed by the man in charge to have thick rubber soles.

From the shadows two nuns walk slowly but with a clear purpose moving down the center of the long hallway. Enroute they pass portraits of long deceased Bishops and Cardinals. The eyes and dour expressions follow their every step.

Some hold portrait lights above the ornate frames. They cast a soft glow over the likeness of those that once held a seat of power here in Washington, DC. And also within the hierarchy of the Catholic Church.

Advisors to Presidents, Senators and Members of Congress.

And advisors and financiers manipulating the truly rich and powerful in this town for decades.

The lobbyists. Men and women who have kneelt at the feet of these church leaders.

These are portraits of church officials, men whose imprint on society in America is unbreakable Despite the clear and undeniable separation of church and state.

Coming closer into view are the two nuns, Sisters of Mercy who still retain the old dress code that limits exposure to just their faces and hands.

They appear solemn in their task.

One carries a tray. She's younger if one could guess with only limited evidence such as the eyes and hands.

The tray holds a tea pot, dry toast, the Washington Post and the Wall Street Journal.

The other, short with a slight bend to her posture indicative of some age perhaps above fifty.

They stop in front of a large oak door. Six raised panels. Handmade and varnished to a soft satin gleam.

The brass handle is brightly polished to the point that one would dare not touch it with a hand not gloved for fear of leaving even the smallest of smudges.

The shorter, older nun knocks twice on the door.

Inside the office is Archbishop Joseph Mendoza. A man feared by those who don't even know him.

While she waits for a response the taller nun grabs a glance at the headline on the right hand lead story of the Washington Post.

"Noah David Ahead in Israeli Polls."

From inside the office a voice is heard.

"Enter!"

The older shorter nun pushes open the door with obvious difficulty. The younger nun follows quickly not wanting to lose a moment in getting the tray to its proper location.

Sister Mary Anunciata, the older one, speaks softly.

"Good morning, your excellency."

She moves closer to Mendoza's desk.

Pointing at his telephone console as if maybe he doesn't know what she is talking about she says.

"The White House call is on line two."

He gives her a long unpleasant stare as the younger nun arranges the contents of the tray now placed on a small table not far from the Bishop's desk but closer to the fireplace.

She arranges its napkin and newspapers exactly the way Mendoza has dictated it be done every morning at this exact time.

She also pulls a medium sized arm chair from a corner. She places it in a precise position where the Bishop can eat. And read the newspaper utilizing the morning sunlight that streams through a large window on one side of the massive office.

She then pours a generous cup of hot water from the tea pot. From the tray she lifts a tea bag.

English Breakfast.

Opens it with a pair of small scissors she has taken from somewhere in her habit.

The tea bag is carefully removed. It is held dangling while she replaces the scissors in her habit along with the spent tea bag package.

She waits a moment.

Then dunks the tea bag into the hot water exactly seven times giving the hot water a faint amber color.

The starched cloth napkin is partially unfolded and placed at the right corner of the table.

The silver serving cover that protects the dry toast is removed and placed on a side-board.

She then brings her hands folded in front, waist high, bowing her head she says softly.

"Your breakfast is prepared, your excellency."

Mendoza looks over at her breaking the stare held on the older nun and nods.

Now a look back at the older nun tells her to leave.

She bows her head and softly says before turning to leave.

"Will there be anything further, your excellency?"

He ignores the question lifting the handset of his telephone and without pausing says.

"Howard! Call me back in exactly twenty minutes."

He replaces the receiver as the two nuns have now left the office closing the large oak door with a thud.

Chapter 6

**State Department
Diplomatic Wing
Morning**

BONNIE BIERSACK has now changed into her Navy Commanders' uniform. She strolls down an interior hallway passing offices occupied by the very well connected and powerful career employees of the State Department. Men and women who have served their country abroad in both pleasant and unpleasant countries. People whose mission is to represent the U.S. in the best possible favorable and caring way.

All this despite the policies that flow from the Oval Office usually occupied with someone who has trouble perhaps spelling "diplomacy."

Just ask the well-known Israeli politician and former military hero Benjamin "Bebe" Netanyahu. Someone who could easily perform the duties of a community organizer while in a coma.

And it's Israel on Bonnie's mind at the moment. While walking she scans the front page of the Washington Post.

Something has captured her attention to the extent that her surroundings including those around her are just a blur.

I don't think she knows I'm right behind her. And admiring her…well, we need to keep this…ah…let's say, diplomatic?

Right. Another sexy hot babe from Ohio.

Maybe someday I'll take the plunge and pay that part of the USA a visit. Have a firsthand look. However, at the moment I need to work on why I can't make that Memorial Day trip "out there" to meet Ma and Pa Biersack.

Maybe I'll suggest a meet and greet via Skype.

"Connolly! Are you following me? Or just staring at my butt?"

How did she know that?

I'm having mental cramps thinking of my days in elementary school where it was a known fact fully substantiated by persons with top secret knowledge. The Nuns could see everything we kids did with their backs to us while writing on the blackboard.

Sister Mary Clair: "Stop picking your nose, Mister Gallo."

Billy Gallo: "I'm not picking my nose, Sister. That's' Jackie. He's picking his nose."

Me: "Huh?"

Sister Mary Clair: "No he's not, Mister Gallo."

Me: "Right, Sister."

A nano second.

She spins around, drilling me a scary look.

Sister Mary Clair: "Did you just give me the finger, Mister Connolly?"

Me: Thinking.

How did she know that?

"So, Bonnie. Gimme the top line on today's news. Haven't had a chance to catch up."

As I say that a cute young staffer drifts by.

After passing behind Bonnie she winks. I return the usual "I'm available" smile and wonder who's paying for those boob jobs young girls seem to be flaunting of late. My guess narrows down the possible benefactors as being the "Weinerites" up on the Hill, a small group of slugs founded by their fallen leader, the photogenic Anthony Weiner.

"She's an intern, Connolly. And a student, emphasis student at Georgetown. Her Dad is someone you don't wanna cross."

How did she see that?

"Okay. I've got it, Bonnie. I'll take you to lunch. Bring the newspaper with you so I have something to read."

She stops short focused on a story on page one.

"Says here that Noah David is surprisingly ahead in the polls."

She stares off in a direction down the hall.

"Jack. Remember that night on the David family yacht in the Gulf of Aqaba?

My juices start to build.

"Moonlight. Warm breeze. We were holding hands. On the poop deck I think."

She gives me a stern look.

"I told you I had a funny feeling about Noah David and the President. Like there was something way too familiar about those two together. Like there was some kind of history between them."

"You did say that the meeting on the yacht was their second face to face meeting."

She thinks for a moment.

"This story points to the possibility of connections to huge amounts of money. That doesn't wash. The laws in Israel are very strict."

I say. "Keep in mind that his father is a very wealthy guy. That could point to the bank accounts. Even off-shore. That guy is capable of paying for the right kind of secrecy."

She makes eye contact. "With religious groups?"

I shrug.

"Part of the Gulf of Aqaba framework deals specifically with Jerusalem beyond its recognition as the Israeli capital. There's fundamental language that addresses issues of solid security for the holy sites. Multinational protection."

I know she's going somewhere with this. But my little brain is having trouble keeping up. This is what happens when you try to look and act smarter than a smart person. Which I do quite often.

And by smart I mean "magna cum laude" smart. First woman ever to graduate from the Naval Academy first in her class.

"You know I recall that the President made some considerable concessions to Mister David that for me seemed a bit odd at the time."

I take a moment to digest this piece of top secret diplomatic Intel.

"I see your point. And while they were a bit chummy on that brief cruise the Secret Service was told to stand back. The same instructions went out to Mister David's detail."

She stops at her guest office door. Looking at me with that "I'm thinking" look she shifts her gaze to the floor. Stuck in "something's not right" mode.

And just like that I remember a piece of background that came to the surface before that romantic cruise with Bonnie on the Gulf of Aqaba.

"Noah David was educated in the U.S. and his mother is American. So maybe they crossed paths in college."

"Hum. Interesting, Jack. Let me know what other secrets you're hiding from me."

She marches into her office. I follow and plop down in her chair. Grabbing a copy of Cosmo leafing through the pages of soft girlie porn, I think it's best to keep certain secrets close to the vest.

Standing on the other side of the desk she scowls down at me.

"Don't you military advisors ever work?"

"Stalking. That's my role here. Things got boring over at the White House after Clinton left office. So I thought it would be a good idea that I liven things up here at State."

I bury my nose in Cosmo but not before asking, "know anyone named Monica in this place?"

"Very funny. Ha, ha. Now how about moving out of my special guest chair that is assigned to my special guest desk that makes me special in this place and let me get back to work."

Not looking up from the Cosmo, "what's this mean? How to pleasure your guy...ten easy tips to get him thinking more about your needs."

I give her a look with a nice smile giving her fantastic body an up and down look and say.

"I think I'll take up thinking."

"Good. Think about where you're taking me to lunch. Then I have to get back to the Pentagon."

I get up and move over to a mirror on the wall. Straightening my tie then wiping some of those funny white things on my shoulders I catch a glimpse of her behind me staring desirously, of course, at me.

"Are you looking at my butt?"

I spin around and she's already got her head in a document on the desk while twirling a strand of that lush blonde hair.

"Gotchya."

She looks at me with a frown.

"Huh?"

"Yeah...huh?"

We both smile at each other. I think something's brewing between us but despite being over forty I'm still stuck in the "non-commitment mode."

I break the spell with something thoughtful and personal.

"So. Like I said. Save me the Washington Post so I have something to read at lunch."

I make a quick get-a-way before she can respond with something romantic and affectionate.

With Jack gone Bonnie spins in her chair facing her LED screen. Scrolling through her address book she finds a name.

She composes an e-mail to Howard Hall sending it over to his private e-mail box at the White House.

Another name is selected from her contacts list.

It gets clicked and now placed in the "To:" box she composes a message to Tommy Trumble, a/k/a, roving government computer nerd, *par excelance.*

Chapter 7

The West Wing of the White House
Morning

The usual silence that surrounds this low level, unobtrusive structure is broken by the sounds of a weed eater Its operator attacks spring clean-up. Other gardeners like the well-aged African-American kind are hunched over weeding and spreading fresh mulch. If one listens carefully the humming of some unfamiliar spiritual dirge can be heard from several of the gardening staff. This explains why Obama was always smiling when he walked through the rose garden.

Posted at the door to the West Wing a Marine Guard stands watch over several black government vehicles parked near the entrance. A Secret Service Agent walks the perimeter of each vehicle. He holds a long device that appears to be a golf club with a large mirror instead of a club head on its end. The mirror reflects the underside of the vehicles he is inspecting.

Inside the West Wing a meeting is underway in a small conference room alongside the Oval Office.

It's nicely appointed with Ethan Allen furniture. A new sofa replaces an old stained sofa from Arkansas.

It's been rumored the room was re-decorated when George W. Bush moved into the Oval Office in 2001. The new White House staff concluded that Clinton spent too many late nights alone in that room and it needed to be freshened up.

Sitting around the table are three men.

Gilbert Gonzmart (R-FL), President of the United States. Known to his close friends as "Gilly." But more to the point of his heritage, he's a second generation Cuban American. And his given name is Gilberto Gonzalez-Martinez. The son of a Cuban-American who escaped to South Florida accompanied by most of his family in the early 1960's. He had just the clothes on his back despite having been the descendant of a highly successful family from Havana in the luxury hotel business.

Caesar Gonzalez-Martinez built a fortune in South Florida as a real estate developer. The profits and well-developed connections from this family empire opened many "political" doors for his son Gilbert now President of the United States.

He succeeded President Melissa Callen who decided not to seek a second term but to marry Doctor Andres Devendorf and move to Texas.

To the President's left is Howard Hall known coldly by his close friends as "the Hump." His slight frame wrapped in an odd looking pin-striped suit and colorful tie speak volumes about his otherwise feminine tendencies. He is a personal assistant to the President for political affairs but usually kept in the background for a variety of obvious reasons.

Only the Secret Service knows he vacations on Fire Island, New York which has earned Hall the Service's private code name "Nancy."

To the Presidents right is Franklin Hennessy, United States Senator from Connecticut. He's tall and powerfully built with a take-no-prisoners personality that belies his Irish heritage.

Hall speaks directly towards a speaker telephone that sits in the center of the table.

"Your excellency. The President has joined us."

Hall eyes the President carefully signaling him to go easy as the man on the other end is not in the best of moods this morning.

The President gives Hall that look that says it all. He *is* the President.

Then aimed at the speaker. "Your excellency, good morning. And please excuse my delay. Matters of State tend to disrupt my –"

"- Gilbert! Where are we this morning with the agreement?"

The three men all exchange glances knowing that this conversation could be somewhat dicey.

The President tries again.

"The agreement is n hold, your excellency."

Office of Archbishop Mendoza

Archbishop Mendoza stands at a window with tea cup and saucer in hand and gazes towards the lush gardens. They surround his exclusive office and residence near the campus of Catholic University.

His tone is tinged with a strong dose of annoyance.

"Your efforts disappoint me, Gilbert. I want this matter done. Am I clear? It's absolutely imperative it be finalized before the Israeli elections."

He takes a sip of his herbal tea.

"Noah is in place. There's no turning back."

From the Archbishops desk the speakerphone comes to life with the voice of the President.

"We're close. Very close. But more time is needed."

Mendoza smirks before taking another sip of tea.

This time the speaker phone carries the voice of Senator Hennessy.

"Your excellency. We have an added new concern being whispered around the Capitol by the House Speaker.

Speaker Glassman is whipping support for further review of the agreements' implications on our military aid to Israel. We're topped out at four billion. But it could go higher."

Mendoza spins at the speaker phone with fire in his expression.

"Speaker Glassman is worried about his re-election chances. Those special interests in New York. That Jewish constituency he's so afraid of lately. Don't give it any further thought, Franklin. I'll take care of his...*special interests*."

Mendoza sits at his desk staring at the speakerphone.

"Well, gentlemen?"

The West Wing Conference Room

The President takes a moment before he leans into the speakerphone.

"I had a thought. Perhaps the Prime Minister will sign a "framework agreement" in the interim. While we work out the final details."

Mendoza's voice is firm.

"Committing the parties, Gilbert?"

The President relaxes just a bit showing some confidence with his thoughts on the matter.

He eyes both Hennessy and Hall giving them the signal to listen but not speak. He taps the table several times with his fingers loud enough for Mendoza to hear.

Then with a firmness as if he's on the right side of the issues surrounding current events in Israel, he says.

"The Israeli election is this Sunday as we all know. And are following closely."

He pauses.

Mendoza speaks.

"Get on with it, Gilbert."

The President frowns at the speakerphone.

"We know from our intelligence on the ground over there the Prime Minister is looking like a loser. His spending is more erratic. His speeches give him the appearance of someone desperate to keep his job. He may not be the right choice for the job according to our intel."

The President smiles feeling that Mendoza should be impressed with his insight into the Israeli elections.

Mendoza jumps in.

"Gilbert. Tell me something I don't already know. You think the money I'm investing with Noah's father is not without strings?"

The President takes a long moment. His thoughts vary from how to end this conversation to how not to sound stupid.

"Your excellency. The Prime Minister will have no choice but to sign a framework. He'll perhaps be able to sell it to the Israeli voters as something that further strengthens the relationship with the United States. It's something the Israeli population has been clamoring for since the dreadful Obama days."

Silence.

The three men just stare at the speakerphone for an eternity.

Then Mendoza speaks.

"The wording of this so called framework? Does it meet my specifications, Gilbert? And you know I'm including the plans for Judea and the surrounding desert."

The President takes a moment.

"The new Prime Minister will have unilateral authority. He will have the power to designate security and development in any form he deems as essential."

He pauses waiting for a comment.

Then in the absence of comment.

"He will have the authority also to transfer territory control at his sole discretion. Void of any parliamentary delay. The current Prime Minister will see this framework as an absolute power grab. He may just like it."

Silence.

Then Mendoza speaks.

"Redeem yourself, Gilbert. This week!"

Click.

The call is disconnected.

And all three men just stare in silence at the speakerphone.

Hall sighs but like a sigh of defeat.

Senator Hennessy is the first to speak.

"Mister President. I'll handle Commander Biersack your Naval Attaché and contact at the Pentagon. She'll need to be briefed as she is pulling the loose ends together."

The President eyes Hennessy very carefully with intense concern.

Then stands.

"Howard I want the Israeli Prime Minister in on a secure conference call in the Situation Room Friday morning. Let the Secretary of State know. He can make the call to the PM. It's a matter of National Security. For both of us. He'll understand. Based on the last conversation with the PM the Secretary and I had two weeks ago."

The President marches briskly from the conference room back into the Oval Office.

Hennessy and Hall lock in eye contact wondering what in the world that means.

Chapter 8

State Department
Bonnie Biersack's Guest Office
Late Morning

TOMMY TRUMBLE is thirty something and a characteristic nerd. Obese, insecure, eye wear outdated by decades and he lives with his mother. He also drives a beat-up Volvo.

He of reminds you of that guy who takes your order at Subway but will somehow manage to screw it up despite your clear instructions. Then thanks you with a smile filled with crooked yellow teeth.

What most people don't know is that Tommy Trumble can hack his way into the most secure servers on the planet. He can upset the balance of power inside and outside the government.

What people also don't know is Bonnie is his fantasy girlfriend. And he will do anything to win over her affections.

And it's likely Bonnie knows this little secret.

Which is why I stroll casually into her office once I learn she has summoned this lumpex.

Now I'm not jealous. But sometimes women go for that guy who will dazzle them with brainy stuff. Women see it as a potential ticket to fame and fortune. Maybe the guy will land a software job that pays six figures including seven figure stock options.

Her only consolation will be to wear a blind fold, ear plugs and latex gloves while in bed with Mister Egghead.

That ought to smooth over the rough edges.

I find Bonnie leaning over Tommy who's seated at her computer. From my vantage point she's obviously giving him a "feel" for 1st base as she pokes her breast into his shoulder.

I need to create a diversion.

"Okay you two let's not get too close. We need to leave room for the Holy Ghost."

I remember that line from a dance I attended as a teen at *the* Mary Louis Academy for *loose* girls in Queens.

Okay. I'm kidding about the loose part. But those Nuns would step right up to you while you were dancing with whomever and say that.

I jump into the fray.

"So Tommy! How fast did you travel to get here once Bonnie, that strikingly beautiful Naval Officer standing behind you, asked for your help?"

I get strange looks from both Bonnie and Tommy.

"Jack. Tommy is tracking the source of that e-mail I got at home this morning."

Hum. Likely excuse to cop a back door feel.

Tommy jumps in. "Bonnie the message is clean. No viruses. So we can assume it's from a legitimate source."

"Inside or outside the government, Tommy?"

"I'll know in a minute Bonnie. But whoever this guy is he's got your home information. Probably a stalker."

I say under my breath, "probably you know who" as I point at Tommy.

Bonnie didn't like that. I can tell from the look she just gave me. I'm good at reading her looks.

"I'll ping the servers we use here at the Fed agencies. See what turns up."

"Will it tell you if I'm still on the FBI's most wanted list, Tommy?" I say with some worry.

I give Bonnie a wink as Tommy slowly turns and gives me a look that says "huh?"

I quickly change the subject seeing that Bonnie is not that thrilled with me at the moment.

"So whatdaya think? Legit or just some scam?" I ask.

"What I don't get is the statement 'by Friday.' She twirls her hair with an index finger giving this some more thought.

"And I'm the messenger."

I add. "You didn't send it. You got it. Remember?"

She thinks some more holding a stare on the message in front of Tommy.

"And the Abbey? What's that? And who in the world is the Prince?" She's stumped.

Tommy taps away at the keyboard, says. "Gosh. Is this like secret spy stuff or something, Bonnie? You know I can help you out there. They sometimes call me over to that CIA place in Virginia to fix stuff."

Now here's Tommy realizing he has perhaps made it to 1st base. Although it's questionable if he even knows what he's accomplished. That is, trying to impress a hot blonde who is well out of his league.

He turns to her.

"I think I see stuff I'm not supposed to see."

I offer. "Which means someone is going to kill you then feed your body to sharks Tommy."

I give him a sympathetic smile.

He breaks a sweat.

Bonnie elbows me in the ribs.

"Idiot."

She sighs.

"Someone must have my home e-mail address. Someone in the government."

She takes a moment to think long and hard.

"Being part of DIA should keep me anonymous right?"

I eye her carefully thinking it may go wider then that net. So I ask.

"Family? Would anyone give it out?"

"No. My dad is particularly sensitive to those issues. Ex-Marine Corps Colonel. Doesn't trust anyone."

Marine? Okay. Now I'd better come up with a solid reason why I'll be unable to make that trip out to Ohio. As a former Naval Officer I'm very familiar with that Marine motto – "Semper Fi" – which means "kick ass and take names."

Tommy adds.

"It doesn't necessarily have to be someone you know Bonnie."

"Huh?"

"Well. You know a good hacker with your IP address which could easily come off a web site you visit say like Amazon or Facebook. They could then have a peek at your e-mail files."

"Oh?"

"Then put messages on your screen that look like e-mails. You know while they're having a peek."

I can't resist.

"You mean like a peeping Tommy?"

Tommy now turns at me with a scowl.

Somehow I think he's filing my obnoxious behavior so he can hack into my computer and leave unwanted messages. Like, 'I'm gonna tell everyone you're gay."

I need to behave myself.

Bonnie says. "There is no hidden agenda. The Gulf of Aqaba agreement is all about Jerusalem. Very straight forward and remarkably simple for this type of agreement."

There seems to be a hidden agenda causing some consternation on the part of whomever is annoying Bonnie via e-mail. I can only conclude that he or she has got a beef with not only the President but everyone involved. Now I'm beginning to realize that whatever Tommy Trumble, ace computer hacker, can uncover goes right to the security of the President and his close advisors.

Like Bonnie.

I need to change my approach with Tommy.

"Tommy! How about a pepperoni pizza?"

Now he's smiling at me.

"With extra cheese, Mister Connolly?"

"Yeah. Whatever. You're the man."

He gives me a thumbs up and is back hitting the keyboard.

Bonnie paces away towards her window.

"The agreement is a 2000 year leap, Jack. I know I need to expose whoever this messenger is. And turn him into...who *do I* turn him into, Jack?"

"How about the religious right?"

"Be serious. I have four days until Friday to find this slug."

"And to think he even blessed you, Bonnie. Which, by the way, I think is even telling unto itself."

She zeros in me. "What do you mean?"

I'm thinking on the fly here. "There has to be a religious connection. You said the main focus is Jerusalem. That's a part of the world, or Israel, that involves the world's major religions."

She says slowly. "So, one or more may think they're being given less than then a fair shake. And now wanna make trouble thinking there's a hidden agenda. Which means there is someone who's looking to take more than his fair share of the pie."

If she keeps thinking like this it'll be like an awakening of sorts. I'm sure glad she's the smart one here. I just have to keep feeding her straight lines.

She continues her thought, staring off into nowhere.

"But why send an anonymous message? Why not just come out and say what he or she wants."

Okay. She's got me there. Which is why we have Tommy.

But I needlessly have to let Tommy know who the smart one is in the room just in case.

"You're the intel genius, Bonnie. Remember, you figured out that enemy rouge submarine problem without being anywhere near it."

Tommy spins in his chair right at us.

"Enemy rouge submarine? Was I supposed to hear that?"

Both Bonnie and I respond.

"No!"

She grabs a look at her wrist watch.

"I've got a Sodality meeting tonight over in Arlington. Marymount University. It's only about ten minutes from the Pentagon. Maybe you should join me. We'll pray together for some insight."

I give her a dumb-founded look.

Then, "since when did you get all religious on me?"

Smiling at me, she says with confidence.

"My fifteen year reunion at Chaminade-Julianne High School in Dayton last spring. Remember? I told you I was going."

I scratch my head.

"Huh?"

"Jack. It was truly a spiritual experience. It made me whole again. I haven't felt that way since weekly Mass at school back then."

"...okay..."

I come up with another dumb-founded look. I'm getting good at those looks. I use 'em to throw her off.

Now she gets a little preachy.

"It's a prayer group, Jack. You may get something spiritual out it. We always have an interesting guest speaker."

Quick. I need a really good excuse.

Fortunately, Tommy jumps in to save my butt.

"Here's something, Bonnie."

Bonnie moves back over to just behind Tommy, and another shot of a 1st base feel for the unsuspecting Tommy.

She zeros in on the computer screen.

"The Abbey?

So. What's that mean, Tommy?"

"I filtered the possibilities, ya know things that would connect 'The Abbey' as a religious place of interest. And narrowed it to places where some people may use."

"Good. What'd you find?"

"Monasteries, schools and seminaries."

As soon as Tommy mentioned schools, a bell went off in my little brain. I'll need to check it further before I fill in the dynamic duo here.

Bonnie says.

"That's a start, Tommy. We'll have to get more on who sent the e-mail. Try to make the connection to one of those places."

She turns at me.

"Jack, why don't you be a gentleman and take me to lunch?"

"I promised Tommy a pepperoni pizza. I was thinking of sharing."

Ignoring that, she says "someplace expensive, Jack!"

Before I can comment, her admin on loan from State, Todd, sticks his pretty face into Bonnie's office. By the way, you should know he's a little light in the loafers.

"Bonnie, love. Senator Hennessy called. Needs to discuss some concerns about the agreement with you up at his office on the Hill."

"Concerns?" She holds an anxious look on me.

Chapter 9

Residence of the Archbishop
Washington, DC
Late Afternoon

MONSIGNOR ROGER SCHNEIDER carries his 50ish well-toned and hard frame easily down the dimly lit hallway. There's no sign of any change from his days as a linebacker on the famed Notre Dame football team. His pace is somewhat more than casual. His expression unreadable. He holds a Fed Ex envelop in one hand at his side.

He stops at the large oak door. And takes a moment to think.

His knock is firm. Only two raps.

From the far side.

"Enter."

He pushes the large door with ease, closing it softly behind him. He enters the massive office of his boss, Bishop Mendoza.

The office is darker than usual. The result of heavy drapes being pulled to partially conceal sunlight from the outside.

The dark, somber office is in contrast to the single desk lamp on the Bishop's desk. At the moment it conceals Mendoza's face.

He continues to focus of the papers before him as Monsignor Schneider approaches the desk. Mendoza does not greet his right hand man.

A heartbeat.

"Your excellency. A Federal Express package from Madrid."

Mendoza's head snaps up. His hand now extended, but not reaching Schneider.

The Monsignor hands him the package.

Mendoza attacks it with a sharp letter opener. He draws out several documents. He lays the papers before him. He reads several pages quickly before settling back in his chair.

Monsignor Schneider, waiting patiently, clasps his hands together as if in prayer.

"Anything further…your excellency?"

Without looking up, Bishop Mendoza says.

"We'll leave here at five fifteen sharp for the Sodality conference at Marymount University."

"Yes, your excellency. I will make the arrangements with your driver."

"Fine. That'll be all, Roger."

Monsignor Schneider bows ever so slightly, and quietly leaves.

The large oak door closes with a noticeable clunk.

With that, Mendoza's eyes dart towards the door with a look of annoyance.

A moment passes before he returns to carefully reading the documents from Madrid.

After reading them through several times he lays the pages before him on his desk. Then leans back in his chair giving its contents serious thought.

He now swivels to face the LED screen of his computer.

A few keystrokes. He has pulled up his e-mail screen. He's ready to compose a message.

From his contacts list, he selects a name.

Click.

It appears in the "To:" field.

The subject is intentionally left blank. There's no indication of "copies," both open and blind.

He begins to compose his message.

When finished he reads it aloud to himself while reclining in his chair.

"My cousin, Elbano Spinnetti in Caracas, Venezuela, will complete the transfer as noted in your communication. Please fulfill at your end tomorrow, the very latest, as time is of the essence. Yours always in the name of Christ, our Lord and Savior. Mendoza."

A moment.

The mouse pointer is positioned on send.

Click.

Swiveling to his left, he zeros in on something on the far side of his office. Developing a pleasant smile, he stands and strolls across the large ornate Persian rug. He stops close to the far wall.

On the wall hangs a 2 foot by 4 foot oil portrait of a man in the robes of a Cardinal in the Catholic Church.

A small brass plate beneath the portrait ID's the subject as Antonio CARDINAL Pulgar.

Mendoza reveres the portrait for a long moment. He admires not just the quality of the painting, but also of the well-known and highly regarded Cardinal who sits on a council of prelates in Rome.

A council that governs the day to day workings of the Vatican.

A powerful group of men. Whose responsibility is to see that the Holy Father and the Vatican – commonly referred to as the Holy See - functions with the appropriate governance that members of the one billion plus Catholics around world come to rely upon.

Men whose decisions will affect the actions of every Catholic around the world, from the Pope on down.

Bishop Mendoza clasps his hands in prayer. Then kneels before the portrait.

"Soon...very soon my dear friend and mentor. Together, in Rome...side by side...in the Sistine Chapel. Together we shall take our Church into the twenty first century. And with it the leadership we have both been praying for the last forty years...

"...to re-consecrate our Church, and take back that hallowed ground in Judea. The land of our Lord, Jesus, the Christ...

"...return the land to the proclaimed chosen people. The land of Israel. It has and always will belong to our Lord and His followers. Like you and me, of course...

"...Blessed be the Lord, Jesus the Christ."

Clinging to the gold cross in his left hand he makes a slow, spiritually filled *sign of the Cross*.

Chapter 10

Madrid, Spain
Early Evening

Two young priests walk quickly down Calle Ramon in the fashionable Rincon de Espana neigborhood, a residential district of central Madrid. Passing several obscure doorways, they turn into a covered entry way that leads to a large hand-carved mahogany door, the main entry point to an expensive looking four story brown-stone style building.

The taller of the two priests takes a key from his pocket. He inserts it into a brass lock. He opens the large door with some effort. They both vanish to the inside.

The door closes with a thud. A small brass plate outside to the left of the door lock reads "Opus Dei."

Sitting at a desk that perhaps dates back to the Crusades by the look of it, is BISHOP FEDERICO JESUS-RUIZ.

Bishop Jesus-Ruiz is well into his eighties.

Over his shoulder are several signed photographs of Popes, personally addressed to the Bishop, and dating back to John the 23rd.

The Bishop reads a set of documents presented to him by one of his young assistants. It was printed off an e-mail screen in the outer office.

The documents represent correspondence from his fellow brother in Christ and leader of the Opus Dei movement in the United States, Bishop Mendoza.

After an extended time frame, he depresses a button on his desk.

He leans back.

Almost immediately the door to his darkened office opens with a creaking sound. It closes softly.

A young priest in a neatly pressed cassock moves quietly to a spot in front of Bishop Jesus-Ruiz.

"Yes, your excellency. May I be of assistance?"

Father Tomas Lorenzo waits patiently for his boss to respond.

"Tomas. You will need to visit our banker, Senor Ugarte, first thing tomorrow morning. Give him instructions to transfer five million U. S. dollars to our Israeli account at Credit Swiss in Geneva."

Tomas takes the documents from the Bishop.

"Yes, your excellency. As you so wish."

"Thank you, my young friend."

"Good night, your excellency."

As Father Tomas Lorenzo turns to leave, the Bishop gives him a small wave.

Once the Father is gone, Bishop Jesus-Ruiz grabs the cross at his chest. Closing his eyes, and with a troubled expression adding to the deep aged lines of his face, he makes the *sign of the Cross* and begins to silently pray.

Chapter 11

The West Wing
Howard Hall's Office
Late Afternoon

HOWARD "THE HUMP" HALL is not a very well composed individual.

Not only is he clearly not qualified to be working in the West Wing, the seat of power on the planet, he's probably not qualified to be working at anything beyond packing groceries at Kroger.

Yet his relationship with the President, which goes back to their days at boarding school, has afforded him a position of power and responsibility.

It is well beyond what any HR placement executive would suggest.

What one would, however, suggest is that Howard Hall must have some dirt on the President. Loyalty has its rewards. But not to the extent presently demonstrated in the position held by Hall as a "special assistant" to the President of the United States.

Those in the know who thought the appointment of Valerie Jarret as Obama's "special assistant" in 2009 was well outside the margins, are now baffled with Hall's appointment.

Sitting at his desk, he breaks a sweat holding a stare on his telephone consol. The President has ordered him to make a call to the Secretary of State, something he dreads having to do.

He dials, and after several minutes he's put on with the Secretary.

After a curt moment of small talk with the Secretary he delivers his message.

"Mister Secretary. The President is *ordering* you to make that call to the Israeli Prime Minister. My e-mail a short time ago to you clearly indicated such."

Pause.

"The fact that you are not ready to do so is of no interest to me...rather to us here...."

Pause.

"Thank you...sir...and good day to you as well...sir"

He disconnects.

Leans back. Still focused on his telephone handset.

Then.

"Shit."

Chapter 12

Jerusalem, Israel
Evening

From a hilltop just south of Hebrew University, a small group of nine American tourists from Clarion, Pennsylvania stop to listen to their guide. They represent the "Walk in His Footsteps" Sodality from Holy Angels Roman Catholic Church. They shift their focus, under the control of a tour guide, to a building just slightly to the east of the University.

The Knesset, located in Giv'at Ram, Jerusalem, is the seat of power here in Israel. It houses the government's parliament. And the politicians who wrangle over both domestic and foreign policy in this war-torn country.

Further in the distance, about two miles, is the old city. A place whose dusty dirt paths provided sound footing for Jesus, the Christ, and his disciples over 2000 years ago.

Visible from the Sodality members' vantage point are walls that enclose the Christian quarter. To its right, the Armenian quarter. The guide goes quiet for a heartbeat. His talk then focuses in on a non-descript office building structure near the Knesset.

The Prime Minister's Office

The PRIME MINISTER, a large, tough looking Ingrun tribe man in his mid-fifties, replaces the handset of his telephone. He looks both pensive and disturbed. He places his hands together on the top of his desk. He takes a moment to reflect on the conversation he has just had with the U.S. Secretary of State. His eyes move over to a man in his late thirties seated on the other side of the PM's desk.

AVI DREYFUSS does not appear to be in a 'happy to see you' mood. As a matter of fact, he's downright pissed.

The PM speaks softly, but with reserved conviction.

"We will sign a framework version of the agreement on Friday morning. I'll do it electronically."

Dreyfuss leaps from his chair.

"Absolutely not! That's preposterous. You'll be committing Israel to the whims of the Americans. I thought we made our point with that guy Obama several years ago. We can't let those bastards push us around."

"They're our friends, Avi."

"The new administration, yes. But there are still some socialists preaching that Obama crap about Israel. There *is* a war on terror. And it's not that far from our front door."

The PM leans back in his chair, giving the bigger picture some contemplation. He's a man of intense intelligence with the ability to understand and compromise for the benefit of all sides. He thinks deeply about the quiet, behind the scenes pull-back in support for Israel's security by the Obama administration. It was done in the interest of not wanting to offend the Muslim world. Little things that went under the radar. With the free world collapsing around Israel, the PM needs to make concessions in the interest of protecting Israel's future in the Middle East.

He knows the Gulf of Aqaba agreement brings unilateral security for Israel's most precious site, the center of the world's religions, Jerusalem.

"Maybe the agreement will be my survival parachute. I need something concrete to put me ahead of Noah David in the polls before the elections."

Dreyfuss, now pacing hard around the PM's office, has more to add to this debate.

"Noah David is a pacifist. So what if his father was a hero in 1967. He's just an old man. With money today. Noah has contributed nothing."

A beat.

He shifts his stance to an aggressive posture.

"He's a nobody!"

Turning to face Dreyfuss, hands out stretched.

"Avi. He's ahead in the polls."

The PM moves over to a window. He gazes off into the distance at the old city. He stares at the Christian Quarter. At the Dome of the Church of the Holy Sepulcher.

Softly, almost a whisper.

"It's a cherished site.

Embraced by practically the entire world. And it's right here. In our backyard. On our sacred soil."

Dreyfuss takes a moment to frown.

"What are you saying?"

"The old city, Avi. Older than time itself."

With some force to his tone, Avi adds.

"And it's ours to embrace *and* to protect. We will not permit foreign troops to protect it."

The PM shakes his head at the lack of wisdom his young aid displays.

He faces Avi Dreyfuss.

"Mr. David, my worthy opponent, has hinted that its relevance to the world will soon bring Israel the respect we have so richly deserved for 2000 years."

"5000 years!"

Avi Dreyfuss makes his point.

Turning back towards the window, the PM contemplates his opponents words.

"What could he mean by that? The voters must have some idea. They've heard it a hundred times the last few weeks."

Still regarding the view from his window, his expression now morphs to one of worry.

"I'm particularly troubled by Noah's bottomless bank account."

Dreyfuss opens a folder he holds in his hands.

"The best we can tell, it's all legal. A variety of religious groups. What the Americans would call "soft money." Funds that meet our rules. Some of it wired from citizens and local religious organizations with bank accounts overseas."

The Prime Minister turns sharply at Dreyfuss, looking annoyed at perhaps what he's just been told.

"Perhaps if my appeal were on religious security rather than on economic stability, I'd be ahead in the polls. The voters know my record with the economy. They need to know my stand on what truly matters to all of Israel."

He returns to taking in the view from his window towards the old city. His eyes shift to a spot south of Hebrew University. To a remote hilltop.

"I'm going to sign the framework agreement, electronically.

Long pause, sitting back down at his desk.

Not making eye contact with Dreyfuss.

"Make the arrangements immediately, Avi."

Chapter 13

The Oval Office
Afternoon

PRESIDENT GILBERT GONZMART has a pensive expression. He sits, pondering several documents on his desk. The documents deal with a variety of National Security issues. Typical of a routine day in the Oval Office.

However, at the front of his mind is the issue of the Gulf of Aqaba agreement. And its implications with regard to National Security.

The President knows it's an over-reach. He knows his legacy could be compromised. Should the security measures contained in the agreement be implemented by whomever is the Israeli Prime Minister, his legacy will suffer.

Which is why he has taken certain precautionary steps. To throw bumps in the road to its ultimate completion. He's no fool. A President's legacy is often not measured objectively for at least a generation after he or she leaves the office.

And for this reason the President weighs his next steps carefully. Not just with the political consequences in mind. But with the careers and lives of a small group of advisors.

Howard Hall strolls casually into the Oval Office, beckoned by his boss and longtime friend. He sits comfortably in one of the power chairs that flank the President's desk. He does not use one of the two chairs that face the desk of the single most powerful man on the planet, chairs reserved for those not part of the inner circle, pursuent with a tactic developed decades ago by the late President Richard Millhouse Nixon.

Howard holds a smirky smile on the President before speaking.

"You handled him quite well this morning."

The President's eyes dart momentarily at Hall. Annoyed that, despite their friendship, he did not get the usual greeting offered by one and all invited into the Oval Office. Such as, 'good afternoon, Mister President.'

"When did you come up with that framework idea?"

The President, ignoring the question, shuffles the papers into a pile. He tosses them face down into a bin that gets emptied only by his National Security Advisor, and no one else. The momentary thought of that moron, Susan Rice, once holding that post gives him a minor chill.

"Howard. I've spent too many private weekends at my summer place in Connecticut with Noah. There's more to that double talker and his father than meets the eye. Time's up."

Hall suppresses his shocked feeling. Not fully understanding where the President is going with this thought. He attempts to keep the conversation on track with the wishes of Bishop Mendoza.

"Franklin wants to be assured that Commander Biersack is not overly suspicious. You know, not asking too many questions. Just keeping the DIA side glued together."

The President looks him in the eye for a heartbeat. Then, shifts away.

"She's fine. Leave her alone."

"Well, you know she's smart and she's pretty. And you yourself know she's not at all naïve."

The President writes into a journal on his desk, deliberately avoiding the tone of Hall's statements. After a moment, he says.

"Push her around just a bit, Howard, and she *will* get nosy. Let's not over-react."

Howard crosses his legs. He takes a more casual position despite sitting at the President's desk. He looks out towards the south lawn. He grins as a special thought over-takes his deceptive little brain.

"She's on her own if this thing unravels. She and her *boyfriend* will be caught in the cross hairs. And not know why."

He turns at the President.

"I just can't figure her relationship with Assistant Director Connolly. There's more there than meets the eye."

President Gonzmart leans back in his chair. He holds a stare on Hall. He's never really liked Howard Hall that much. He has always viewed him as deceptive and self-serving. He's known to manipulate events to his agenda, and at the expense of others. But, Gonzmart was forced into having him on the staff by the money behind his political career. And knowing full-well that the Prince would need a sap as a potential fall guy.

Family money is one thing. But financial power from other sources, namely Bishop Mendoza, while critical to the President's success, has had its consequences.

He thinks for a moment.

"We'll defer to the Prince on that issue."

Hall squirms. The thought of letting the Prince into issues that Hall himself wants to control makes him nervous. Should something go wrong, Hall knows the Prince will likely blame him.

And the consequence are unimaginable in Howard Hall's little brain.

It scares the crap out him.

Hall attempts to deflect the idea by showing the positive side of that relationship.

"We've all benefitted from his generosity, Gilly."

The President glares at him.

"You're the President of the United States, for Gods' sake."

"And I worked hard to get here, Howard. Let's not forget that."

"Well, if Commander Biersack gets in the way because she's nosy, and raises last minute questions about the framework? Well, I cringe at the thought of the Prince's reaction."

The President ponders the statement. He's equally concerned. For reasons he will not divulge to Hall.

"Call off Franklin. He may push her a little too hard. Arrange for me to have a talk with her. Tonight."

He returns to writing in his journal as Hall gives him a questionable look. Thinking, again, something's a little fishy.

"Okay. I understand. But, I'll have to brief the Prince on this. Bring him up to date. More involvement by the DIA might make him anxious."

Hall stands. He turns to leave, when the President drops his pen and zeros in on Hall's back.

"Howard! I'll call Franklin and have him do it. Not you."

He returns to writing in his journal as Hall has turned back at the President, bewildered.

A long heartbeat.

Softly.

"Yes, sir."

Chapter 14

The West Wing
Howard Hall's Office
Afternoon

HOWARD "THE HUMP" HALL really is a deceitful hump.

Despite clear instructions from the President, he's fixed on running things his way. He's a politicians best friend when it comes to leaving the "big guy" untouched. He can see to it that other bodies are left in the wake of a crisis.

He has no friends to speak of. Unless you include "hook ups" arranged years ago by a recently retired arrogant Congressman from Cape Cod.

Nor does he have any visible authority in the White House. Other than being able to follow the President around like a trained puppy follows his master.

The brief discussion with the President moments ago was troubling. Hall was not sure where he stood on the current situation with the Israelis and the Gulf of Aqaba agreement. It seems President Gonzmart's position has now moved from clear to slightly blurred.

And this new position seems to be directly related to that young beauty over at DIA. Jack Connolly's little concubine. A young woman Hall has loathed since first meeting her several years ago. She was assigned to the Executive Branch working as an admin for the National Security Advisor's staff over at the OEOB as a Naval Attaché.

As soon as she caught the eye of the President, Hall knew there was more to her than meets the eye. He was suspicious of her every move. He thought she may just be someone capable of taking down the President in some sort of bizarre sex scandal.

His paranoia was further justified when the President assigned her to the project that became the Gulf of Aqaba agreement. And had her sent over to the DIA at the Pentagon.

In his fully obsessed mind, he thought the President had decided the further away she was from the White House the closer she'd be to the President.

So, he had to watch her every move.

And now he needs to call her with instructions to contact the President later this evening. That in itself is unusual. But Hall will have to twist the instructions so as to put her into a perceived position of defense.

Give her enough to worry about. So maybe she'll back down on her inquisitive nature.

An e-mail from her earlier this morning was troubling. An e-mail Hall deliberately failed to show the President.

In it she was alerting "the White House" through Hall to a question about Noah David's background. Specifically, his connection to the President going back to David's school days in the U.S.

In Hall's mind, this kind of information can send important issues off the rails. He doesn't need that problem right now.

So, what he needs to do is deal with Commander Bonnie Biersack at the Pentagon. If anyone is to go off the rails it should be her career. He's all worked up right now.

But, Howard Hall is a wimp.

He simply cannot bring himself to confront anyone in an adversarial situation.

Especially a woman.

He's a tangible "Nancy."

He punches in her number almost wishing she is not there. Leaving a message is the easy way out of this assignment.

"Commander Biersack," she answers.

She's there. And sounds rather authoritative.

"Bonnie! Howard Hall. Over at the White House?"

"Yes, Mister Hall. How are you today? Did you read my e-mail?"

Hall starts to stutter. But catches himself.

"Yes…yes, of course. I'm looking into that right now. Should have an answer for you later."

"Great. Something else I can help with, Mister Hall?"

"Ah, yes, Bonnie. As a matter of fact there is. The President appears to have several minor questions for you. You know, wrapping up the agreement and all?"

"Oh?"

"Unfortunately, his schedule as such is rather tight. He asked if you could give him a ring in his study later this evening. Say, around ten? Call the main White House number, of course."

Bonnie leans back in her chair.

This request is odd. The protocol would be an e-mail from the National Security Advisor. Then cleared by the White House Communications Director. Then forwarded by someone like Howard Hall.

Her calling the President directly in his private study is way off the chain of command protocol.

Bonnie takes another moment to quickly recall a brief conversation she had with the President. It was in the Oval Office about three months ago. He asked that she be part of a small DIA team that would tackle the final issues of the agreement.

At that brief talk he handed her a note. It was a single page of short issues. He asked for her to check out those few issues before the final draft was prepared. Issues she thought were already addressed. Issues that did not need further research.

At the bottom, was a hand written telephone number. With a note, "my private study number."

Suddenly, she recalls the odd nature of the note.

"Commander! You still there?"

She snaps back to the conversation.

"Yes. Mister Hall. Sorry. Just making some notes here."

"Good. So you'll make that call later?"

"Yes, sir. Of course."

"Fine, Commander. Have a nice day."

He disconnects.

Bonnie takes a moment to recall where she may have put that document.

She checks her briefcase, wondering if the note is in her office at the Pentagon.

Shuffling through a mound of documents she finds that single page document.

Giving it a careful study, her mind wanders off to that day in the Oval Office.

As if an epiphany, she recalls turning to leave the Oval Office. Hearing a noise, she looked quickly to her far left. Coming into the office through a concealed door was Senator Franklin Hennessy, followed by an unusual visitor.

Someone she had not known to ever visit the Oval Office.

Archbishop Joseph Mendoza.

Chapter 15

Taxi Cab Ride
Streets of Washington, DC
Late Afternoon

I should feel special that Bonnie has let me accompany her up to the Hill. She's scheduled to have a little chat with the Senate Majority Leader, Franklin Hennessy.

Actually, I had to twist her arm to let me ride along. I did buy her a very expensive lunch. Although, glancing back and forth between her and the sports section of the Washington Post was probably not very polite on my part. Especially when she asked me to fill her in on the President's school career. I responded by saying Notre Dame looks like a top seed for the fall season.

Okay. The big guy did attend Notre Dame. So, I'm sort of off the hook.

Not!

My biggest problem at the moment is trying to keep a low profile. But, it's her profile that I need to keep in my sights.

Orders from the Director of the Secret Service.

She's aware of my assignment to ferret out potential threats against the President. Given her involvement in what appears to be a delicate issue, i.e. a major shift in our relations with Israel, the hard issue of my assignment involves providing a protective screen around her. We're using shadow agents she's not aware of, as she herself may be in danger.

We have to keep this piece hush, hush.

The world is full of nuts. And they're not just coming from foreign shores. The tide of anti-Semitism in the U.S. has been on the rise. Some it borne by ISIL and al Qaida.

The media, of course, doesn't help by continually harping on the fact that our largest piece of foreign aid goes to Israel. While 4 billion dollars is sizeable, there's a quiet under current in the country that feels it should be pulled back.

Why? Because Obama has convinced the left that we shouldn't piss-off the Muslims. We need to lead from behind.

A secret Obama mantra: "Screw the Jews!"

Which has created another problem altogether involving people like Commander Bonnie Biersack. People who work hard to do the right thing. People who face vile threats only because it involves Israel. If she only knew what comes in over the transom at Homeland Security.

Especially since the origin of Eric Holder's mantra: "Black lives matter."

Which brings me to my current assignment.

Providing comprehensive protection for a mid-level DIA official who really should not be in this position.

The good news is I get to hang with a single, hot blonde. Who is my former main squeeze. Someone who could easily have her choice of any rich power player in this town.

Like the lobbyists, a/k/a lawyers along K Street who charge $650 an hour for opinions that seem to get everyone in trouble. Except, of course, those few who got caught lying and cheating, and are serving time in Federal prison waiting for the current President to hopefully pardon them, in secret.

I glance over at Bonnie who seems to be holding an aggressive stare at the south lawn of the White House.

"I'd offer you dinner for your thoughts, Bonnie. But I'm tapped out."

Looking back at me, she says.

"I wonder why I need to call the President directly tonight. Doesn't that seem strange to you?"

Well, yes, in fact it does. I've had the feeling lately that my protective assignment was not just a gut feel the Director had after his morning tall mocha latte and raspberry croissant. He's such a snob. But he did tackle a mentally deranged bystander. The guy was wearing a small clip-on red bow tie. He went after Obama yelling 'it's me, man. Lewis.'

Like I said, there are a bunch of nuts in this country.

"Hear him out, Bonnie. But I'd stay mum about that e-mail you got."

"...yeah."

I'm thinking the e-mail she got this morning came through some very rigorous firewalls. Unknown to her, I was able to copy it onto a thumb drive and shoot it over to Homeland Security. Our nerds over there are giving it a sweep.

"But I'm still uncomfortable, Jack. Confused is better."

"Right. I'm with you on that point. But the President doesn't need to hear about it. Anyway, he knows we're keeping a close eye on certain security issues."

She gives me a hard look.

"We?"

You see?

As soon as I bring up something she shouldn't get involved with she wants to be involved. I need to deflect that question with something that gives her confidence in the efforts of the people around her, and 'to carry on, with vigor.'

That's what I heard JFK used to say to the hot blondes he escorted (sic) into the Oval Office every day.

"So, how's it feel being the President's female white slave? He likes tall blondes to visit the Oval Office. They're his favorite."

"Huh?"

I'm good at redirecting the conversation into something safe and harmless. Something that would spur on some serious and thoughtful conversation.

Looking out the front window, I smile at the thought of the Secret Service code for when a President wants to be alone in the Oval Office with a hot babe. Turning back at her, I say.

"It's called a Monica moment."

"Grow up, Jack!"

She ponders some more about this call she needs to make this evening.

"And why so late?"

"Bonnie! You're a top notch intel officer. You should be able to figure it out. You don't need my superior, highly trained experience as a Naval Officer and White House groupie."

"Former."

She had to needlessly say that, right?

I lean forward and say to the taxi driver.

"Let us off on the Senate side, northeast, Abdul."

He waves at me while catching my eyes in the rear view. His look is something close to fear. Law enforcement personnel now, as a matter of routine, quickly profile. A taxi driver who appears to be from Sand Land, has dark skin, an Afghani name, an al Qaida membership card duct tapped next to his medallion, dynamite strapped to his chest, we call him, or her, by name.

We know it scares the shit out these guys. As if we have written down everything we know from the short cab ride, plus snapped a few photos with an iPhone.

You bet we have.

Welcome to America, *el terristo*!

Chapter 16

**Office of the Senate Majority Leader,
Franklin Hennessy (R-CT)
Late Afternoon**

We stroll casually into the outer office of the guy who's king of the Hill, a/k/a, the Senate Majority Leader. I can only think of the years of lunacy and misbehavior that flowed from these hallowed chambers. I mean those bizarre days when hop-along Harry was in charge.

Like enacting rules that clearly run roughshod over the Constitution of the United States.

That depends on the party currently living high on the hog in the White House. The guy who occupies this suite of luxury crash pads and cribs here in the U.S. Senate is either absolutely dead-on in his behavior...

...or mentally off the reservation.

There's no gray area to contemplate.

One guy determines the agenda for those lucky 100 who have been sent here by the other 310 million, like me, to make sense of the way our government should behave.

That island in the South Pacific is looking better every day. If Tom Hanks can live there for four years, so can I.

I think.

Well, fish and coconuts are not high on my list of preferred diet choices.

But, what the hell. It was only a movie.

A cute young blonde admin type opens the Senators' door. She gestures for Bonnie to go on in. Before Bonnie has a chance to head for the door, I tactfully clear my throat.

"I think I'll go in with you. You know. Moral support?"

"You have no morals, Jack."

Isn't she special?

"He may be a sex crazed politician, Bonnie. You never know these days. Maybe even a secret member of the Weiner Society."

My reference to "one hung low", a/k/a, Anthony "the package" Weiner, the former Congressman whose "junk" made headlines around the internet a few years back, didn't go unnoticed by the young, cute blonde admin.

I gave her a wink.

She blushes.

Bonnie, not missing the vibe, chimes in.

"Idiot."

"I *was* with you in Israel thrashing out the details of the agreement. Maybe the Senator knows that. He'll probably want my input. You think?"

"No! And the only detail I remember was your insistence that we hurry back to your - "

She stops short realizing the young admin is right there.

Giving her a curt smile, she turns, heading for the door.

"Okay. You win Jack. But speak only when spoken to."

"Right."

Sounds like instructions my mother would give me when we had to pay a visit to my Mom's very rich Uncle

George at his Sutton Place apartment in New York City. He was married to another Venezuelan, Tia Adelina. Now you know why I possess a hot blooded Latin libido.

Walking past the Connecticut state flag, we march into Senator Hennessy's office. He's seated behind a large desk, obviously a gift from a major money contributor like the "Friends of Nutmeg Society."

He's on the telephone, smiling and chuckling every now and then.

Gesturing for us to sit, we grab two chairs that face the dark brown (nutmeg brown) desk. I quickly take the opportunity to eaves drop on his conversation while Bonnie scans the array of photos on a far wall.

It's interesting to note that the photos are placed with famous and not so famous Republicans at or above eye level. While famous and not so famous Democrats are placed along a line that's seems to be even with one's "gold member." The one behind my pants zipper, for example.

He bellows into the phone.

"Now you listen, Governor. You tell those spineless wimps that call themselves legislators to get off this drunk driving trash. They need to figure out how to spend all this taxpayer cash I'm bringin' home."

He chuckles, obviously at some stupid joke offered by the nutmeg Governor.

He adds.

"No, no. I don't want any state building named after me. Some towel head Arab terrorist is liable to blow it up."

He laughs out loud. Then hangs up the receiver.

After a moment, he spins around and smiles at Bonnie. Then shifts is gaze to me.

And for a moment he looks as if he knows me. It's the frown on his high hair line.

Now, we *have* met. And he should know that I have been part of the President's detail going back three Presidents.

But he simply can't place me. So, I make it easy for him.

"Greetings, Senator. Jack Connolly."

He just looks.

Shrugs.

Okay. I passed the "who the hell is this guy" test.

Then, to Bonnie.

She catches the odd moment.

"Mister Connolly accompanied the President, his staff, and I to the Gulf of Aqaba.

Hennessy gives me another look.

And another shrug.

Pointing at his telephone, he says, "drunk driving. You believe those bird brains up there in Hartford. We got bigger fish to fry."

I determine it's my moment to show the majority leader how really smart I am, given the fact that I'm a big shot at the White House. Right?

"Did you know that the shore line in Israel that borders the Gulf of Aqaba is where Moses settled, temporarily, with the Israelites after their escape from Egypt?"

Another shrug.

"Mount Sinai is near-by."

Now a questionable frown from the Senator.

"It must have been a lovely place back then because those dudes stayed about four hundred years."

Holding a stare on him, I think he's contemplating blowing my brains out with one of the twelve guns he owns, cleverly concealed in his desk.

I said twelve guns, right? To be a Republican Member of Congress you're required to have at least one manicured finger for pointing at Democrats on the floor. A fancy pin in your lapel with instructions on the back explaining the secret handshake. And proof that you own twelve guns.

Don't you just love the NRA?

Hennessy, focused on Bonnie now, smiles.

"Commander Biersack. I hear you'll be speaking with the President later this evening."

She nods.

"Good. Let's talk about this agreement for a moment."

He stands, taking a glance out his window. Then a quick, scowl at me.

"Bonnie. May I call you Bonnie?"

He doesn't wait for an answer.

"Your hard work will get recognized. Everyone from the White House and the Pentagon – the DIA establishment - are quite impressed."

Pause.

"A framework will be signed, electronically, this Friday."

Bonnie jolts forward in her chair, temporarily startling the good Senator.

"Friday? Friday? Before the elections this weekend?"

"We're past diplomacy, Bonnie. We need to have a firm grip on our interests."

Hennessy adds.

"I understand this comes as a surprise, but the President made the decision just a short time ago."

I can see that Bonnie is perhaps thinking about what she said to me just moments before walking in here. So, since she's been spoken to, she's about to unload on this guy.

Time for me to step in. I recognize this is usually where a more senior guy tells you what's going to happen if you don't like what he's saying.

"Senator. Commander Biersack has viewed this assignment as fascinating and terribly educational in every respect."

Hennessy just looks at me. I think he's still trying to figure who in the hell I am.

At the same moment I feel the sharp point of a Ferragamo shoe poke me in the calf. Not authorized Naval Officer dress code.

I give her a look.

She gives Hennessy a look and asks.

"Sir. Do you think there's anyone out there who would not want the agreement to go forward?"

Hennessy spins for a look out his window over towards Union Station. Perhaps he's wondering if he should catch the next train back to Connecticut. Or leap across the desk and strangle Bonnie.

My gut tells me it's option one. Only because my amazing street sense screams in my brain. The e-mail Bonnie got this morning is perhaps more a tactic than a red herring.

Hennessy returns to the discussion.

"Bonnie. You've been asked to go beyond your job description and responsibilities. And you've done a fine job."

Another pause. This time for effect.

"But, this matter has some risks given the parties involved. The venue. Jerusalem. An assortment of religious groups. There's an alphabet soup of problems, Bonnie, that may involve a cast of characters who do not wish to cooperate."

Did he say religious groups? Interesting.

My little brain flashes back to Grandpa and Great Grandpa, on Mom's side of course. And the obsession with Catholic Church matters. The discussions back then involved someone connected, via Venezuela, to the family.

Maybe he does know about the e-mail.

Hennessy gives me a look, but, he refrains from saying anything.

Speaking to Bonnie, he says.

"Not wanting the agreement to go forward? You're maybe raising a troubling question, Bonnie."

"I'm merely speculating, Senator. Some of the issues, yes, are open to criticism."

He points the manicured finger at her.

"Be very mindful of your duty to the President. To your country as a Naval Officer with a stellar record."

I give him the finger, hidden, of course, on this side of the desk thinking her future "star" is off the table.

I think Bonnie saw that.

She says with some measure of force. "I am mindful of the fact that religious freedoms cut to one's soul, sir."

"And security comes with a price, Commander Biersack."

Her nostrils flare. She looks as if she may just spring from her chair. He may not have an opportunity to further his point.

"Well I certainly hope not at the expense of a sovereign nation, Senator. That would raise some eyebrows on the world stage."

Not to mention AIPAC, the super strong Israeli lobby that practically owns every politician here in Washington, DC. I'm very impressed with Bonnie's conviction here. She's turning me on. Of course, ever since she brought up that night in the Gulf of Aqaba, the mere mention of the agreement activates the launch sequence. If you get my drift.

"We're done with diplomacy. The President has spent too much of his time on this matter. It's a done deal. This Friday."

Bonnie takes a moment to calm down. She is a respectable Naval Officer.

"Sir. I'm only in favor of seeking mutually rewarding agreements that –"

But he quickly senses her pull back. As the elite in the room, he needs to keep her in her place.

"This agreement will go a long way in stabilizing the region. Sure, there will always be criticism of good things. Liberals throw that crap at us every day."

He leans on his desk, ready to make a substantive point.

"Look at our friend Wayne what's his name at the NRA. The poor guy gets beat-up every day. What a shame."

Why doesn't someone just throttle him. Put the poor guy out of his misery.

"Don't get me wrong, Senator. But I'm being cautious...making sure everyone is happy."

Hennessy holds a hard stare on her. He moves into his desk chair. Shuffling a few papers on his desk, he breaks eye contact with her.

"Your level in the Navy has your career on the fast track for that "star," Commander Biersack."

A moment as he re-establishes eye contact with her.

"Don't screw it up!"

He's back to reading something very important, probably the dinner menu from the Senate dining room.

I grab Bonnie's arm, noting her frozen position in the chair. I indicate that I'm quite sure the meeting has been adjourned.

She follows me out.

Majority Leaders Outer Office

Bonnie has a grabbed a seat at table where she sets up her laptop.

She looks appropriately pissed.

She's probably typing out a letter to Senator Hennessy saying she's left a bomb in his office which will go off if he reads the letter.

I, on the other hand, notice a maintenance worker holding a can of Ortho wasp killer and aiming it at the ceiling.

Buzzing around the light fixtures are several wasps. He's getting them at a distance of at least 15 feet.

"Jack. I need to e-mail Shannon Bream of FOX News. Invite her to the Sodality event tonight."

That name gets my instant attention.

I know her to be one of those hot blonde babes on the FOX News Channel.

Now that piece of news may change my decision. And show up at the Sodality event.

But, I'll play it cool.

As I'm watching the wasp killer guy, Bonnie is up, heading for the door.

"Let's go, Jack."

I follow.

Reading her body language, and once clear of the Majority Leaders prying ears, a/k/a admin staff, I say.

"Politicians are hard to read. What they say is not what they mean. Like when that Senator from New Jersey, what's his name, took a trip to the Dominican Republic. Said it was to thank his primo benefactor, some dirt bag from Florida."

She gives me a questionable look.

"He was really there to thank that guy for the "jail bait" who were there to 'make him comfortable' while on vacation in the DR."

"Huh?"

"I think he said 'I like 'em young, Doc' while he was slugging down another pina colada."

"Huh?"

This got me thinking.

"Bonnie. I need a drink."

"Jack. We need to get our arms around this."

"Okay. They serve drinks at the Warship in Georgetown. In extra-large glasses. Then, how about dinner?"

"We need to be at Marymount."

"I was thinking we could eat at the Warship Restaurant. I'll show you a photo of the warship my Grandpa – on Dad's side - commanded during the big one, WW 2."

Glancing at her watch, while making a bee-line out the door. With the taxi cab stand her destination.

"I'm going. And you've taken me out there before. Remember?"

"Right. I'll call ahead for a quiet table in the back."

"It would be nice if you were to go to the talk with me."

"Well, since you can't hold your liquor, I wouldn't think of letting you drink alone."

She stops short.

And turns to face me.

"The Sodality meeting, Jack!"

Okay.

She can be very illusive at times.

It must a woman thing.

Or an Ohio thing.

I need to find out before this relationship gets too serious once again.

"Are you sure Shannon Bream will be there?"

Chapter 17

Senate Majority Leaders' Office
Moments Later

Senator Hennessy holds a hard stare to the outside, and below. He's got a bead on Bonnie and Jack as they wave down a taxi cab. He fumes at the thought of the conversation he just had with Bonnie. His thoughts bounce from things being on track to things regarding his career that could just run into a brick wall. Things giving the Prince more ammunition to blow the lid off his political aspirations.

Taking a seat at his desk, he grabs the telephone receiver. He punches in a three digit code hard enough to crack the plastic console, should it be breakable.

The special code gives him instant access to the West Wing of the White House. Specifically to Howard Hall's small office space. Space once occupied by a spin doctor from Chicago, someone personally responsible for sabotaging Herman Caine's Presidential aspirations. Giving direction to his dirty tricks guru by proclaiming "we own the Black candidate, not the Republicans." Someone who attempted to go incognito by shaving off his mustache in order to appear on MSNBC. The purpose, to deny any responsibility for the failure of the Obama Administration.

Fortunately, those journalists who are not activists pretending to be journalists, unlike the MSNBC crew, know better.

Ergo, the clean shaved look.

Howard "the hump" Hall glares at the ringing telephone for a long moment. He's perplexed. His caller ID feature has been disconnected.

Finally taking it to his ear, he says, "good afternoon."

Bellowing from the other end, Senator Hennessy speaks.

"I didn't like her tone, Howard! She's developed serious doubts."

Hall wipes a drop of sweat from his brow.

"I can handle it, Franklin. She doesn't know enough to read between the lines."

Hennessy stands, and takes a moment to think this through.

"Careful, Howard. If you wanna knock her off the track, just don't make too much noise. We gotta get through the Israeli election cycle."

He pauses for effect.

"We don't wanna upset the Prince."

This statement sends Hall into a tizzy.

"I said I can handle it, Franklin. She was Gilly's choice. Not mine. So, back off, for chrissakes."

Hennessy develops a smirk, picturing Hall's unstable demeanor.

Then, with some condensation in his voice, Hennessy finishes him off.

"It's still in your hands, Howard."

Click.

Hennessy disconnects.

Chapter 18

Marymount University
Arlington, Virginia
Evening

Archbishop Joseph Mendoza stands at a podium looking particularly regal.

This, of course, is not by accident.

He scans the audience of less than one hundred.

His minions. At least that's his attitude. They are here to hear him.

And, perhaps learn.

His take-away is more about his performance than what the audience of sodality members from a University religious group takes away.

Their religious fate is in their hands. Not his.

But, he makes the best of the situation, not to terribly distort the message. He is, in fact, a man of the cloth. And needs to not cross that fine line that could make some of the brethren uncomfortable. His staff has meticulously pre-approved the group before him. But, he is still suspect of one or two "unfriendly" journalists who may have snuck in.

His largest concern is a certain publisher of the New York Times who has openly lodged criticisms of the Catholic Church. He ran absurd articles on the front page, slamming the Church, and the Holy See in Rome.

Mendoza knows that his boss, the Cardinal who oversees the mid-Atlantic region, reads every major newspaper. And is glued to cable news each evening.

After a brief pause he concludes his lecture.

"My friends. Our Church has come too far to be selfishly idle in thought and action where it involves the earthly life of our Lord, Jesus the Christ."

Looking almost sternly at the group, a mix of men and women, and several nuns who flank the group on both sides. His tone turns a bit forceful, accented by the reading light that casts a mysterious light and shadow combination on his hard face.

To his right, Monsignor Roger Schneider sits. Stoic. His serious expression locked onto his boss. Every now and then, a quick, almost imperceptible glance at the audience. Hopefully unseen by the Bishop.

"Your obligation…no, your right…your right in Baptism and confirmation as His followers is to walk in His steps…in His land…the land we all know as Judea."

A long pause.

"The land of *our* Church, my friends. The land soon to be the centerpiece of our future."

A moment before Bishop Mendoza takes several steps to his left. Then bows his head in obvious reverence.

This is the cue for Monsignor Schneider to rise and address the group.

Bonnie, seated in the first row, turns for a look to the rear of the room.

I catch the look from her and immediately smile, giving her a thumbs up. Luckily the guy next to me, I think his name is Abdul, remembered to wake me when Mendoza was wrapping up his inspirational talk.

At least that's what the guy next to me said. Inspirational. But, I was careful not to be seen.

You see, I know that guy. Going way, way back to my reckless, lust-filled youth, and before.

My Grandfather, Don Mateo Segui, and my Great Grandfather, Don Pedro Segui, were close, very close, confidants of the marvelous Mendoza when he was a young parish priest on Long Island.

Father Mendoza's connection to our family goes back to Don Pedro's relatives in Venezuela. Those who did not emigrate to Spain prior to World War II.

On his feet now, Schneider says.

"Please stand for the Bishop's Benediction."

Everyone stands and I do likewise, short of garnering a boatload of nasty looks.

Abdul does the same as I thank him for waking me at the right moment. Despite his dark skin, Mediterranean nose, the Banana Republic outfit, and the bulge in his pants which could easily pass for a suicide bomb, I doubt his name is Abdul.

No further comment on the bulge in his pants.

I hear the good Bishop say something truly spiritual, then raise his hand, blessing us all with whatever powers he possesses.

Good Karma, I think.

I hang loose for a moment waiting for Bonnie's high sign. A signal for us to make a quick get-a-way. The one and only thought on my mind at the moment.

Rather than signal for me to move towards the exit, she walks over.

"So, Jack. Were you moved?"

Without thinking, I say, "yeah, to sleep."

Rather than comment with something of a foul nature, she moves her gaze over towards the Bishop. He seems to be holding court with a group of religious zealots.

Monsignor Schneider, who I know to be a decent, down to earth guy, based on certain intel which I'm not at liberty to divulge, is standing at the Bishop's elbow.

He looks as if he needs a couple of Tums chewables. Going from a death star linebacker at Notre Dame to his current role in life surely took a leap of faith...pardon the pun.

Bonnie now mumbles.

"He's a Saint. Very generous. Powerful. A Church leader I truly admire and respect."

At which point Mendoza's gaze locks onto Bonnie. His eyes say it all. 'Get your cute butt over here.'

Well, maybe not exactly that, but close.

A thin smile crosses his hard features now. And she returns the favor.

Then a knowing glance at me.

Shit!

She says to me. "Want to meet him?"

"He bites. I have that on very high authority, Bonnie."

She sighs.

"Do you go to Church daily...or at least on Sundays?"

"Daily?"

"I didn't think so, Jack."

She gives him a small wave. Then says to me.

"Tell him you admire his point of view...and don't forget to kiss the ring."

She walks towards Mendoza.

Standing rock solid in place, I ask.

"Kiss the what?"

Now what? He's gonna reveal my connection. I'm screwed. I should have checked the program details before agreeing to be here. I could have said to her…"sorry, Bonnie, love, but I need to feed my parakeet tonight!"

But she's already in front of him, hand extended.

"Your excellency. Wonderful presentation. Thank you so much."

He simply smiles and gives her a slight bow of the head.

"I'd like you to meet a friend. Jack Connolly.

Mendoza now offers me his hand…palm down…crap.

But, instead I just give him a military hand shake.

"Mister Connolly. How long has it been?"

I feign stupidity. Which is rather easy for me, as Bonnie frowns hard at me.

"Your Grandfather, Don Mateo, I trust is well? I'm certain he would have enjoyed my little talk this evening."

Despite my erratic Catholic grade school disciplinary record, I am standing face to face with a high official of the Catholic Church. Back then, no sensible person would permit me to do this. Something about being caught on several occasions giving the nuns the finger.

Those women had no sense of humor.

Anyway, he was okay with shaking my hand, although Bonnie gave me one of those "looks." His smile did quickly evaporate.

"Mister Connolly?"

Being of Irish decent and coming from a family that very rarely holds back during charged conversations at the dinner table, I take a moment to give his provocative glare some serious brain time.

I cave.

"Fine…well…my Grandfather is very well, thank you."

On the one hand, I'd like to provide what I would term as constructive criticism of his many interesting homilies. On the other hand, Bonnie is standing right here between us. To be completely honest, I would like to have sex tonight.

The wrong thing said would definitely change that dynamic.

What a freaking dilemma.

Beat-up a high Church official?

Or sex!

Men are simply wired to think just this way. And no other way.

I take a mediating shot in the dark.

"Well…controversial…sort of…"

Bonnie's eyes go wide, but it's a questionable wide look.

Mendoza frowns. But, not that badly. And asks.

"May I ask in what specific way, Mister Connolly?"

Okay.

The good news is that he didn't order Monsignor Schneider to put me in a head lock and pummel me to death with that heavy gold cross around his neck.

Now I need to be a lot smarter than I look. Or, at least, appear to be at times. Which, by the way, is not that often. But, don't tell anybody.

So, I search for a moment in time back when I was a smart-ass elementary school student solely engaged in lusting after anyone wearing a skirt.

Of course, not including those dreadful nuns, nor my gay friend, Terence, who I think wanted to wear skirts and high heels to school.

We were just school yard buddies.

Nothing else.

Really.

In a moment of stunning enlightenment, I respond to the Bishop.

"Israel. The holy sites. I believe they all belong to the Catholic Church. But…at least in a symbolic sense…I think."

He has now locked onto me with those penetrating eyes. Eyes that have been given notoriety by those in the media that have interviewed this prelate.

"Mister Connolly, you speak of the cornerstone of our faith. What has existed for more than 2000 years. I'm impressed with your...belief."

"Thank you...sir."

The quick look from Bonnie alerts me to the fact that "sir" was not proper etiquette.

Now, do I grab his right hand and kiss the ring? Or just move on?

I move on.

"I have been there. Compliments of the United States Navy. Quite the place."

He gets a little preachy with me.

"I would suggest another visit, Mister Connolly. While there, take the time to walk in His steps. The footsteps of our Lord and Savior, Jesus the Christ. You'll see it is far more than symbolic, my friend. And here I thought we taught you well many years ago."

Turning to Bonnie.

"Am I not correct, Commander Biersack?"

Back to that frightful glare at me.

"But, it's perhaps time to examine your conscience, Mister Connolly. Through the Sacrament of Reconciliation we sweep clean our past. Both thoughts and actions. We bring our spiritual, faith filled minds to present day. And do what's right."

Bonnie, showing signs of some trepidation in her voice, responds.

"And trusting that the origins of our faith are in those steps, your excellency."

Mendoza smiles broadly at Bonnie's comment, much the way a professor would complement a student on a brilliant statement in class.

Bonnie told me that once in college she had a similar experience with a professor, fortunately someone who was not a man of the cloth, who had praised her highly in class.

Then proceeded to invite her up to his private office for a special assignment that would lead to extra credit.

At that encounter the "special assignment" involved a routine of groping, kissing and un-zipping.

And not with her hands, but his.

She did get an A.

Maybe there's more to the story. You think?

Not.

What I do *know*, from my experience in the Secret Service, is that kind of incident on college campuses is more the rule rather than the exception.

Turning back at me, he continues to preach his sermon, choosing his words carefully.

"I'm confident responsible authorities will guarantee unilateral and unencumbered access."

Pause.

"For all faiths, of course."

A heartbeat.

"Forgiveness of ones sins is contagious, my friends. Sins of our ancestors included. We identify the virtue that will help us displace the sin. Chastity counteracts lust."

He holds on me for along moment. I suppose he hears Bonnie's confessions. You think?

"Temperance uproots gluttony. Generosity counterbalances greed. Diligence displaces sloth. Forgiveness and meekness offset wrath or anger. Kindness replaces envy. And humility supplants pride."

I'm hoping that Bonnie's not taking copious notes.

If so, her Naval career will likely be followed by donning a chastity belt, throwing away the key, and joining some remote order of nuns.

Without waiting for my brilliant thoughts on his politically incorrect and bizarre hidden agenda – it's in the eyes, as always – he adjourns our little chat.

"Time for evening vespers at my personal chapel."

Giving Monsignor Schneider a hard look.

"Roger! Bring the car around."

Schneider bows ever so slightly, and departs the room.

Now the big guy zeros in on Bonnie.

"Commander Biersack, this was certainly a pleasant evening I hope for all."

"Thank you, your excellency. And, yes, it was indeed."

Giving me a weird look, he says.

"Mister Connolly. I hope we meet again."

With that, he spins on his soles, and heads for the door.

I thought that maybe I'd get to shake his hand. Or even kiss the ring. Or, at least say *adios, big guy,* which may not have been spiritually correct.

Bonnie gives me a look. Then says.

"Your Grandfather?"

I shrug.

Better to keep the family secrets inside the family for now. Anyway, if I start to spill my guts about Mom's side of the family, I'll likely be cornered into that long weekend Bonnie is planning out in Dayton, Ohio.

Watching him leave, she says.

"Well, I'm not so sure he likes you. As a matter of fact, I'm certain he doesn't."

"Hey. It's been decades. He needs to warm up to me again. Anyway, I was wondering."

She turns, and gives me that look. The one that signals 'think before you speak'.

But, you know me.

"Did you catch those eye teeth? I'd say were talking fangs, you think?"

"Watch it, Jack. He's a Bishop. Anyway. It's been decades? You need to fill me in. I think you're hiding something from me."

Shit!

I need to get her pissed off about something else. And off this 'how do you know Mendoza' crap.

"Well, you must admit, that crap about allowing all religions full access to Jerusalem. As long as no one else - read here Jews, Muslims, and everyone else but Catholics - screws things up...or words to that effect."

Bonnie sighs heavily.

"It would have been a good idea for you to have listened to him more closely, Jack."

Then...

"Where are you taking me for dinner, Jack?"

Phew!

She's hungry.

Left brain dominance saves me.

Oh, right. A dinner date, with the possibility of sex later on.

Maybe.

Actually, prospects are looking somewhat dim at this point. I need to deflect the question with an incendiary, but thought-provoking question.

Looking around the room, I ask.

"Didn't you say Shannon Bream from FOX News was going to be here covering the event?"

Turning back to Bonnie, I note she's halfway to the door.

Shit!

Chapter 19

Bonnie's Alexandria, Virginia Home
Late Evening

Bonnie paces in her simple, but mid-western tasteful, living room. In her hand she holds firmly onto a cat toy, every now and then giving it an unintentional squeeze.

"Skippy! Skippy!"

Her foot kicks a bright fluffy yellow ball by accident. She quickly bends for a look under the near-by sofa.

No Skippy. On her feet, she sighs, doing close to a one eighty. A glance at her watch informs her that it's close to eleven pm.

She walks back into her bedroom, slowly, eye-balling every possible hiding place her cat can be.

No Skippy.

At her desk, she grabs her iPhone, looking at it with a degree of trepidation.

She punches in the number she knows will take her directly to the President's private study.

"Yes," says President Gonzmart.

"Good evening, Mister President. It's Commander Biersack."

"Ah, Bonnie. I hope I haven't kept you up too late."

"Oh, no sir. Not at all. Just looking for...well, I hope it's okay to call so late. The time just got away- "

He doesn't wait for her to finish her thought.

"Listen, Bonnie. I have an issue with Section E, paragraph J-19. I've noted a comment. I'd like your opinion."

Bonnie sits back in her chair trying to focus on that part of the Gulf of Aqaba agreement in the absence of a copy in her hands. The President knows a copy would never be in her apartment pursuant to a litany of National Security issues.

Her best guess about section J-19 is that it deals with who can sign on behalf of the parties.

It's a no-brainer. Why this question?

"Yes. Sir. I understand. I'll be over first thing to – "

"I've got your secure e-mail address here. It's on its way. Don't bother answering by e-mail. Anyway, thanks for your time, Bonnie. Send over your thoughts tomorrow, first thing. With the Joint Chief's brief."

He quickly disconnects.

Bonnie takes an eternity to just stare at her iPhone.

Then she spins at her laptop, running her fingers across the touch pad. It comes to life.

And there it is, front and center, on her screen.

The e-mail from the President of the United States.

She didn't even have to open the app, nor select the message.

It just simply appeared.

She gives it a quick read.

"Huh?"

Chapter 20

The White House
OEOB Office Complex
Sub-Level 2
Late Evening

The room is small and dark.

Soft voices can be heard coming from an array of speakers along one wall.

Once one gets used to the darkness, one would be able to make out three or four people seated at audio consoles.

At one station a voice can be heard referring to someone as "Bonnie."

The conversation is soft.

And brief.

Then, a disconnect.

Followed by the soft hum of a dead line.

The console operator flips a switch, and the humming is quieted.

He notes the elapsed time of the call on a single sheet of paper. It includes the callers' name and number. The number and person called. And a notation indicating a digital marker.

He folds the paper, placing it into an envelope.

A short distance from the operator, a man appears, gently tapping the operator on the shoulder.

The operator turns slightly, handing the envelop to the man standing behind him in the darkness.

The man standing holds the envelop giving it a long stare, and saying softly to the operator.

"Have the disk placed in my office safe no later than mid-night."

The operator nods his understanding.

A moment passes before Howard Hall turns away from the operator.

Hall leaves the darkened space.

Chapter 21

The Pentagon
E Ring, DIA Suite
Commander Bonnie Biersack's Office
Morning

I'm standing here at the window looking down on several hunched-over men dressing-up the mulch beds around this place. Gardening was never my thing. Probably comes from those days as a youngster when the "Admiral", a/k/a, my Dad, would order us out of the house on a Saturday morning when he was home from deployment. Our mission was to engage in those wonderful chores like cutting the grass, weeding the flower beds, raking the gravel driveway, tying my little sister to the dog run.

Okay. Not that last thing. But we were certainly tempted. She always found a way to get off yard duty. Usually it was an excuse about having to do the piles of homework heaped on her by those nuns at school.

Actually, I knew she was in her room on the telephone talking to one of her dopey friends about who was the cutest boy in school.

As far as the homework excuse was concerned, I could never use that one. Mom and Dad knew my homework was always up to date, and on time.

Really, it was.

Actually, I had the perfect solution to the weekend homework problem.

A cute girlfriend.

First it was Jackie. Then Linda. Then one of the Judy's in my class, which one I don't recall. Then the one who was well developed early in life. Her name was Karen.

And that was just the 7th grade year.

And they were all smart as a whip.

And liked the idea of referring to me as their 'boyfriend' – at different times, of course.

Ergo - homework problem solved.

I turn back towards Bonnie, whose focused concentration is on her LED screen. I take in the spacious office.

"You know, Bonnie. I kinda like your office here at the Pentagon better than that hovel they let you use at State."

Still focused on her LED screen, "unless we're protecting them at Embassy's overseas, they have no use for the military. Hillary set that tone in place. Remember Benghazi, Jack?"

Frowning, I comment.

"You're gonna go blind."

She sighs.

"I can't concentrate."

I walk over to her, placing my hands on her shoulders. I give her a thumbs only massage to the back of her neck. I'm trying to be as compassionate as possible.

"Maybe it was something he ate."

"He was an inside cat, Jack. What was he doing outside on my deck?"

Thinking, I ask.

"No signs of a break-in?"

She folds her arms as if the thought makes her nervous.

"I wouldn't know, Jack. I don't know. My home? Invaded?"

A heartbeat.

"Lucky I wasn't home. The Alexandria PD would be carting off a dead body this morning. And I don't mean mine."

Right. I know she owns several seriously dangerous weapons. I've seen the sharp-shooter awards she won at the Naval Academy."

I'm not sure what I could do for her at this point. I feel for her loss. And wish that I could be more helpful. I drift back towards the window to think.

Bonnie comes back to life, stating firmly.

"I need to focus...clearly, on who the messenger is. That's my mission."

I zero in on her, gratified that at least she's prioritizing her tasks.

"Look. You figured out everything about that renegade submarine several years back when we were at Camp Peary...together...very together."

She glances sideways at me, not wanting to go there. I'm sure she probably has never forgotten the amazing sex. It was during the time I spent with her on those lonely weekends. Free of my job at the White House. You think?

But, I need to ask anyway.

"What about the President's request from last night?"

"Done. I sent over a simple one paragraph statement in the JCS pouch. It really did not change the agreement. Odd that he would send those comments to me. It was nothing."

She sighs again. This time, it's followed by the issues she sees as crucial to finding the messenger.

"No Abbey. No messenger. No nothing."

She bangs her fist on the desk. It startles me.

Then, it hits me. I take a few steps towards her.

"Not long ago, the President took a trip, as I can vaguely recall, to Connecticut. Not a campaign thing, just a personal trip."

Bonnie gives me one of those skeptical looks as if I'm orbiting a different universe. A common occurrence.

"Go on line and pull up a bio on the President."

"Why?"

"I think something in his past will connect to Connecticut."

Still staring at me, now very skeptical, she says.

"What makes you remember that?"

"Memory school. It's a secret."

Turning back to her computer and working the keyboard, she asks.

"Why is everything with you a secret?"

"I can't tell you. It's a secret. You do know that we are the *Secret Service*. Right?"

She whispers, "…Jesus."

Banging away at her keyboard, I notice that she has developed a very sly smile.

I ask.

"What?"

Still smiling, and working the keyboard, she says.

"I know when -- or is it how -- to get you to come clean, Mister Assistant Director Jack Connolly. I will explain on our planned trip to Dayton, Ohio."

Crap! It's I go. Or give up sex forever with this gorgeous babe.

I'm confident I'll make the right decision.

Reading the President's bio, she says.

"I know most all of this stuff."

I point at the screen.

"There. Read that section. Education."

She moves closer to the screen, and starts to read.

"The President graduated from The Abbey in 1973. An exclusive prep school for boys in New Milford, Connecticut. From The Abbey, he attended Notre Dame University in South Bend, Indiana, then onto Harvard Law School."

Bonnie sits back, thinking.

Then, "the Abbey is the key to his past. Meaning who?

Thinking back on that e-mail from the messenger, he, or she, specifically referred to the Prince."

"The Prince, obviously." I respond.

"But is the President the Prince?"

"I doubt it, Bonnie. But, both are definitely connected to The Abbey. I feel strongly about that."

"Yeah. So do I, Jack."

After a moment.

"This bio also confirms what I think I already knew. Senator Hennessy and Howard Hall were classmates of the President at that time…interesting."

I see the wheels turning now, very quickly. She's onto a break through. I need to pay close attention to whatever it is she feels has to be done.

This messenger nonsense has got her in knots.

And it's going to have me in knots if she starts to make rash, unilateral decisions about her next move. Like organizing a search party to look for this dude…or dudette.

Which may include me, and perhaps even Mister Potato Head, Tommy Trumble.

Due to the sensitivity of the Gulf of Aqaba agreement, Bonnie could inadvertently put herself in danger should some of the actors involved here be a bit shady.

Maybe I'll suggest a cooling-off period. Say a day trip into the Virginia countryside for instance. Like a visit to wineries in the Charlottesville area.

I hear there are several very nice Bed & Breakfasts in the area.

By the time we get back, maybe the dust would have settled. And the agreement will be a done deal.

And my job at protecting her safety will be noticed by the President. He will undoubtedly award me with high praise and future assignments that involve palm trees and beaches. I sense I'm getting carried away with myself. So I turn to Bonnie and ask.

"Hey. How about a nice long lunch in Georgetown where we can plan a long-weekend getaway starting, say tomorrow?"

I'm not sure she heard me as her eyes are still glued to the computer screen.

"Hey!"

I give her a gentle poke in the arm.

"Huh?"

"So, whatdaya think, Bonnie?"

"Huh?"

I give her a nice smile.

"So?"

"Did you say something, Jack?"

Oh, brother. I'm doomed.

"That's it. I've decided, Jack."

Okay.

"I'll catch the shuttle up to La Guardia Airport. Rent a car. And drive to New Milford, Connecticut."

Really.

My head drops to my chest.

"Jack! You need to go with me. I can't do this on my own."

Really.

"So. Are you in?"

More than you know, babe.

Chapter 22

Senate Majority Leaders' Office
Morning

SENATOR FRANKLIN HENNESSY is pissed.

Holding a telephone in his one hand, he shuffles documents on his desk with the other.

"A cat, Howard? That's your idea of knocking her off the track? Get on her now, you jackass. She can't dig any deeper. We have only three days...tops."

Leaning back, he gives his wimpy friend, Howard Hall, on the other end a short listen.

Interrupting Hall, he says.

"I have to get onto the floor. Durbin is making his usual bullshit speech about Republicans being evil. Call me tonight. We'll need to see the Prince in the morning."

Hennessy slams down the receiver.

"Sonofabitch."

Howard Hall's White House Office

Hall, visibly agitated, hangs up the telephone. Then wrings his hands in a nervous gesture.

Dealing with the power players of Washington, DC, especially the ones he's known for ages, is one thing. But to be called a jackass is downright insulting. Thinking to himself that one day he plans to get even. He's not sure how. But he knows his close friend, President Gonzmart, will always stand by him.

They have a long history together. Going back to The Abbey. There are things he knows that no one else knows. Things, incidents and private matters, a few little white lies, that could bring the President down in a heartbeat.

While he's not about to use his trump card, he's comforted by the fact that it's there.

He breaks a sweat knowing that he still must deal with Hennessy, and the Prince.

They both scare the crap out of him.

Studying an e-mail on his laptop, he goes deep into a devious thought.

He grabs his telephone, punching in seven numbers.

A moment.

"Henning? Find that moron friend of yours, Pellicane. Our friend Miss Biersack is going to The Abbey on some sort of snooping exercise."

He listens for a moment.

"Yes. New Milford, Connecticut. Today.

Pause.

"I want you two to do something about her. Am I clear?

He listens.

"God dammit. Just do it!"

He slams down the receiver.

Chapter 23

The Abbey Prep School for Boys
New Milford, Connecticut
Afternoon

I maneuver the rental car to a parking spot behind one of those boxy Fed Ex trucks. We're near the entrance to the school campus.

I'm presuming that if you're not somehow connected to this place, you're liable to get towed. In the absence of a parking permit, I hear students will go out of their way to notify the administration of an illegally parked car on the campus.

Said students will likely get a commission on the towing fee. They promptly use it to buy more weed.

But don't tell anyone. I know that having attended a boys private boarding school in my youth.

Bonnie and I get out from the car and walk through the main gate. Checking out the young boys here I quickly notice a similar dress code. But, combined with varying degrees of neatness.

Ties seem to be optional. But not back packs.

In my day you had to carry a bag similar to an over-night carry-all. The Marist Brothers would be encouraged to see you navigate the campus, lugging a bag obviously loaded-down with books giving the impression you might not make it to your next class, nor even up two flights of stairs.

"That Connolly kid must be doing extra work," I would often hear the Brothers say to each other.

Little did they know that my bag had a sparsely filled-in composition book, and four bricks that I had lifted from our neighbors' front walkway late one night.

Of course, no one ever learned why Mister Stein, our neighbor, didn't see the missing bricks. He had fallen, broken his leg in three places on his front walkway while running to catch the 6:57 L.I. Railroad train into Manhattan.

Interesting.

The boys on the campus, while talking, pretend not to not even notice us. They are perhaps carrying on insightful and highly erotic conversations about the new crop of hot babes over at Saint Gertrude's School for girls. It's just down the road about a mile. But, I know better. I catch several of them giving Bonnie that "eye candy" look boys do when faced with a gorgeous woman that's beyond their reach, so to speak.

A Prep school snobby persona has many definitions. One being the failure to notice those in your immediate vicinity. Like within arm's length. Like perhaps someone beneath your station in life.

And, of course, someone older, and who's not part of the school administration.

I stand there as if suffering an attack of *"déjà vu."*

"Look familiar?"

That was Bonnie.

And I think she's deliberately breaking my chops.

She dressed in civilian clothes. For the trip up here from Washington, DC, she chose not to wear her tight fitting, well-tailored Naval Officers uniform. She knows it's a turn-on for most young men. And older men, as well. I now see that most of these boys can't keep their eyes off of her.

Suck it up, fellas.

Again. I've got to stop saying things to her during sex that will come back to haunt me. And, yes, everything does look familiar here.

"Doctor Shannon said he would find us between classes if we mill around the quad, whatever that is. "

She looks around.

"Let's walk down this way."

We walk through an archway that connects two buildings. We're now out in an open area that seems to be connected by walkways to other buildings on the far side.

"Commander Biersack?"

The voice of a man comes from our left side.

This guy is right out of central casting.

Prep school headmaster.

A pleasant chap. Slight British accent acquired at Oxford, but not overdone. Bow tie, mandatory, of course. Tweed jacket, tailor made with suede elbow patches...now really? And suede shoes. Probably Brooks Brothers, but I wouldn't tell them.

Doctor J. Butler Shannon fits the bill perfectly.

"Doctor Shannon? Bonnie Biersack. Thank you for seeing us on such short notice."

He grabs Bonnie's hand, holding it gently.

"My pleasure, indeed, Commander Biersack. I was looking for a woman in a Naval Officers uniform."

She points over at me.

"Jack Connolly, sir. He's with Homeland Security, sir."

I add to the introduction, "I asked Commander Biersack not to wear her uniform, sir. Didn't wanna send your boys into a tizzy."

Shannon looks as if he didn't get the implication.

Gay, you think?

We shake hands. But Shannon is noticeably silent, looking me over very carefully.

Then, "we've met, Mister Connolly?"

Just what I need. For him to remember that I had accompanied the President just a year ago as part of his detail.

And I do remember, of course, clearly. But, keeping up the charade is essential. You see, I must keep certain information from Bonnie. It's part of the over-all strategy, for some reason unknown to me, as ordered by the President.

"I'm sorry, Doctor Shannon. But, no."

Shannon looks a bit befuddled.

"Oh. Well. We get so many visitors here to our school I just simply cannot remember everyone. It's enough to remember my boys' names."

He chuckles, while I'm thinking this guy is most definitely unforgettable.

Bonnie says "what a beautiful setting, sir."

"Our boys find it to be a delightful atmosphere for learning. And the parents certainly hope they mature before heading off to University."

Now here I would point out that the parents hope their super bright and marvelous, dope smoking boy gets into a good college. That followed by a good job at which time they will be able to pay back Mom and Dad the outrageous tuition this place charges.

But I bite my tongue and add, perhaps, a more thoughtful comment.

"Lucky there's a girls school right down the street."

He chuckles.

I think he likes me.

I hope for not the wrong reasons.

Bonnie, on the other hand, gives me that look.

"Where would be a quiet place to talk for a few moments, Doctor Shannon?"

"Let's walk this way. It's in the direction of my next class."

"You teach as well, sir?" Bonnie asks.

"Oh, yes, my dear. Must get into it with my boys, you know. They need to see the juices flowing. I let them tap into my brain with whatever is on their young minds."

Sex!

Okay. I need to be a little more respectful. Get my little brain out of that rut where it spent most of my rebellious youth.

Although, I am now convinced this guy is a little bit light in the loafers.

As we walk across the quad, most of the young fellas recognize Doctor Shannon with a little wave, or even a "good morning, sir."

Shannon just nods in their direction, the privilege of being in charge.

Since they seem to be showing some respect for Bonnie and I as we're walking with the BMOC (big man on campus) they offer us a smile as well.

Aren't they special young boys?

Although I did turn to look back at a couple of fellas after passing us, and noticed they were locked on Bonnie's cute butt, salivating.

I smile at them.

And give them a thumbs up, including a wink that says, been there, done that, suckers.

They give me the finger.

"You sounded quite rushed on the telephone, Commander Biersack."

Bonnie says, "sorry for the short notice, sir...but."

She sighs, looking towards a large statue in the middle of the quad.

"Doctor Shannon. Could The Abbey have any connection with the politicians who are involved with the Gulf of Aqaba agreement…I mean on both…or either side?"

Shannon lowers his head, and grunts.

"That's a strange question, Commander Biersack. I'm not sure if I even understand the context."

He stops and looks right at her, almost as if making a firm statement of fact.

"Nothing comes to mind."

He continues, now walking at a slightly faster pace.

A young student hurries past, "good morning, sir."

Shannon nods as Bonnie looks back at the young man, taking note of the blue and white skull cap on his head.

"Jewish…sir?"

"Ten percent of our boys are Jewish, Commander Biersack. The parents embrace our environment. The combination of academics and discipline, of course."

He pauses, giving Bonnie a nice smile.

Whispering.

"The ones with deep pockets, you know."

Looking in several directions, as if to point out someone, he says, "I'm sure you would recognize the names of some of our boys, Commander. We draw from a very influential crowd, both here in the States, and over-seas."

We walk slowly towards the center of the quad.

"Although, we have had some concern over those of the Muslim faith. Fortunately, we have a dedicated and heavily financed parents and alumni council. They bring in specialists in religious education, including the finest therapists. Men and women who spend time with those boys who, shall we say, need re-direction."

He smiles at Bonnie.

I, on the other hand, think brainwashing.

Forty grand a year, huh? That's what I'm told.

That gets your little towel head camel jockey-in-training kid, or yarmulke wearing, snot nose smart ass pushed into Christianity.

I wonder if Doctor Shannon passes out copies of the United States Constitution that these boys can stick under their pillows at night. You think?

We have now reached the center of the quad where there is this almost frightful looking statue about ten feet off the ground.

It's bronze, and the person it depicts is rather stern looking, not at all friendly, and cloaked in what appears to be a cassock.

My recognition is instantaneous.

Bonnie's gaze is frozen on the face as her eyes meet the eyes of the person in the form of a bronze statue. Then, an audible gasp as she suddenly realizes who it is.

I, on the other hand, wonder if she's seen the ghost of some long lost relative. Perhaps the black sheep of the family. Whomever, it has sent a chill through her body.

Doctor Shannon steps alongside Bonnie, smiling with obvious delight.

"Our largest benefactor, Commander Biersack."

He faces her.

"Archbishop Joseph Mendoza. Headmaster from the late sixties to the late seventies. A magnificent man. Truly someday will be a Saint."

I step up for closer look, feigning interest, of course. And he's looking right at me with evil in his eyes.

I should've kissed the ring.

"The trustees commissioned this piece of art, and deemed it be placed in this spot where all of us here at The Abbey pass-by each and every day."

I wonder how many boys sneak out here late at night. Hide behind Mendoza's likeness. And take a few puffs from their bongs.

"You may know of him, Commander. He's the Archbishop of Washington, DC, and…"

He takes a moment to look around as if not to be overheard.

"Soon to be elevated to Cardinal by his holiness, the Pope."

He steps back just slightly. His cell phone rings. He grabs it from his leather case, noticing the caller ID, and grunts.

Before answering he says to us while now viewing the Mendoza likeness, with true, unabashed admiration…

"Soon to be a Prince of the Church."

Chapter 24

The Abbey Quad
Moments Later

DOCTOR SHANNON had walked off several yards from Bonnie and I to take his call. He strolls back towards us after finishing his cell phone call.

"I'm so sorry. One of the trustees looking for me to review a nephew's admissions paperwork."

"Does that paperwork include financial statements?"

Doctor Shannon chuckles a bit. "Why of course, Mister Connolly. Why wouldn't it?"

"Just curious, that's all."

I don't like the look Bonnie is giving me. I best change the subject. Bonnie and I have tucked away Doctor Shannon's last statement about Mendoza being elevated to a "Prince" in our brains for discussion later.

Doctor Shannon focuses on Bonnie for a moment.

"Something troubling you, my dear?"

"Huh? Oh, no sir. Just thinking..."

Bonnie quickly regains her composure.

"...actually we've met. Archbishop Mendoza and I."

She refocuses on Mendoza's likeness.

"The Marymount University Sodality."

"I'll tell you a little secret, Commander Biersack. Something I'm truly thrilled about."

He shivers a bit.

"He's promised The Abbey twenty million...after the big day in Judea...he truly is a Saint. You think?"

Judea? Why did he say Judea?

I step in for a closer look at the inscription. Reading out loud, I want to make sure Doctor Shannon picks up on the one missing element.

"Alumnus...trustee...benefactor..."

Turning back at Doctor Shannon, "but nothing about being Headmaster for, what, ten years?"

It appears both Bonnie and Shannon have ignored my little discovery.

Bonnie asks.

"That's a hefty donation, Doctor Shannon. How is he able to re-direct a large amount of Church funds to this school?"

"Oh, dear. Not Church funds, for Lord's sake. Don't you know his family is extraordinarily wealthy?"

Bonnie nods a negative.

"Billionaires. That's with a capital B, my dear. His grandfather was *the* oil baron of Venezuela...1920's...1930's."

While Bonnie computes this new piece of information, Shannon steps closer to us, lowering his voice.

"No, it doesn't say Headmaster. I recall his tenure ended abruptly back in the late seventies. I was first form, you know, back then."

I catch Bonnie's frown.

I resolve her query. "Freshman...it's a preppy thing. You're from Ohio. You wouldn't understand."

There's that look again.

Doctor Shannon takes a nano second to look around, again, for eaves-droppers.

"There was this incident - apparently? Well, one of the trustees back then. A wealthy Jewish man. Sought to have Father Mendoza removed. Placing blame for the..."

Shannon appears to be a little uncomfortable.

"...distasteful behavior on the part of several of his boys."

I ask, "what incident?"

Shannon brushes off my question with a wave of his hand. Clearly not wanting to provide the "distasteful" details.

I press further, "so the trustees fired him?"

"Oh, no, Mister Connolly. Fire a Priest? God forbid. He resigned on his own. Apparently he discovered the noble trustee in question was having a secret, shall we say, *liaison* with the schools largest benefactor. A wealthy woman, no doubt."

Shannon stands a little closer.

"I trust you understand this is all hush, hush."

"On my word as someone who works for a political operative, sir." I add.

There's that look again from Bonnie.

"So, anyway. Let me continue. There's not a single shred of evidence about this incident in the Bishops file. He has a stellar record. A well respected former Headmaster."

He stands tall, giving us a smile.

"I've personally checked his file."

I think I'd have a problem with someone who rifles through private personal files. And probably late at night. Then pass on the information to complete strangers.

Like us.

And this guy is here to educate the future leaders of our country?

In the distance a bell rings.

"Oh. That's my signal. Have to scoot. I teach third form social studies. Today we talk about Venezuela. The Bishops' home country you know."

He turns and fast walks away.

"Junior year. Third form? Get it?"

Bonnie ignores me.

She calls out to Shannon, "thank you for your time, sir."

He yells back over his shoulder, "feel free to snoop around. Any of our boys will gladly help. We're all gentlemen here, you know, Commander."

Bonnie moves to a concrete bench facing the Mendoza likeness.

I follow and sit beside her watching the young boys run for their classes.

"So, I get it. They teach conspiracy as a science *and* a life style at this place."

She points at the Mendoza likeness.

"The Prince. We found the Prince, Jack."

Right. I'm glad she's paying attention to my insightful observation.

"Well, Bonnie, I would say it's time for us to pay a formal visit to the aforementioned and hugely adored Archbishop Joseph Mendoza."

"He's not the messenger, Jack."

I check the surrounding area for eaves-droppers. My guess is Mendoza probably has this entire place wired. I'm getting paranoid. Looking at his likeness I suspect he hears every word I say.

Shit. I should've kissed the ring.

Bonnie jumps up.

Turns, heading for the main entrance.

"Let's go, Jack."

Uh oh. Now what?

Chapter 25

The Abbey, Main Entrance
Moments Later

Try keeping up with a much younger, well-toned, hot blonde who's on a serious mission.

Hot blonde is the key here. Which, by the way, is enough for a forty something, ex-Naval Officer. Did I mention I spent a significant amount of my career under water in a submarine with 130 other sailors?

And I mean the male kind of sailor.

Regardless of the age difference, you push the envelope. Which is precisely what I'm doing now.

I can't be sure what jolted her superior brain. But it must be downright serious. One moment she was contemplating the Mendoza likeness back in the quad. And the next moment she's off at a sprint for the rental car.

I catch up, and key the remote lock.

As she goes for the door handle, I have to ask.

"I hope this is about being hungry for lunch."

"No. Get in!"

I move around to the driver side, hop in, and ask.

"Where to, Inspector?"

"The New Milford Library."

"Library? What's a library?"

"Very funny. They have old issues of newspapers going back decades. Usually on microfilm."

I start the car and pull out onto the street. I'm thinking maybe I'll head for that girls school down the street. It's near lunchtime and perhaps some of the young women students, a/k/a, jail bait, will be in the crosswalk.

You do know that in most places you must stop for pedestrians in a crosswalk.

It's the law.

Except South Beach. It's in Miami, Florida.

If you stop there for a closer look at the parade, it's akin to, say, bending over in the weekly group shower. You know, that all-purpose, government funded community "bath." The kind you find in Federal prison while doing three to five for humping jail bait.

Driver beware!

Anyway, I note a suspicious black sedan pull from the curb 30 yards behind us. I can't quite make out the occupants. Maybe two guys. Wearing shades. In the front seat.

They're either tailing us. Or they're drug dealers. Having just made a sale to a few polite school boys back at The Abbey.

My extensive training and superior street sense tells me the latter is perhaps unlikely.

"Take a left here. Are you watching the GPS, Jack?"

I hang a quick left, not wanting to respond to the my back-seat driver companion, a/k/a/, Bonnie Biersack. I don't want to alarm her to the presence of our sudden company.

The black sedan has made a left as well. It's now tailing us at about 70 yards back.

Or, more precisely, out of range for a small arms attack. Unless, of course, they're heavily armed with RPG's.

We cruise into New Milford, a typical quaint New England town. The cars are parked head in, at an angle, rather than parallel. I figure it must be one of those towns where they eliminate the parallel parking course in Driver's Ed. Probably not enough time given the need to use the same car for sex education, a more popular course.

I spot the Fed Ex truck seen at The Abbey turn a corner in front of us.

I pull into a spot on Main Street. I watch in the rear view mirror the black sedan rolling past us. I casually watch it pull into a space about a half block away.

"There. That's the Library. Let's go."

Bonnie points off to her right at an old brick building which is, without question, the Library.

The faded black letters over the doorway is a dead give-a-way.

It reads "Library."

"I never would've guessed."

There's that look again.

We both exit the car. We walk towards the Library door.

I take a quick look over my shoulder at the black sedan. Not wanting to be obvious, and stare.

Two occupants. Still wearing shades. They're looking our way.

The passenger looks vaguely familiar. I can't be sure who without a closer study.

I file this piece of Intel into my little brain. And follow Bonnie into the Library.

In the Library

Now the lady at the front desk could easily pass for my great grandmother. Stern looking. Gray hair in a tight bun. Wearing old fashioned calico. And granny bifocals.

Bonnie asks. "Old editions of the local newspaper, ma'am?"

The old broad is curt.

"Archives. Downstairs. On those machines. You can search by date, if you know what you're looking for, Miss."

Bonnie asks, "machines?"

This is where my superior street sense kicks in.

"I think she means computers."

She ignores me…again. So I refrain from commenting on the fact that we probably *don't know* what we're looking for.

"Thank you, ma'am."

She spins for the steps downstairs.

"Let's go. This could take a while."

Following Bonnie down the steps I suddenly have a sense of *déjà vu*.

"I haven't done this since my senior year in Prep School. We would hook up with the girls at Rosemary Hall."

Bonnie thinks for a moment. Then…

"Did what? Library research for extra credit?"

I smile. A distant thought pings around my perverted mind.

"Went off to a quiet corner with Jackie Rupert in the village Library. We had a copy of Chaucer's Canterbury Tales."

"Did you read it or just look at the pictures?" She asks with a sarcastic tone to her voice. She gets that from me, no doubt.

Although, I must admit, I don't recall there being any pictures.

Bonnie finds a free computer. Sitting quickly, she attacks the keyboard.

"Sit in front of the one next to me, Jack. You check 1973. I'll check 1974."

At this point I'm afraid to ask what I'm supposed to be looking for while skimming through 40 year old issues of a local newspaper.

I hope there're lots of pictures.

Later

I've lost track of the time. Mainly the result of reading insightful reports on the huge success of the local ladies club monthly covered dish picnics. I gotta meet this Miss Petie Balsam who, according to the numerous reviews, has a wiz-bang recipe for a deep dish turnip, tuna, and lima bean casserole.

Despite the sickening thought of such a dish, the reviews would make Julia Child blush.

Now that I've completely lost my appetite for anything, I turn to Bonnie and comment.

"I'm yearning for a barf bag."

"Huh? What have you been doing?"

"Got anything, babe?"

I'm quick on my feet.

"Yeah. Maybe. April 25th issue, 1974. Buried on the second to last page."

I scan the page and note the headline that jumps out at us.

"Headmaster Resigns. Sodality Disgraced."

Bonnie starts to read the highlights of the story.

"Certain fourth form members of the Sodality were allegedly engaged in homosexual activities. While it's just speculation, interviews with school officials and selected students seem to confirm parts of the story. Although solid evidence is still missing."

"Fourth form. That's seniors. I'm just saying."

Bonnie ignores me.

"There's no mention of who, Jack. But it appears that Mendoza has covered up most of the incident with some convoluted spin."

"So why resign?"

"Listen to this, Jack...Board member and trustee, Caesar Gonzalez Martinez, also known in the greater Miami, Florida area as a successful and powerful developer..."

She turns to me.

"The President's father, right, Jack?"

I nod.

"...made serious and extremely vocal accusations of a cover-up. And also informed the Board that he would withdraw his annual hefty contributions to The Abbey if the whole truth fails to come out."

I, of course, know of the President's connection to The Abbey. But I had no idea that connection involved contributions. Including a few gay students – presumably - and, more importantly, to the aforementioned Archbishop of Washington, DC, Joseph Mendoza.

"Jack. We need to get a copy of this story."

"Right, chief."

Time to check in with Madame Librarian.

I walk up stairs to the old broad's desk. I indicate our need for a copy.

She says, "I'll come down and take care of that for you."

We both head back down to Bonnie, who continues to stare at the story.

The Librarian sits at the computer and keystrokes the instructions. Bonnie has moved over. But watches.

"Jack. We need to find a year book."

"Right, chief. I'm on it."

The Librarian, ease-dropping, says.

"Upstairs. Reference section."

A printer on a distant table whirs to life. The Librarian moves to collect the copy. I can't help but note she has printed two copies of the story. One of which she hands to Bonnie. The other she keeps.

She moves back up the steps to her guard post without saying a word.

Interesting.

Bonnie and I head for the reference section.

"We need 1974. Hopefully there will be information on the Sodality members from that year."

"Chances are they're all serving hard time in a Monastery somewhere."

Bonnie sighs. Then continues with her insightful thought, despite my interruption.

"From there we should be able to get our hands on the alumni directories. They may give us current addresses and phone numbers."

"And current boyfriends, you think?"

"Idiot!"

Now I should mention that while I find this little expedition interesting, I understand Bonnie's objective here. Which explains why I'm on-board. I also understand dealing with powerful politicians connected to powerful and influential money, you take a chance. It involves opening a new window on a potential problem. A problem that's somewhere between maybe no problem, and perhaps harmful to your well-being.

Like ending up missing, i.e. Jimmy Hoffa.

Or dead.

Again, which explains why I'm here.

Not to mention the two suspicious individuals outside who may have an interest in what we're up to.

Things are definitely getting interesting.

We find the 1974 year book for The Abbey rather quickly. And, luckily, an alumni directory.

Bonnie sits and pages through the issue. I gaze out the window hoping to regain an appetite. I can see the Fed Ex truck swing around, making a U-turn to cover the opposite side of the street.

"Jack! Here it is. A picture of the Sodality members from that year."

I stroll over and have a look at the photo.

The photo illustrates five young men. Perhaps teenagers. On closer examination, the dress code of these young men suggests a photo taken in the early 1970's. They stand, posing in front of a small, yet well-appointed alter. The trappings in the background easily identify this worship space as Roman Catholic.

Bonnie reads the caption.

"Franklin Hennessy, Howard Hall, a Richard Cerzanski, a Malcolm Lamb, and…oh, God, Jack…look!"

"Huh?"

"Noah David."

"You mean as in Noah David, the current candidate for Prime Minister of Israel? Bonnie, do you mean that Noah David? A Jewish kid part of the Sodality?"

We both stare at the photo for long heartbeat.

I then add, "but no President Gilberto Gonzmart."

"Apparently not a member, Jack."

Bonnie leans back, deep in thought.

I, on the other hand, have considered Howard Hall to be a little light in the loafers. So, the news story has legs.

"Jack. Check the alumni directory."

"Right, Chief."

I page through the book to the class of 1974.

"Okay. Cerzanski, Richard Anthony…hum…killed in Lebanon…Beirut. With all those Marines."

I give her a look.

"Likely not the messenger."

"Jack!"

"Sorry. Wanted to see if...okay, let's move on."

I flip through more pages.

"Lamb, Malcolm Donald...unknown."

"Huh? Unknown? How could he be unknown?"

"Probably doesn't wanna be known, Bonnie."

"You mean he doesn't want to be found. You think, Jack?"

"Sounds plausible. You're getting smarter by the minute. But we need someone who knows how to find people who don't wanna be found. And we need that person yesterday."

"Okay, Jack. Think about that. I need to use the rest room."

Bonnie leaps from her chair, making a bee-line for the ladies rest room.

I get up, walking over to the Librarian to ask for a copy of these pages. I glance out the window and stop in my tracks.

On the far side of the street I spot twiddle dee and twiddle dumb hovering around that black sedan.

Also known by those in the Service as Henning and Pellicane.

And here I thought they were stuck in China with an insane woman named Julia. That was shortly after the last time I had a confrontation with those two morons in Texas and South Carolina. But, now that I give it some thought there was some mention of their return to the states. They were absolved of any connection to the attempted abduction of former President Melissa Callen.

I'm not so sure I agree with that conclusion. But, be that as it may, they're here in New Milford, Connecticut. And I don't think on a tour taking in the spring color changes.

I hand the book to the Librarian.

"I would like copies of the pages I've marked. Thanks very much. Please tell my friend to wait here. I've got an errand to run."

I head for the rear door. I'm out, walking quickly around the old building.

I'm not visible to Henning and Pellicane. So, I move down the sidewalk. But I can see them about 200 yards away.

Between us is the Fed Ex truck.

I move onto the truck into what would be a passenger seat area.

The driver, seated in his seat, looks over at me and winks. Then back to his chore at writing on a tablet.

Why did this guy wink?

I'll deal with that later.

Right now I need some help.

"Hey, man. How's it going today?"

"Slow, man. You?"

"Look. I need a small favor."

He stops his writing. And peers over at me. This time, no wink.

I remove my wallet and flash my Secret Service badge. He takes a moment to read it twice. His eyes widen.

"No shit. For real, man?"

"Yeah. Look. See those two dudes over there. Around that black sedan. Wearing shades?"

The Fed Ex guy looks. And sees. And nods.

"I need you to take this truck and block them in. Then get out. And walk into the Library. Okay? Tell them you'll be just a minute. Don't take any crap from them. Just wink. And bolt into the Library."

The Fed Ex guy looks at me. Then over to Henning and Pellicane for a long moment. Then back to me.

"They're not gonna shoot me, are they?"

"No, no. Of course not. They're not armed. Just a couple of dopes wanting to pester my charge. Are we cool?"

He nods a few times, like he's all in. Then…

"I aint gonna get shot, right?"

Now I gotta be a PR guy.

"Look, what's your name? I will personally make sure you get a special commendation from the President himself."

The Fed Ex guy thinks for a moment. Then says.

"Okay, man. I'm in. I did vote for the guy."

He hands me a business card with his information. I take it and head back to the rear door of the Library.

Barreling through, I spot Bonnie up front with the Librarian. She, of course, doesn't look happy, having to spend a few extra minutes with the old bird.

I go for the front window for a look to see if my plan is in place.

The Fed Ex driver has moved his truck to a spot where Henning and Pellicane's black sedan is blocked in, unable to leave until the truck moves.

I watch as the driver bounds out of his truck.

Henning is clearly calling after him.

The Fed Ex driver, being the stand-up guy I figured he'd be, shouts something back to Henning over his shoulder. And winks. What a trooper.

Henning stops. Looks for a moment. Then gives the Fed Ex guy the finger.

Nice.

"Where were you, Jack?"

"You ready to go yet?"

"What?"

At this point the Fed Ex guy comes through the front door of the Library.

Stops and smiles at me.

No wink.

I give him a thumbs up

"Well played, my man. You're the best."

"Cool. When do I get that letter from the big guy?"

"I guarantee it will be in the mail tomorrow."

I pat him on the back, grab Bonnie by the hand. And bolt out the front door.

We jog over to the rental.

"Hop in, Bonnie."

Once in, I back out of the head-in space. Shift to drive. And accelerate down the street. We pass Henning and Pellicane now in full view of Bonnie.

Bonnie holds a stare on those two. Then asks.

"Hey. I think I've seen those two dudes before.

I try to be uninterested.

"Who?"

"You know…I think they work for Howard Hall doing some advance work…or something."

"Really? What would they be doing here in New Milford, Connecticut?"

Bonnie has now turned, looking hard through the windshield.

Putting her super-charged brain into that intel mode she's so good at. She's faster and smarter than a Dell laptop.

I can see she's computing all the facts of the last several minutes. I know her. I'm clearly in a bind now.

"What the hell's going on, Jack?"

"Nothing. Nothing, really."

She's still thinking.

She trembles.

"Am I in danger, Jack?"

Chapter 26

**Main Street
New Milford, Connecticut**

Henning stares down the Fed Ex guy, who's about to take a dump in his pants.

"Look, man. I was just following orders. Ya know, that guy was Secret Service, man. Had a badge."

"And you know that badge was legit?"

"Hey. I'm just a driver. Fed Ex don't pay me to check badges, man. You gotta a badge? So, why don't you just chill?"

Henning grabs the hand grip on his Glock .378 strapped to his belt.

"Yeah, big shot. I have a badge."

The Fed Ex guy breaks a sweat.

"Look. All he said was to block your car in. Run into the Library. That I'd get a personal commendation from the President. That's it."

Henning seethes.

Then backs away, saying to the Fed Ex guy…

"Get the hell outta here."

The Fed Ex guy leaps in his truck, fumbles for the keys for a moment. After starting, he leaves rubber pulling out.

Henning moves over to Pellicane. He's standing on the sidewalk taking in the pretty skirts strolling up and down Main Street.

"Some nice MILF in this town, bro."

"Lighten up, Pellicane. I 've gotta call that Nancy in the White House. He's not gonna like what I have to say."

Henning takes several steps away while punching a number into his iPhone.

A moment.

"Yeah. It's me. Things didn't go as planned. They slipped away from us."

Pause.

"I know what to do, Hall. I got the pizza guy on ice. He's waitin' for my call. You know who I mean, right?"

Pause.

"He can handle it. Alright? Jesus H Christ. Chill out, man. You're gonna have a coronary."

Henning disconnects.

Pellicane has to needlessly say...

"More love and kisses from Howie?"

"We gotta get that dyke a boyfriend."

Chapter 27

Connecticut Countryside
In the Rental Car
Moments Later

The silver Chevrolet rental speeds down state route 7 in western Connecticut. There's little traffic. The new spring bud colors are popping all over.

I remember my dad always talking about the best part of Prep School in Connecticut was the springtime. And the subtle change from winter to spring. He attended the Kent School, somewhere near here. He had my application into the school within a month after I was born.

He was a planner.

By the time I was to enroll, tuition costs had been out of reach. Only sons and daughters, the likes of Kennedy's, Bush's, crooked Wall Street bankers, and Arabs with oil wells, could make the cut.

Bubba Bill Jefferson Clinton of Arkansas would have been accepted had he not claimed his middle name was in recognition of the third U.S. President, Thomas Jefferson. It was, in fact, in recognition of Jefferson Davis, the President of the Confederacy.

Connecticut Yankees are not that stupid.

"You're not in danger. I'm just cautious."

I need to keep Bonnie calm. Not let her unravel. Although she appears to be sitting next to me. She's fidgeting with her iPhone.

"You know, Jack. I've concluded that the Sodality was a cover for something truly evil."

Trying to see that she looks carefully at all sides of this bizarre issue, I add.

"Or, it just brought them together by coincidence."

"Huh? You once told me you don't believe in coincidences, Jack."

Like I've said before. I need to undo most things I've said during sex. But, maybe not that one. I don't believe in coincidences, really. So, she may be on to something.

She continues.

"Mendoza protected them. He resigned rather than expose them. There had to be a price of some kind."

"Perhaps a secret pact. That's more likely. If Mendoza had control of those boys, he'd be in a position to get their cooperation."

Bonnie gazes to her left, spying an old church that could likely date back to colonial times.

"Jack. Who would not want the Gulf of Aqaba agreement to work? It truly coalesces religious freedoms."

I give this a little brain power, concluding with my usual conspiratorial theories involving crime.

"Maybe all of them, Bonnie. They're all in on it, one way or the other."

"Yeah. I'm on that page."

Really? I'm beginning to rub off on her.

Interesting.

"Well, Jack, we now know that Mendoza is the Prince."

I'm thinking that Mendoza has always considered himself a Prince. This would explain why the messenger, who must clearly know Mendoza, referred to him as the Prince. Must be an ego thing with the guy. Although with the kind of wealth we know he possesses, calling himself something he is not yet is perhaps a side effect of his personality.

Given that brilliant Freudian analysis, I must say there is perhaps a small criminal effect in play here. Why would Bonnie attract the interest of two thugs like Henning and Pellicane?

Obviously, it's the connection with The Abbey, and a couple of swell fellas from Washington, DC. As Bonnie suggests, the common thread, i.e., the Gulf of Aqaba Agreement, points to trouble in the kingdom.

Which brings me back to Bonnie's intuitive question. Is she in danger?

My gut says yes.

But, I'm not sure yet as to why.

Bonnie looks over at me.

"Penny for your thoughts."

You don't wanna know, babe. But...

"Do you think there may be something out of place with the Agreement, Bonnie?"

Bonnie ponders that thought. Then adds.

"Well, you know there are religious fanatics out there of all stripes. Not just the Muslim Brotherhood, or Hezbollah, ISIL, or those Iranian screwballs."

"How about inside the Catholic Church?"

"Bite your tongue, Jack Connolly."

"I'm just saying, some of the facts lead to Mendoza, soon to be a Cardinal. A Prince of the Church. Someone with extraordinary power."

Bonnie goes off into deep thought mode.

I try to change the conversation to something different.

"I think we can make the last shuttle back to DC."

She snaps back. "We have to find Malcolm Lamb."

"Okay, I'm good. We'll call alumni in the AM."

"You think there's a hidden agenda, Jack?"

"If that's a possibility it goes all the way back to the 1970's, and The Abbey."

That I'm certain of.

Bonnie sighs before coming to a conclusion.

"So the big ugly finger points to the Bishop. Deep pockets. The American dream. If you want it, just buy it."

"I never thought you to be the cynical type. How about metaphorical?"

She grunts.

I continue with my thought.

"A Super PAC?"

It's like a light has gone off in her brain.

"Yes. And the Supreme Court has made that all the more possible."

I think my brilliance is rubbing off on her. It's good to be older and wiser.

Bonnie pivots at me.

"Do you think it's a coincidence that Gonzmart and Hennessy ended up in positions of enormous political power?"

Sometimes she can be a slow learner.

Women.

What can I say?

"First of all, you know my position on coincidence. Secondly, the aforementioned hypothesis is not possible, vis-à-vis, the Gulf of Aqaba agreement in the absence of including the current rock star of the Middle East, Noah David."

Notice how I cleverly put together all the pieces from what we have learned today.

After a long moment, Bonnie opens up.

"Jack. I'm scared. I saw guys I know back there. Henning and Pelicane."

Chapter 28

Bonnie's Home
Alexandria, Virginia
Early Morning

It must be very early in the morning. The sun coming up in the east. I hear the faint sound of birds chirping in some sort of sing-song fashion that could easily get quite annoying after a while.

But, I don't care.

I'm getting to sleep-in, for once, after a long day yesterday up in the nutmeg state, a/k/a/ Connecticut. Home to Vince McMahon, the WWF honcho who has made millions bringing wrestling, home of the "smack down," to the family TV room.

A sport that involves a bunch of tattooed, hardened, over-weight, tight butt morons in speedos playing fake rough house on a canvass mat.

Isn't America wonderful?

Then there was the, ah...work out last evening with my new main squeeze, Bonnie. A work out that gave new meaning to the girlfriend/boyfriend "smack down."

I, of course, remembered to think twice before revealing anything that could be repeated back to me at inappropriate times.

Which means I must be getting comfortable in this relationship.

And I think Bonnie is feeling the same about me.

Although, I need to be careful about going too quickly. I'm still faced with that proposed weekend in Dayton, Ohio with Ma and Pa Biersack. I'm still working out a clever excuse. Last nights' activities may have set me back somewhat.

As I go to roll over with more pleasant dreams about our budding love affair, I hear a faint, yet noticeable "click."

It's a familiar sound. One that I've heard before. But in my current semi-conscience state I'm having trouble connecting the dots.

Then…I get it.

And quickly flip onto my back.

Open my eyes.

And I now find myself staring down the barrel of a 9mm Glock handgun.

Which, I think just might be my handgun.

Bonnie is now screaming at me.

"Who are you? Answer me! Who the hell are you?"

I raise my hands in a defensive gesture as my eyes have noticed the safety has been flipped off.

Ergo, that clicking sound I heard a moment ago.

"Bonnie! Please! Let me explain. I can explain. Just…just…please, point the gun over there. The safety is off-"

"I know the safety is off. I turned it off."

I quickly compute the pressure needed to pull the trigger and conclude that she has more than the strength to do so.

And in her current agitated state, may do so accidently.

Secret Service Agents have their handgun trigger pressure settings rolled down from the manufactures recommended factory settings. They're set for sport shooting before leaving the factory.

Defending the President of the United States, and other high level charges in the midst of a gun battle, is not a sport.

It's the real deal.

"Talk fast Connolly, because I'm about to pull the trigger."

"Okay. Okay. Let me get out of bed –"

"Stay where you are! You need to explain the e-mail."

I frown hard.

"Another mysterious e-mail?"

"Right, Connolly. Except this one is not so mysterious. It mentions you by name. You are Jack Connolly, right?"

Now I'm confused. I mean I am who I say I am. And she's known me for what, four, five years?

"Bonnie. Let me see that e-mail. Maybe I can make some sense out of it."

"It's a trick. Don't you play any tricks on me, Connolly because right now I'm having trouble putting everything that's gone on the past few days into a clear picture."

And I can assume her mind is out on some ledge right now doing just that. I need to stay calm and get her to show me that e-mail.

"Right. I understand, Bonnie."

"Get up! Slowly. Sit on your hands."

"Right. Good call."

She backs away, but still holding me in her gun sights.

I get into a sitting position on the bed, my hands tucked neatly under my butt.

She moves over to the laptop, not taking her eyes off of me. She manages to print off a copy of the notorious e-mail.

Grabbing it from her printer she gives it a quick glance. Then throws towards me.

Not being a paper airplane it drifts to the floor about halfway between us.

"Pick it up! Slowly!"

She's so rattled now I'm almost afraid to read the incriminating document.

But I take it. And read it...twice.

"Holy shit!"

"That's all you got, Connolly?"

It's not from the same guy that sent her an e-mail several days ago. And he, or she, is connecting me to a group that is out to sabotage the Gulf of Aqaba agreement.

And, like a bolt of lightning, my quiet, revealing conversation at Starbucks with Monsignor Roger Schneider, Archbishop Mendoza's side-kick, comes sharply into focus. His talk with me the other day was a warning, of sorts. And my connection to the Monsignor needs to remain confidential at the moment. His role runs along the edge of danger to this willing partner.

The tone of the new e-mail clearly outlines what I don't want Bonnie to know. It's now obvious that one of our concerns – i.e., myself and the President – was I could be used as a wedge between him and Mendoza.

It's a long story that will take a while to explain. I promise to make it all clear.

Soon.

But, right now I need to get Bonnie off "that ledge."

She is holding my Glock, safety off, pointed at me. And as any good Naval Officer will tell you, she knows how to use it.

It is safe to say that I've perhaps been used to unknowingly foster the development of some far reaching, outrageous plan the good (sic) Bishop has hatched.

Emphasis, "unknowingly."

A plan he had perhaps hatched many years ago using the influence of his family's enormous wealth, and the convenient, long term relations with my Great Grandfather, Don Pedro, and Grandfather, Don Mateo, two men – father and son – who, while apparently in possession of secretive and confidential facts, have a connection with the Holy See in Rome that, I've been told, goes back to World War II.

Mind you, what I know is sparse in comparison to what is truly going on in the Bishop's short circuited brain. There's certainly more to Mendoza's plan to reclaim Judea in the name of the Catholic Church.

As a youngster, I was exposed to very bizarre conversations that had little meaning in my little brain.

A plan that somehow is connected to the lost cross.

The cross Jesus died on 2000 years ago.

Before I go any further, this related - aforementioned above - but not relevant part of the current messy state of affairs is put on the back burner.

Here and now in Bonnie's home, is a more relevant situation.

She has a gun pointed at me.

And she's pissed.

Without preamble for her benefit, or a detailed explanation, I look at Bonnie.

"Bonnie. My job is to protect you."

Her eyes widen.

A heartbeat.

"My best guess right now is that e-mail has come from a co-conspirator. Someone close to the Bishop. Someone who's trying to use me to drive a wedge between us."

"It says there's a long term connection between Mendoza and your family. Something that was clear to me when the Bishop asked about your Grandfather and Great Grandfather."

She creases her brow.

"Fess up, Connolly. Now!"

Well trained submarine Commanders, like myself, are able to handle tense, near deadly situations like this. At this point I would usually grab the nuke key from the chain around my neck and lock it into the weapons firing panel.

Of course, there's always a second officer, the nuke Commander, with a key. Both are needed to fire the nuke.

In this case, I'm it.

All alone.

"Okay, Bonnie. Here's the story."

She's breathing heavily. Maybe she'll hyperventilate, and pass out.

Maybe not.

"My Great Grandfather's family, the Spinetti's of Caracas, screwed the Mendoza family out of ½ their oil fields. About 60 years ago.

It's been a McCoy's verses the Hatfield's situation ever since.

"How?"

"My Grandmother, many years ago, and after way too many Martini's, told me that Elbano Spinetti, a close great uncle, delivered a suit case full of cash to "El Presidente" in Caracas."

"A pay-off?"

"Right. Transferring certain drilling rights from the Mendoza cartel to the upstanding, generous and charitable Spinetti family."

She slowly lowers the weapon.

A long, thoughtful heartbeat.

Then…

"So…you mean we're both in danger, Jack?"

And there you have it, folks.

A clean get-a-way.

By yours truly, Jack Connolly.

Chapter 29

Residence of the Archbishop
Washington, DC
Archbishop Joseph Mendoza's Office
Early Morning

The huge office is dimly lit. The drapes pulled only partially that cover the floor to ceiling windows on two sides.

The silence is deafening.

Until the large, heavy oak door suddenly creaks for a nano second. Then crashes open. It's being pushed easily by Monsignor Schneider, Mendoza's aide.

Schneider stands to the side, holding the door open.

A moment passes before Bishop Mendoza parades into the office.

In arm chairs near the stone fireplace, Senator Franklin Hennessy and White House advisor Howard Hall leap to their feet.

Hennessy says firmly, "good morning, your excellency."

Hall nods at the Bishop accompanied by a thin yet tight smile looking as if the proverbial cat got his tongue.

Mendoza stops and faces the two. Eyeing both individually with a level of disdain. He shifts his eyes down and to the right.

"Leaves us, please, Roger."

Monsignor Schneider exits pulling the door shut with a noticeable thud.

Mendoza strolls over to a window. He takes a moment to enjoy in the budding colors outside his office.

Then…

"Sit."

Both men sit in chairs that are angled towards the chair the Bishop uses for such encounters.

With his back still towards Hennessy and Hall, Mendoza speaks in a soft, yet firm tone.

"I'm so very close, boys. My day is almost here. That special day we have been planning…and praying for, together."

He turns, now facing these men whom he's known for forty years, or more. A thin smile develops.

"As a family, no? And it's so close I can actually touch it. Feel its divine spirit through my entire body."

He's back to gazing out the window.

A moment passes before he speaks again. Yet this time the tone has changed.

"I'm upset about what I'm learning from my…sources."

Hall squirms. Hennessy crosses his legs.

"Do either of you know what I have learned?"

Hennessy answers with a stroke of confidence.

"We had our men on the girl…and her companion…on both while in New Milford."

Mendoza spins hard at the two, his stance threatening.

"Well, Franklin, next time you might consider using a Fed Ex driver to supervise your little mission. Or perhaps a seventy year old librarian."

As Mendoza turns back to the window, Hennessy and Hall make eye contact knowing it's gonna get ugly.

"What do you think she now knows?"

Hennessy shrugs, then answers.

"Perhaps only that we were all at The Abbey at the same time. Nothing that's not already public information. I can't see what damage that could cause."

Pause.

"They wasted their time, your excellency."

Speaking with his back to both, Mendoza casually asks.

"And what is it that you two have learned?"

Hennessy and Hall are silent, not fully understanding Mendoza's question.

He clarifies.

"Nothing about her friend...and lover...Connolly?"

Howard "the Wimp" Hall starts with a slight stutter.

"He was a military advisor, assigned to the executive branch. Now with the Secret Service."

Mendoza glares at Hall.

"You both should know, at least by now, and after all these years, my connection to Mister Connolly's family."

They both shrug.

Hall reluctantly asks.

"Then...you must know who put Connolly in place?"

Mendoza spins hard at Howard Hall, with fire in his eyes.

"I fully expected you to track every move Gilly makes in the White House."

He glares hard at Hall.

Obviously, you've failed me, Howard."

Hall slides lower in his chair as Mendoza steps closer to the two men.

"More importantly, gentlemen, Mister Connolly, as Assistant Director of the Secret Service, raises some serious concerns for me."

Both sit in silence as Mendoza takes a cigar from the humidor on his desk, including a clipper and solid gold lighter. He clips the cigar, then flicks the lighter, lighting the cigar with several long puffs, blown in Hall's direction.

Hall looks as if he may puke any second.

Hennessy chimes in.

"Perhaps just a routine assignment."

Mendoza glares at Hennessy who now uncrosses his legs.

Mendoza exhales, then speaks, having now settled into his oversized arm chair facing Hennessy and Hall.

"I'm suspicious about Mister Connolly's *attachment* to our Miss Biersack. I don't see Gilly making that assignment. Those decisions are made well below his position."

Another exhale.

And Hall turns away.

"Who else can assign agents?

Both men facing Mendoza, shrug, either not knowing, or simply afraid to respond.

The Bishop gives more thought to possible scenarios as he puffs away. He does think about calling the President but dismisses that idea. It may get Gilly thinking too hard about possible unintended consequences that may surround the agreement. He's hoping that the signed agreement and the election of his personal surrogate, Noah David, will deflect any misgivings about the agreement.

He certainly cannot allow Howard Hall to return to the White House, asking questions about Mister Connolly. That would definitely raise eyebrows within the Secret Service.

And it may, perhaps, put Mister Connolly on further alert to be particularly focused on not just Miss Biersack.

Still, there is a loose end that needs to be tied up. But the Bishop is not happy about that at this late date.

He asks.

"Why would they suspect Miss Biersack to be in danger?"

Hennessy offers.

"I still say it's a routine assignment."

"DIA has their own security force, Franklin. You're not thinking this through."

Hall jumps into the conversation.

"I can't see where she knows too much. I think we're worried about nothing."

Mendoza bites hard.

"Don't think, Howard. It's not your strong suit."

Mendoza stands and moves to his desk where he grabs a folded piece of paper. Unfolding it, he walks back to the two and hands it to Hennessy.

"What's that headline say, Franklin?"

Hennessy reads it to himself, then grabs a quick glance at Hall. Then, a soft read.

"Headmaster resigns. Sodality disgraced."

He folds the paper as if not wanting to read further.

Mendoza sits in his chair saying.

"They left New Milford with a copy of that story."

Hall has buried his face in his hand.

Hennessy says, "that was forty years ago. It has no significance today."

"Franklin. It all depends on how nosey Miss Biersack gets. Wouldn't you agree?"

Hennessy thinks a moment. Then adds.

"She can't link Noah David to any of us. That part you've handled brilliantly all these years. And Malcolm Lamb? He hasn't been heard from in years. Maybe longer. For all we know, he could be dead..."

"No one will find Malcolm...I've seen to it...personally." Mendoza smiles to himself as if having accomplished a rather clever cover.

But Hall needlessly has to ask.

"So, your excellency, you do know where Malcolm is?"

Biting hard again.

"What I do know, Mister Hall, is it's none of your business!"

Mendoza stands and moves back to his desk, sitting hard in his executive chair. He shuffles various papers, not looking at either two gentlemen.

"Howard. I want the girl dealt with. I worry that she's smarter than we think. Certainly smarter than you."

He gives Hall an evil stare. Then…

"My special piece of equipment, Howard?"

Hall takes what looks to be pen from his pocket, handing it to Mendoza, he says…

"It's a Zip Gun. Loaded with a 22 caliber round. Made of plastic. It'll burn…easily –"

"- place it on the desk, Howard."

Mendoza gives the weapon a look, but does not touch it, except to roll it over with his pen.

Hall wipes a bead of sweat from his forehead.

"Your excellency, I'm not sure –"

"- that will be all boys. Roger is waiting to show you out."

Leaving, Hennessy mutters "your excellency."

The door opens with a creak.

It closes with a thud.

Bishop Mendoza's eyes dart at the door.

Chapter 30

Bonnie Biersack's Home
Alexandria, Virginia
Morning

Why is it that women take so long to get themselves together in the morning? Or at any time, for that matter?

I did it in less than 15 minutes.

That was more than an hour ago and I'm still sitting here in Bonnie's kitchen having almost finished a pot of coffee.

But I did take the opportunity to map out my day. It's gonna start with a stop at HQ, that is Homeland Security. And to find out why those two morons, Henning and Pellicane, who linger around the White House on occasion pretending to look busy while catering to Howard Hall's every whim, were in New Milford, Connecticut yesterday.

Those two are suspicious to begin with. But their connection to Howard Hall, an alumnus of The Abbey School, is even more highly suspect.

I'm beginning to connect some of the dots.

Perhaps the President's idea of secretly assigning me to keep close tabs on Bonnie is more telling.

I'm not sure who knows of this assignment, other than the Secretary of Homeland Security. But that e-mail this morning is more trouble. Someone at HQ needs to have it traced. Although, Hall's men following us yesterday would naturally confirm that Hall either was in on the assignment, or has been told by some other source of my current mission.

My gut tells me it's the latter.

But who?

Once again, my superior street sense instinct points the big ugly finger at the Prince, a/k/a, Bishop Mendoza.

On the surface, the Gulf of Aqaba agreement fits nicely into the past and current narrative about Jerusalem offered by the Catholic Church. There should be lots of happy folks at the Vatican right now.

Then there's the other e-mail from the so called "Messenger."

While it seems authentic and serious enough in tone and direction, it could be a red herring thrown into the mix to knock off the Pentagon's effort at getting this thing done.

Bonnie's right about one thing.

We need to find this guy named Malcolm Lamb.

I'm giving this more thought while fingering Bonnie's over-sized car key.

"Don't press that red button. My Honda Accord will start."

She sneaks up behind me, kissing the top of my head.

I grab her, putting my arm around her thin waist.

"Ditched the biker image, huh? I sure liked that sexy outfit."

"No. I use the bike and the black leathers to escape. Kinda makes me feel more wholesome. You think?"

I get stuck in fantasy heaven while she breaks away to clean out the dishes in the sink. Standing, I bring my coffee cup over, and grab her waist again.

"Bonnie. I'll catch up with at your office. I need to make a stop at Homeland Security. I wanna check out that e-mail."

She takes a moment to glance over her shoulder at me.

"I also wanna know why Henning and Pellicane were in New Milford yesterday."

She turns to face me, a disturbed expression enveloping her pretty features.

"You're leaving me alone, Jack?"

I take her in my arms and give her one of those Jack Connolly smiles.

"You'll be okay. I promise."

After a peck on her forehead, her looks still a bit unnerved, I move away, folding my suit jacket over my arm.

I look at her, this time seriously.

"Bonnie. Just be aware of what's going on around you. You know, that extra sense?"

I smile.

She frowns.

I give her another kiss.

This one a little more passionate.

Hopefully, with good things to come later on.

Like maybe this evening?

You get the picture.

I step back.

"Now, I'm serious. Be very aware. Got it?"

She folds her arms.

Thinking, as her eyes cover the kitchen.

"Okay. I got it."

I head for the door.

She asks. " Is your gun loaded, Jack?"

Holding the door open, I stare down at the floor for a moment thinking that just maybe I've scared the crap out of her. I should've just taken a softer approach, knowing how fragile these Ohio woman can be.

Looking right her, "Bonnie, like all weapons law enforcement officers carry, there's always a round chambered, and my safety is transformed not to work."

It hits her. The weapon pointed at Jack earlier was "live."

Outside Bonnie's Home

Jack leaps into his ride. Fires up the 4.5 liter engine, and peels away from the curb as a pizza delivery van rolls slowly down the street.

Jack doesn't notice it in his rear view, focused on his iPhone as he careens down the street.

The side of the van is cleverly marked:

"My Cousin Guido's Pizza"

"Cheap Delivery"

"You Betta Call…Now!"

A phone number, in a smaller size, is printed on the Van's side panels.

"101-448-6261"

Underneath the phone number, someone has used a magic maker to carelessly write the corresponding letters to the keypad numbers.

"Hit-Man-1"

Its driver, GUIDO, stops on the street, but in a spot where he can see the rear end of a Honda Accord.

He gazes with a hapless expression at the Virginia Tag on the Honda.

It reads: B SERIUS

He scratches his head.

Then shrugs.

He continues slowly down the street to an open space about 50 yards away from the Honda. He pulls in, hitting the curb and scraping his wheel rim.

A dog barks from the front yard of the house opposite Guido's van.

Guido exits the van, leaving the engine running. In his hands, a 16 inch pizza box, although not in an insulated pocket bag.

In his other hand he carries an average size brown paper bag.

Walking towards the Honda as if searching for an address, he suddenly stops alongside the Honda. Bending down, and placing the pizza box on the sidewalk, he acts as if re-tying his shoe. A moment before he slides his arms, head and torso under the car, brown paper bag in hand.

Down the street, about halfway between the Honda and Guido's van, the dog starts to bark. This time with a degree of alarm.

From the front door of the house opposite the van, a woman quickly appears at the front door, having swung it open in a fit.

"Faydra! You dumb animal. Get inside! Right now!

The dog stops its barking. Looks back at the woman, then a look down the street at Guido.

A moment passes before the dog trots into the house.

The woman slams the door shut.

She can be heard yelling at the mutt.

By this time, Guido has surfaced from beneath the car, and proceeds back to his van.

Passing the house where the dog resides, the front door suddenly opens, startling Guido.

The woman appears, rather annoyed, standing on the front porch searching for something.

Guido stops, and holds a stare on her.

Then the woman shouts over her shoulder, into the house.

"I don't see that god dam thing. You come out here and look for his toy."

"Ecuse me, senora. You know 228 Henry Street, si?"

The woman takes a moment to look him over.

Then, using her thumb to point behind her.

"Henry's two blocks over."

Guido waves his thanks, and smiles.

As he turns to walk towards his van, the woman calls after him.

"Hey! Chico! You got a pizza there?"

Guido, who has now lost the smile, stops, and with his back to her, takes a nano second to think this through.

He turns, smiling once again.

"Si."

"How much?"

Guido shrugs, not wanting to answer.

"Come on, Chico. By the time you find 228 Henry it'll be cold. The customer's gonna tell ya to take a hike."

Guido shrugs again, pointing at his van.

"Hey! By the way. What the hell were you doin' under that girls car up there? You drop somethin' or what?"

And it's at this moment that Guido has made a decision about this annoying woman.

A woman who has perhaps seen something she should not have seen.

He walks towards her short walkway while reaching into his waist band at the small of his back.

"You wanna a Pizza, Senora, si?"

"Yeah. You got that right, Chico. Come on in."

Chapter 31

Crossing the Potomac River
Alexandria, Virginia
Morning

Pizza!

Why am I thinking Pizza?

It must be something subliminal.

It's not even the post breakfast time frame when I should be thinking about that third cup of Joe and not Pizza.

Anyway, it'll come to me.

What's coming to me is perhaps a stop at that Starbucks up Massachusetts Avenue where all the cute co-eds from American University hang out.

It *is* on the way to Homeland Security.

I gotta get off this trend.

One of these days I'm gonna slip-up and say the wrong thing to Bonnie.

As you probably know I've done that before.

And not just to Bonnie.

Usually those confessions come during or right after sex.

Right. Bad timing, I know.

As an old acquaintance once told me he has given his wife instructions should he ever stop admiring pretty young women she was to throw him in a pine box and bury him.

He's deathly afraid of losing his "mojo."

Anyway, I'm on my way to DHS. I need to get my arms around the fact that Henning and Pellicane are tailing us. And why. Then, find out who's behind that new e-mail.

I can only surmise that someone in the White House is behind both. Clearly someone who's likely not all that pulled together. No one with half a brain would employ Henning and Pellicane for any kind of work.

Those two bozos must have the goods on someone.

Maybe even pictures.

They were cut loose from their unplanned visit to main land China several years back. That was after the assassination of President Giordan. It obviously indicates they have some serious connections.

Which is why I say it's the White House.

But not the President.

He doesn't fit that profile.

So, the tail must have something to do with the President's assignment, given to me several months ago, to protect Bonnie. The tail being ordered by some big dog with connections and power.

But the President, I now think, knows more than he's let on with me.

I'd swing by the Oval Office for a chat, but that's not something you just simply decide to do on a whim.

On the other hand, I do know the President is a big fan of Pizza.

You see, I knew there was a Pizza connection to this puzzle.

Chapter 32

Suburban Street
Alexandria, Virginia
Morning

Bonnie bounds down her driveway from the rear entrance to her home on the second level of a two story house. Her purse is slung across her chest.

She holds the electronic keys to her Honda Accord in her hand.

Pointing at the car, several feet away, she squeezes. BEEP...BEEP.

She jumps into the car.

Keys the ignition to one click.

Waits a moment.

The sound of a woman's voice. "Alarm disabled."

And now a continuous buzzing sound.

The sexy voice, sans the Japanese accent, is always a pleasant sound, in Bonnie's opinion, each morning.

Sometimes she actually says "thank you, ma'am."

She looks to the right, and down on the floor.

"Shoot. Get it together, girl."

The buzzing, on a 30 second timer, stops.

She separates the bulk keys from the ignition key, leaving it in place.

Bonnie leaps out of the Honda.

Using a separate soft pad locking key, she points it at the car over her shoulder as she fast walks up her driveway.

BEEP...BEEP.

Bonnie vanishes around to the rear of her home as a Fed Ex truck has pulled up the street. It stops, and now blocks Bonnie's car.

The Fed Ex driver bounds from his truck with several packages in hand. He races across the street and onto the sidewalk. He proceeds to sprint down the street and out of sight. He's vanished.

Moments later

Bonnie walks quickly down her driveway from the rear door. Reaching the sidewalk, she stops suddenly, noticing that the FedEx truck has blocked her car in. She looks up and down the street for the FedEx driver. Not seeing him she throws her arms up in the air. She turns back, running to the rear of the house.

Moments later

Bonnie, atop her Suzuki 650 Savage motorcycle, roars out of the driveway turning quickly around the FedEx truck and heading away at an accelerated speed.

The Pentagon

So here I am sitting in Bonnie's DIA office at the Pentagon waiting for her to say something.

She looks exhausted.

I lean forward, getting closer to her, and look to say something encouraging.

"So, any more earth shattering ideas, Bonnie?"

"I'm out of ideas, Jack. I'm tired of making telephone calls."

She stares at her watch and I'm hoping she's thinking about getting something to eat because just sitting here watching her work is like sitting outside and watching the grass grow.

"Jack, he just can't disappear."

"Well maybe, he's just dead. You think?"

"If he were just dead, Jack, the alumni directory would say so."

She leans towards me, giving me that pouty look she usually does when she wants something special from me.

"And you're telling me that we cannot go to the Secret Service for help, Jack? I thought you were some sort of big shot at that place, right?"

Okay, things are getting a little dicey. I certainly cannot fill her in further on my very secret mission. I mean, I do have strict instructions from the President. The folks who know what's going on with her have to be kept in a very tight circle. Which at the moment I think only involves the President and yours truly.

"You got that right, babe. This whole thing has not been officially sanctioned by anybody."

She jumps to her feet. Leaning on her desk, she glares at me.

"What do you mean officially sanctioned, Jack?"

Oh boy. I may have accidentally stepped in it.

"Look, Bonnie. I need to focus on my job which is to protect you. Do you understand?"

"So let me get this straight Jack. If I disappear, I really didn't?"

"Yeah. Sort of."

Bonnie walks around her desk. She heads over towards the window. With her back to me she says, "Jack, I'm not letting you out of my sight."

Now I've got to keep the moment light. Can't get her too worked up or else she'll go out on that ledge again. So I think of something rather appropriate.

"Well, Bonnie, if you do disappear, maybe you'll run into Malcolm Lamb."

Bonnie spins quickly looking at me with a strong, frightful scowl. She relaxes.

"But Jack, everyone is known."

I get up and walk towards her, grabbing both her hands.

"If Malcolm Lamb is alive, and presumably he's an adult, he must have an ID, right?"

I think about that for a moment, considering the various ways we at the Secret Service would go about doing a background check.

"You know Bonnie, I think the IRS would be one place that would be able to at least hunt him down. They know every known, living and breathing Malcolm Lamb in the USA. If we could figure out a way to get them…"

Just like that, she "open palm" smacks me on the chest.

"Yeah, Jack! You're right. You're right"

"Huh?"

"Come on, Jack. Let's go. We're wasting time here."

And with that she makes a beeline for the door. She's out of her office and down the hallway.

I follow, trying to catch up with her.

"Bonnie! Where we going to now?"

"We're going to find a man of my dreams!

And to think all this time I was it.

I jump into the elevator just as the door begins to close.

Chapter 33

**Department of State
Employee Cafeteria**

So here we are standing at the State Department in their employee cafeteria. I'm alongside Bonnie. She's scanning the tables occupied by at least several hundred people. She's looking for this "man of her dreams."

I can't help but notice these wannabe diplomats of all ages keep glancing over at Bonnie. Maybe she likes that. It's why she just keeps standing here looking around. But actually I don't think so. She's looking for this mystery man.

I think she has found him because she tears off to my left at a fast pace.

I follow, commenting, "I hope he's worth it, Bonnie."

Typically she ignores me.

She has now stopped at a table occupied by a loan person. Someone who is clearly overweight. Someone who prefers to outfit himself at Sears, Roebuck and not Brooks Brothers, as is the custom here at the State Department.

Bonnie sits at the table across from this nerd.

I use the term nerd loosely. But confident that I'm not too far from wrong. It is perhaps the cheap taped-together glasses and the pocket pen holder on his shirt that gives him away.

"Bonnie. Is this him?"

"Yeah. Sit down here Jack!"

"Bonnie, I think you may need a shrink."

Looking at the amount of food on this nerd's tray I'm inclined to look around. I wonder who will be joining him for lunch. I point out the food, about to say something when Bonnie smacks my arm.

"Jack, this is Tommy Trumble."

Tommy, of course looks over at me, with an expression that says he's not aware of who I am nor what am I doing with Bonnie. If he only knew

"Hey, Tommy. I'm Jack Connolly. Nice to meet you."

Tommy shifts his focus to Bonnie.

"Hi, Bonnie. Having lunch? I eat here every Wednesday. It's burger day, you know?"

Tommy Trumble, my new straight man. I can't resist.

"So, Tommy. Let me get this straight. You cram in all five days of the week every Wednesday?"

Bonnie whacks my arm.

"I know you are here every Wednesday, Tommy. I've seen you here before. But, I've never had the nerve to come and sit with you. I feel so ashamed."

Is she really hitting on Tommy? I can't believe it. But, as I look over at Tommy he is now flashing a great big smile. She has made his day. Now she reaches over, putting her hand on his arm, and it's a huge arm. All blubber.

"Listen, Tommy, honey. I really need your help. And you are the only totally cool guy who can help me.

Oh brother, I'm going to throw up.

Tommy, still smiling very broadly, points over at me.

"You mean not even him, Bonnie?"

Bonnie shrugs, smiling at Tommy, she says. "Who? Him? Jack? Tommy, please, be serious."

Meekly, Tommy says, "okay."

"Now here's the deal, Tommy. I need to find someone... someone who is really important but is hiding somewhere. I need to know where he lives, where he works...whatever you can find. But I need to find this guy. It's very important for what I'm doing right now."

Tommy thinks for a moment.

"But doesn't the DIA have the resources to find people, Bonnie?"

"Oh, you know the drill, Tommy. Politics and all that nonsense. It just makes me sick. I can't get anything done most days. I'm stuck with having to use my own devices to solve gigantic problems. You do understand now, Tommy, don't you?"

Meekly, Tommy says, "okay."

"Now I realize several government agencies have all kinds of information, right?"

"Right, Bonnie. The IRS is the very best."

Tommy leans in towards Bonnie. He whispers.

"You know, Bonnie, they know everything."

He winks.

"Yeah, I know. I've heard a lot of very bizarre stories about what goes on inside the IRS. They've done some very nasty things to people who didn't need to be targeted because of their political views. That's just awful Tommy."

Tommy, jamming another burger into his mouth, gives her a thumbs up with his free hand.

Bonnie inches closer to Tommy, whispering.

"You'll need to get into the IRS personal data files and retrieve information on the guy I'm looking for."

"What?"

That was me. Jack.

"What?"

That was Tommy.

As a sworn federal law enforcement officer I now feel is my duty to handcuff this gorgeous, near genius, female naval officer and cart her off to the brig. Unfortunately, I don't have my handcuffs with me. The other problem would be that if I did handcuff her I somehow have misplaced my handcuff key. Therefore, I would be unable to set her free if she got really upset. Which is entirely likely.

So I need to initiate Plan B.

"Bonnie! Are you simply, no make that completely out of your freakin' mind?"

"Look, Jack. Tommy. It's our only chance. We have to find this guy."

"Oh, I don't know Bonnie. I mean, I can get into the IRS personal data files. But if I get caught I don't know what they would do to me."

I, of course think 'jail time', big guy.

"Tommy. You work over there, sometimes, right?"

Tommy nods very slowly.

Then meekly he says "okay."

"Tommy, I work over at the Pentagon. It's like exchanging information. Right? Agency to agency. Except this is an issue of national security. We need you to play an important role here in helping us all solve a great big ugly problem. If I had to wait and go through proper channels or, let's say the FBI, we'd all probably be dead by then."

Tommy sits perfectly still just staring at Bonnie.

"I need Tommy Trumble."

Tommy, looking quite nervous, shifts his huge frame around in his chair. Looking off into the distance, he's thinking very hard.

Then looking straight at Bonnie, expressing a sly deceptive smile, he asks…

"I could be like a spy, right Bonnie?"

Now my only reaction is to roll my eyes. I sigh quite noticeably. Bonnie darts a very lethal glare right at me then turns back towards Tommy.

"Tommy, you'd be my very special hero."

Tommy blushes, and tries to hide an embarrassed smile.

"So Tommy, will you do it?"

Tommy once again squirms around in his seat, thinking hard with a bizarre expression on his face.

"Okay, Bonnie."

Bonnie sits back in her chair, folding her arms, and smiling broadly.

"Great. I knew I could count on you, Tommy. You are simply awesome. Now, all I have is a name. And an approximate birth year."

"Oh sure, Bonnie. That's no problem."

"Great. I'll write it down for you right now."

Bonnie grabs a piece of paper from her pocket, and Yanks a pen right out of my shirt pocket.

"Hey! Bonnie, that was a special Christmas gift from my nephew, Brady."

Bonnie studies my pen very carefully. She frowns very hard. Then looking at me with questionable features. She says.

"A Spiderman pen? Please!"

Bonnie writes on the piece of paper at the same time telling Tommy what she is writing.

"His name is Malcolm Anthony Lamb."

She hands the paper to Tommy who now studies it very carefully before looking back up at Bonnie.

"No Social Security number huh, Bonnie?"

"The only thing we know, Tommy, is that he attended The Abbey Prep School in New Milford, Connecticut."

Tommy thinks for a moment.

"Well I sure hope there is just a few of those guys."

"That's okay, Tommy. It's certainly better than what we have right now."

Once again Bonnie leans back in her chair. Arms folded. And smiling broadly. After a moment, she turns at me and winks. I would like to wink back but I'm not sure if that's a good idea considering she has just asked Tommy Trumble to violate certain national secrecy regulations.

So we both turn our attention to Tommy who has now proceeded to devour a double cheeseburger all at once.

I guess doctors have to weigh this guy one leg at a time.

Chapter 34

Internal Revenue Service
Main entrance
Early afternoon

Tommy Trumble makes his way up the steps to the entrance of the huge IRS office building. He squeezes his rather large frame into the revolving door. As witnessed by several bystanders, they see that he takes up the entire space in the revolving door.

After a moment the door spits him out. He stumbles haphazardly towards one of the main entrance guards A fella he knows as Officer Wilson.

Tommy forces a smile. He knows he's not where he is supposed to be. He gives officer Wilson a little wave.

"Hey, Tommy. What brings you here again this week?"

Tommy, visibly rattled for just a moment, regains his composure.

"Oh, nothing. No, nothing. I mean, I have a quick little job. Shouldn't be long. You know, just the regular old job.

Nothing special. Just kinda checking up on something or other, or nothing, or, you know. I got nothing to do. Just thought I'd stop by. Check on bad stuff, I mean, no bad stuff, and, you know, just make sure all the wheels are turning in the right direction, you know. Nothing big, just a little thing, so, you know. Not much. Just the usual stuff. You know."

Officer Wilson takes a very long moment to just stare at this bizarre computer nerd.

"Okay, Tommy. Let me just punch you in to my computer here."

Tommy leans over Wilson's desk to get a better view of his computer screen.

After a moment, Tommy finds it necessary to provide some special computer input to Officer Wilson.

"You know, if you use your tab key it goes faster."

Wilson stops. Looks up at Tommy. And says.

"I like it my way. But, thanks."

Tommy, still focused on Wilson's computer screen, develops another thought.

"You know, officer Wilson, you don't have to backspace. Change your macro to insert. It goes faster."

Wilson stops. Looks back at Tommy. Then says.

"Thanks Tommy. I'll remember that."

Tommy needlessly has to add.

"Use all caps. It goes faster."

Once again, Wilson stops entering data into his computer. And now gives Tommy a rather tough look as if he just wants to clock this guy.

"Thanks."

Tommy smiles. Wilson reaches over to his printer and grabs a document. He hands it to Tommy.

"Here, Tommy. Here, just take this pass. Turn it in when you leave. And don't forget. Okay?"

Tommy takes the pass and stuffs it into his pocket, grabbing his canvass briefcase and says.

"Okay. Thanks."

Tommy starts to amble over towards the elevator. Wilson shakes his head. His eyes follow Tommy. He mumbles "weirdo."

IRS Data Room

Tommy walks from the elevator towards a specific data terminal. It's a place he is very familiar with. He crashes into the chair with a thump.

He takes a moment to catch his breath.

Tommy takes time to examine the personnel in cubicles all around him in sort of a stealth manner. He hopes nobody saw him come in and take a seat in his usual cubicle.

He figures there are about 15 to 20 different people at workstations in cubicles in this room. He, of course, knows most of them. But trying to keep a low profile, he decides not to stand and wave or engage in any pleasant hello's.

Thinking that nobody knows he's here despite the loud noise he made slipping into his chair and dropping his bag on the floor. He faces the LED screen, laying his hands on the keyboard.

He looks left and right. He listens for any possible people that may be approaching his cubicle. A moment. He begins poke away at his keyboard.

"Tommy? What in the world are you doing here today?"

At that moment all of Tommy's roughly 285 pounds are propelled about 3 inches out of his seat. His thick, nerdy glasses almost come off of his face. He catches them just in time. Sweat on his forehead begins to form in large drops.

"Ah. Mr. Meyer. Ah. Well, ah, I have… I forgot to clean a file, last Monday. Just thought about it, sir, you know just sorta hit me in the brain a few minutes ago. Okay?"

Tommy offers Mr. Meyer a toothy smile.

Mr. Meyer takes a heartbeat to just stare at Tommy.

"Well, okay, Tommy. But I would like to know when you're here. Got it?"

"Yes, sir. Absolutely, sir."

He smiles broadly, and says.

"I'm here."

"Tommy, I mean before you get in that chair."

"Yes, sir. Yes, sir."

Mr. Meyer walks away, shaking his head, mumbling "weirdo."

Tommy watches Mr. Meyer leave the area, waiting for him to be out of sight.

He turns back to his keyboard. Shaking badly, he begins to type, mumbling to himself.

"Okay. Lamb, Malcolm Anthony. Search by year of birth. 1955. Secondary search. 1956."

"Hi, Tommy. How's my big hunk-a-love, sweetheart?"

Tommy's heart has stopped. He knows it's not beating. He turns white. Now, he looks to his right, over a narrow table. It's Lisa. Blonde, and incredibly gorgeous. Shaped like a fashion model, and voluptuous.

"Oh! Hi, Lisa. How you doin'?"

"Fan-tastic. I brought you some coffee, sweetie."

Lisa leans over the narrow table. It's, of course, an exaggerated move. And it's cleavage galore. Up close and personal. In Tommy's mind, it's a 'holy cow' moment.

Tommy's heart stops, again. His eyes lock onto almost heaven. And she knows it. She's playing with him.

"I'll check back if you need a refill, lovey."

"Okay."

And it's a sweaty okay. She turns. And lap dances back to her cubicle.

Tommy starts to mutter to himself once again.

"Oh man, I'm coming apart. Some spy. Okay. Get a grip. Enter, search."

Tommy now leans back in his desk chair watching the screen. Sipping his coffee, he notices literally thousands of files running quickly across the screen. Finished, his eyes go wide.

"37! Oh, monkey poop. Now what?"

Once again leaning back in his chair, he's thinking as he surveys the area around his cubicle. Then it hits him. An epiphany. He leans, hands on the keyboard.

"Oh, yeah. I got it. Search parameter. Living only. Search. You dummy. She doesn't want a dead guy right?"

Tommy now leans back once again in his chair watching thousands of files run frantically across the LED screen. After a moment his eyes go wide once again.

"35! Double monkey poop!"

Now Tommy stands, looks across the top of the cubicles. And in the distance he sees an IRS worker waving an IRS form 1040 in the air. And, it's another epiphany.

"Search parameters. Active names. That's 35. Search on IRS form 1040. Now let's see. Let's check from the year 2000 to the year 2013. Charitable contributions. Any match to the Abbey Prep School, New Milford Connecticut. Enter search."

Tommy leans back, pushing his chair into the aisle that separates the cubicles. He sees the very sexy Lisa coming his way. He pulls himself back in, grabbing his coffee cup off the desk and pouring its contents into the wastepaper basket. He then pushes himself back out into the aisle.

Lisa approaches, swaying in a very sexy manner.

"Need a refill, cutie pie?"

"Okay."

Tommy gives her a very friendly smile.

She leans in. He looks. Once again, it's cleavage heaven. She pauses, realizing he just loves the view. She takes his cup. And moves away. As she's walking away Tommy takes his glasses off, wiping off a large amount of sweat. Lisa returns.

"Here you go, sweetie pie."

"Okay."

Once again, she leans. He looks. She turns. And it's another lap dance back to her cubicle.

On the way back she glances over her shoulder at him and winks. At that moment she grabs her breasts. And pushing them towards the middle. She runs her tongue over her lips. Then winks again at Tommy.

Tommy goes into a semi-paralyzed state. His tongue hangs out almost to his belt. And at that moment his computer dings. Tommy snaps back to reality. Spinning in his chair to face his LED screen, he once again mumbles to himself.

"Okay. Okay. Good. One match found. Print fast. Fast."

He taps his fingers on the printer command, and the laser printer spits out a copy. He grabs the paper and stuffs it into his briefcase.

Tommy is now up and makes a beeline for the elevator, pressing the down button. He turns. Leans against the elevator doors looking back towards the area of cubicles. He catches Lisa staring at him. He smiles. She blows him a kiss. And at that moment the elevator doors open and Tommy crashes backwards into the elevator. The doors close.

In the lobby Tommy rushes from the elevator to the front door. He hurries to get out of the building as quickly as possible.

About 20 feet from the front door Tommy rushes towards his car. Then, a voice.

"Hey, Tommy! Hold up."

Tommy stops short. Drops his briefcase. And his hands and arms go straight up into the air. He breaks a sweat.

Officer Wilson approaches Tommy from behind.

"Tommy, you ran out with the visitors pass. And put your hands down. You're not under arrest. It's only a piece of paper, not some bloody files." Wilson grabs the pass from Tommy's pocket. Shaking his head, Wilson walks back to the front door of the IRS building.

Chapter 35

The Pentagon
Defense Intelligence Agency
Bonnie's Office

So, here we are again in Bonnie's office at the Pentagon. I've decided to chill out and relax. I sit at her desk with my feet propped up listening to Bonnie.

She paces back and forth. She reads this very interesting information that Tommy Trumble has provided to her.

Information that he lifted from highly confidential files at the IRS.

Information that will likely get all of us long sentences in Federal prison. And with my luck, I'd get some 300 pound black dude for a bunk bunny.

Tommy stands in a corner closely watching Bonnie. She paces, and asking questions.

Bonnie stops, and thinks for a moment.

Then says, as if to no one.

"Malcolm Lamb. It appears he's a Benedictine brother. And lives the life of a cloistered religious individual in a monastery somewhere buried in the Blue Ridge Mountains of Virginia."

I think about that for a moment. Considering that a man of the cloth, a cloistered Benedictine brother, would certainly have very little to do with this agreement. Especially with the President, Bonnie, and the entire DIA and State Department already working on it.

But then again I think of my old buddy, the Prince.

And what comes to mind are perhaps issues that Archbishop Mendoza has cleverly put in motion.

So I simply need to let Bonnie know where I stand with regard to this problem. And, of course how brilliant my observations have been.

"You see, what did I tell you Bonnie."

Bonnie appears to ignore me. We all know it's not important what I think.

So what else is new?

She says, "this has got to be him. Tommy I think you have found our guy."

"There was only one match, Bonnie, on all the tax returns. It actually turned out to be quite easy after I was able to narrow the search."

I note that Tommy appears to believe he is now king of the hill, top of the heap, 'A' number one, as Sinatra would sing.

He decides to provide even more information to Bonnie on how brilliant he is in scouring through highly confidential tax records of, let me see, 300 million Americans?

"Charitable contributions. That's what did it Bonnie. I checked charitable contributions to The Abbey Prep School in New Milford, Connecticut going back almost 10 years."

Now with that comment I slowly move my feet off the desk and sit up straight.

He has not only crossed the line. He has gone head first into an area that will get us all in deep pooh-pooh, i.e., ...you know what I mean, right?

"Tommy! You mean to tell me *personal tax returns?*"

Tommy puffs out his chest, smiles broadly at me. He's looking like he is now the new "man."

Now smiling…

"I helped write the search software for the IRS. What'd ya think, Bonnie? Is that cool or what?"

My brain is in quick compute mode. I need it there so I can completely understand what he has done. Not to mention the fact that he has most certainly left "computer finger prints" all over the IRS files he invaded.

But I don't dare bring that up at this point.

It may upset Bonnie.

And that means trouble for Tommy.

And trouble for me.

The "no sex" kinda trouble for me.

Oh, and Federal prison time trouble, as well.

So, I simply say…

"Tommy! You mean that my tax dollars pay your salary?"

Tommy looks at me as if I'm some sort of bug that is landed on Bonnie's desk.

Smiling he says to me.

"Yeah."

Tommy then shuffles his feet a little bit. Sticks his hands in his pockets. His shoulders droop.

"But, you know, not very much money. I have to live with my mother."

Bonnie spins away from staring out the window and now looks at us, and says.

"Hey, it's already 1:30 in the afternoon. Get your things together, Jack."

I stand up, looking at her.

"Okay. Where to, Inspector?"

"We're going to search for that Benedictine Monastery in the Blue Ridge Mountains. Let's jump in your car, Jack, and roll. Tommy you get onto my computer. Try to find the location of a Benedictine Monastery somewhere in the Blue Ridge Mountains of Virginia. Start from Winchester, Virginia, and work your way down to Roanoke. It's got to be there somewhere. Jack and I will head out Route 66. Should take us an hour to get to the Blue Ridge Parkway.

Tommy has come back to life.

"Yeah. Good. That's really cool,. I'll get right on it, Bonnie."

Tommy moves over to Bonnie's desk. He starts pounding on the keyboard.

As Bonnie and I head for the door, Tommy says to us. "Can I come with you guys?"

Both Bonnie and I stop, turn, and jointly answer him. "No!"

Tommy looks as if he has been rejected by the human race – the normal ones – he is a nerd, you know.

Bonnie, of course, notices this. She moves over to him, grabbing his big arms, she kisses him on the cheek. She backs up, saying.

"Tommy Trumble you are my hero. Thank you, very, very, much."

Bonnie and I head for the door, me pulling her through before Tommy can say anything else, like, bring me back something to eat!

Chapter 36

Avondale Campus, The Archdiocese
Washington, DC
Late Afternoon

MONSIGNOR ROGER SCHNEIDER strolls casually down the quiet hallway. He stares at a text on his iPhone. But he's also focused on being as quiet as possible as he passes by Archbishop Mendoza's office door. His glance askance at the door is rather telling at the moment.

There's a genuine dislike for the Archbishop.

But his selection to be Mendoza's right hand man was a promotion sought after by multitudes of priests around the country. Clearly, someone of importance interceded.

The Washington, DC Archbishop presides over a prestigious school, Catholic University. He is also the key man between the hierarchy of the Catholic Church, and the leaders of the most powerful country on the planet.

Working at the right hand of the man who holds this esteemed position in the Church gives one immediate and preferential access to whomever and whatever that individual so desires.

For Monsignor Schneider, the best tables in the finest restaurants that Washington, DC has to offer is, perhaps, the ultimate prize. Something he never experienced growing up on a farm in rural Indiana. Working on the farm from sun up to sun down was the norm. And sitting down at the family dinner table each evening, enjoying his Mom's outstanding meals, was the closest he ever got to fine dining.

And when he wasn't working with his Dad on the farm during the summer and fall months, he was also playing football for Sts Peter & Paul High School.

He was not only an outstanding player. He was the physical and moral glue of the team. A player with the strength, discipline and moral character for a team he lead to three State Championships as Captain.

And that won him a full ride to Notre Dame where he excelled as both an All American player, and an honor student. Notre Dame was his first and only choice after High School.

He turned down an NFL draft offer to play for the Oakland Raiders, a team in need of an outstanding linebacker. A job that went to Hall-of-Famer, Howie Long. He chose, instead, to accept an offer to enter the Franciscan Seminary.

That rural, family oriented upbringing, the solid Christian education at Notre Dame, and the sparse, yet structured life with the Franciscans, provided him with a strict moral character that has come to define his life.

Monsignor Schneider stops in the hallway.

A moment passes before he types in a message response.

"Mister Connolly, I will continue to monitor critical conversations from here, understanding fully your serious mission. Text me 24/7 with whatever you need. My device is always no more than arm's length. Good luck & God bless. RS."

Chapter 37

A Monastery
Hidden in the Blue Ridge Mountains of Virginia
Late Afternoon

I stop the car at the main entrance. Two huge concrete pillars flank the long driveway. The heavy iron bar gates are wide open, obviously expecting somebody, but I'm not sure it's us.

I glance over at Bonnie, noticing that she is taking in the beautiful grounds.

"Good. The gates are open, Jack."

"Oh, look at that, Bonnie. There's a sign. And it reads no visitors."

"We didn't come this far, Jack, to be turned away by a silly sign. So hurry up, let's go."

"Right. Check the trees on both sides for snipers."

We wind our way up the long, curvy gravel driveway to what appears to be at least a 100 year old English tutor structure. The only sounds we hear, besides the car engine, is the crushing of gravel as we drive towards this imposing structure. I stop the car. And shut down the engine.

"Okay. Let's get out, Jack"

Somehow I have an uneasy feeling about this place. It's likely either my superior street sense, taking in this medieval structure, or my extensive training as a Secret Service Officer. One or the other tells me we should turn around and make a quick getaway.

However, I am giving our next move some consideration. But, Bonnie is out of the car doing a 360 degree turn, taking in the property.

She walks towards another iron gate that has been left open. Clearly the folks in this place are expecting someone. Maybe some nuns from a convent in Waynesboro. It could be dance night.

I note the monastery has a very medieval look to it. Perhaps several hundred years old. It's interesting to note that it can't be hundreds of years old as we are in the Blue Ridge Mountains on land once occupied by Indians. Or rather I should say, Native Americans.

I strive to be always politically correct.

Someone sure went to the trouble to make this place look ancient.

The two story structure has several doors that open into the courtyard. At the far end there is a large stone archway that leads, to what looks to be, another courtyard.

I turn, facing Bonnie.

"It's very quiet."

"It's a monastery, Jack."

"What do you think they do here?"

"Think."

"I'd fit right in."

"I don't think so, Jack."

I stroll around the courtyard, keeping a safe distance from the perimeter walls. I'm looking for what could be an entrance, or at least some way to contact the inside world. It's the quiet that's gnawing on my nerves.

And something else is poking at my brain.

"Bonnie. I get the feeling that we're being watched."

And for a nano second I think Bonnie has that same weird feeling.

"No. It's maybe prayer time. Your know, perhaps they're gathered in the chapel seeking guidance and wisdom from the Holy Spirit. Monks do that, you know, Jack."

Or maybe they've spotted us and the big guy is passing out AK-47's and ammo, telling them to take their assigned sniper positions.

I casually glance up to the second floor windows, then the roof.

No sign of trouble...yet.

"What are you looking for, Jack?"

"Laser sights."

"Huh?"

I point over at several benches along one of the walls, indicating that we should sit.

"Let's talk about which door we should bang on, Bonnie."

"I wish there was at least a door bell, or a knocker on one of these doors. Don't you?"

I wish we could just high-tail it out of this place. It's beginning to creep me out. And I have a gun!

As we head over to the benches, a door, somewhere behinds us, has closed with a thud.

We turn, and notice a rather elderly monk in dark brown robes walk slowly in our direction. His hands are concealed inside the robes. His body bent forward, and his gait indicates an obvious limp.

His concealed hands light up my little brain.

My suit jacket is open. My side arm is at the ready, clipped onto my belt.

Bonnie notices the slight movement of my right hand. She whispers.

"Jack!"

"He needs to show me his hands."

"No, he does not. This is not what you think!"

The elderly monk gets to within ten feet of us.

He stops.

He raises his head, first looking at Bonnie. Then at me.

A silent moment passes. And I wonder if these guys are allowed to speak.

Then, he answers that question, as if he heard my thoughts. I try to figure out which door he came from.

"I am Father Ambrose. A Benedictine Monk. I am the Superior here. We don't allow guests."

You see, I said we were not expected, right? Best I do not say anything at this point. His hands are still not visible.

And Bonnie is wearing those pointed expensive Ferragamo shoes. She'll kick me, for sure. Again, she needs a talk on Naval Officer dress code guidelines.

For my benefit, of course.

Bonnie immediately steps up to the challenge.

"Father Ambrose. We're here to see Brother Malcolm Lamb."

Father Ambrose raises a surprised eyebrow. A task perhaps made more difficult and unexpected due to his advanced age. I think that Bonnie has struck a nerve. I hope the poor guy doesn't keel over dead from a heart attack.

"We don't receive guests here, Miss."

He should have referred to her as Commander, but I'll let him slide. But introductions are in order.

"Your Superior...ness. This is Commander Bonnie Biersack, United States Navy. And I'm Jack Connolly, United States Secret Service."

Bonnie, this time gently, elbows me.

"You must forgive me, but we simply do not receive guests here at the monastery."

Bonnie asks, "does Brother Malcolm live here?"

"Again, I'm sorry…but we do not reveal the names of any of our residents. Now, if there is nothing further, I must return to my duties. You do know the way out?"

Bonnie sighs heavily.

"Father! It's very important that we contact Brother Malcolm. It's a very sensitive matter that I'm not permitted to discuss with anyone but him."

Very good, Bonnie. Turnabout is fair play. He's not giving up secrets, so you're not, as well.

The good Father is not a happy monk at the moment.

He stares down Bonnie for a long heartbeat.

"Are you family, Miss?"

"No, Father. We're from Washington, DC , and we're here on official National Security business. We're confident that Brother Malcolm can help us with a very serious issue."

If this guy buys her line, that is, slipping in the term, "National Security," then he probably does not pray enough.

"Our residents live in general isolation from matters of government. Perhaps the provincial office in Boston can help you."

A loud "gong" comes from a point up on the roof, capturing the attention of Father Ambrose.

"I must go now. Vespers starts in thirty minutes."

"Please, Father Ambrose. We believe he's here. And we know he can help with information that will head-off a plan that could disrupt religious freedoms."

She certainly knows how to lay it on thick, right?

"Miss Biersack, our priests and brothers live a very unique life. Strangers are not welcome into this holy life of ours. Now –"

"– Father! Miss…Commander Biersack has spent untold hours hunting down Malcolm Lamb. Only because of the importance of her mission. A mission fraught with danger and mistrust, both here in the U.S. and abroad. She can't let this effort go unresolved with you stone-walling the mission."

Father Ambrose looks quite pissed at this point. So much so, that I wonder if there is a weapon in his hands buried inside that dirty brown cassock.

Before he has time to pull out a switch blade, and knife me in the heart, I whip out my ID. I flash it in his direction.

Out comes his hand, grabbing my ID with more force than I expected. Rosary beads *do* strengthen one's hands.

He examines it for a long moment, obviously never seeing such credentials.

He hands the ID back to me, pointing to an area behind us. A long, uncomfortable looking bench.

"Wait over there!"

He then turns quickly as Bonnie and I grab a long look at the utilitarian wood bench up against a stucco wall with vines creeping all over. It's about 20 feet away.

Bonnie gives me a stern look.

I give her friendly wink.

We turn back to address the Superior, but he's not there.

We did catch the sound of a thud somewhere. I simply cannot identify the door he went through.

We walk over to the bench.

"Pleasant fella."

"They don't have much contact with the public, Jack."

"Coulda' fooled me."

"It's a committed way of life...very utilitarian. Much like the Franciscans. A special calling."

"So, let me get this straight. No babes! No booze! No baths."

She sighs, "idiot."

"You didn't catch a whiff?"

"Oh...that was him?"

Sitting on the old wooden bench, I take in the surroundings again. It's pretty. Classic, in some old fashioned way. But too quiet for my liking.

"So, Bonnie. Vespers?

"A prayer service. Together, as a community. They pray like that several times a day."

"So, not a game show."

There's that look from her…again.

"How do you know all this truly enlightening stuff?"

She sighs. Then…

"Elementary school…the Baltimore Catechism…Nuns."

I look quickly away. Momentarily startled.

"Nuns! I don't wanna know, Bonnie. How 'bout we change the subject. Baltimore, huh? You think the Orioles will go all the way this year?"

Bonnie is in deep thought, far away someplace.

"I respect and love the Church, Jack. Nuns have given me a reason to revere how children are brought into the fold. At a very young age we were given the reasons and tools to live as Jesus did 2000 years ago. When you give this serious thought, you can't help but understand the entire pro-life movement. It's so clear."

She turns to me.

"Abortion is not correctly defined by those who support it. Nor does the media understand."

She scans the monastery.

"It's simply murder, Jack."

I take a heartbeat to contemplate my experiences in elementary school. Bowing my head, I begin softly.

"I have a different take on those women, Bonnie."

My mood has turned dark.

"Okay. What happened, Jack?"

I lift my head and turn away from her.

"I was maybe ten or eleven years old at the time…my brother Bobby was a year younger. We would walk over to the school playground after dinner…it was late spring and still daylight."

I make eye contact with her.

"We lived only a hundred yards from the school. My great grandfather, Don Pedro Segui, donated the land and built the school for the parish on Long Island. The land was in the family for generations, part of an inheritance from the Venezuelan arm of the family. I think they found a way to hide money from the Venezuelan government."

I take a moment to gather my thoughts, as well as scan the monastery roof. I am a bit paranoid.

"It was only eight acres, and a single story, eight classroom building with a cafeteria and some offices, initially."

"Jack, it's simply wonderful that he did that."

"Great grandpa needed a sizeable charitable donation for tax purposes, so I'm told. Plus, the pastor of our local Church, your pal, the charming and personable, Father Joseph Mendoza, somehow caught wind of the "issues" south of the border."

Bonnie thinks for a moment. Then…

"Oh…I see."

"Yeah. Really. Mendoza put the arm on Don Pedro. And he got his school, touting the accomplishment to the Bishop as if he was a genius at bringing parishioners into the fold, as you say."

"Was the school named for Don Pedro?"

I give her one of those looks that means 'get real, Bonnie.'

"Not even a mention anywhere to be found."

"Sorry."

"So, Bobby and I are on the playground that night. We knew the guys would throw those pink Spaulding balls against the building during recess. And so would the girls. Except the girls threw like girls, with the balls ending up on the flat roof."

"The girls played ball, also?"

"Sure. The ones who wanted to get picked-up by the guys so they could show-off their training bras after being walked home from school."

"Jack!"

"Anyway, one night Bobby got a bright idea. Get up on the roof and collect the balls the girls threw. And I could stand look-out for the Nuns. They lived in one of Don Pedro's old houses on the grounds. He donated it as a place for the Nuns to live. It had termites."

"Did you have some sort of signal?"

"Of course."

Pause.

"I would yell Penguin…Penguin…"

"Jack, really?"

"Now there had to be dozens of balls up there."

"Thrown by the girls, not the guys, huh?"

"Right. Except those balls guys threw, aiming for the back of a Nuns' head, also ended up on the roof."

"Please!"

"Well, Bobby is up on the roof, out of sight for some strange reason, when I notice two Nuns walking right at me at a fast pace. You do know they only travel in pairs, right?"

Bonnie wants to poke me in the eye.

"Armed with rosary beads and a ruler, they stop inches from me. Sister Mary Agnita, the principal, and Sister Mary Arthur. Or better known as Rocky Marciano and Adolph Hitler. Today they would probably be known as Hilary Clinton and Elizabeth Warren."

Bonnie sighs, once again.

"In my face, Rocky, Sister Agnita, asks, Mister Connolly, where is your brother?"

Bonnie says.

"When they get all formal like that I bet you knew you were in trouble."

I must admit, this hot babe is one sharp piece of…

"So, I cleverly respond by saying 'well, Sister, I think he may be around here someplace. Ya know, maybe on the swing set behind the school.' Well, she didn't buy it. And then, the unexpected happened."

"What, Jack? What happened?"

"Whack! She nails me. Full hand to my left cheek. I was dumb struck. Then scared shitless. Because if my Mom found out that Sister hit me, she would immediately assume I committed a serious crime, like swearing at the Nuns, placing me in time-out for life."

"Wow! So Bobby's on the roof. And you get whacked. The humanity of it all."

I notice Bonnie covering her mouth, laughing.

"Bobby never got in trouble. Do you have any idea how humiliating it is, Bonnie, to get slapped by a Nun?"

Then…

It's a gravelly voice. Off to our left, maybe 15 or 20 feet away, says…"I do!" And it startles both Bonnie and I.

I presume this is the guy we're after.

BROTHER MALCOLM LAMB is perhaps in his mid to late fifties. But looks many years beyond that. He's tall, with an unkempt head of salt and pepper grayish hair. A scraggly, short beard. He wears a cassock, much like Father Ambrose. It's covered with an extra layer of filth. I note his hands, arms folded in front, but not concealed by the cassock. And the obvious telltale sign of a heavy smoker. On his right hand the yellow stained index and middle fingers.

Good! No weapons that I can see.

But his expression is threatening.

Not at all welcoming us for afternoon tea and crackers.

Bonnie and I are now on our feet, staring at him, wondering who makes the next move.

Brother Malcolm opens the dialogue.

"I was twelve years old. She hit me. I hit her back. Knocked out her, actually."

He clasps his hands together, as if to pray.

"She lived. And I was sent away to boarding school in Connecticut." The Abbey, to be more precise."

So this *is* our guy.

Great. We're making progress.

Bonnie can't wait to question this guy.

"Brother Malcolm, -"

"How did you find me?"

"Brother. We need your help. It's imperative that we -"

"I have absolutely no desire to help, nor be involved in whatever it is you're looking for, Commander Biersack."

So, we can quickly conclude that the good Father Ambrose filled in the mad Brother Malcolm about his uninvited guests.

"We've been to the Abbey, Brother. Recently. Very recently."

Malcolm's expression changes. But just slightly. It appears to have maybe softened.

"We learned things from the past that are perhaps connected to the present. Maybe you can fill in some of the blanks for us. Please, Brother."

Brother Malcolm takes a prayerful moment.

"The Abbey is the past for me. Please understand that."

"But you still make contributions, Brother. Why?"

His eyes widen, doubling in size.

"My family inheritance is nobody's business."

Bonnie takes a moment to study Malcolm.

"We know about the Sodality."

Brother Malcolm, with fire in his eyes, turns at Bonnie, and placing severe emphasis on his words, says.

"I said...the past is the past. And that's final."

Bonnie is not buying any of it.

"The Sodality has lived on...in some ways...with those who you know or knew well, who are involved in certain government activities in Washington. Hasn't it?"

Malcolm's stare, one filled with intensity, holds on Bonnie's eyes. He's searching for something there. What, I don't know. But he could explode at any moment.

Bonnie looks to calm the situation.

"I'm involved with an agreement that will affect Jerusalem. The Holy sites scattered throughout Israel. Perhaps the long term fate of Christianity in the world."

Brother Malcolm's eyes have now darted away from Bonnie. Like he's suddenly afraid to look her in the eye.

Maybe he knows. Maybe all this is not something he's involved with, but somehow, he is.

His body language is telling.

And Bonnie has picked up on this vibe.

"There's a hidden agenda, Brother."

Studying his surroundings, he takes a moment to check the time on his wrist watch. Then, a noticeable sigh.

"Not here. Follow me!"

He turns quickly, heading for an archway that leads out of the courtyard, away from where we had parked.

Bonnie and I follow.

I poke her arm. Then say quietly to her.

"Bonnie. I'm armed."

She says something under her breath. I can't quite make it out. But I think she said something like move on...or was it moron?

Sometimes she's just so hard to figure out.

Chapter 38

Benedictine Monastery
Garden Pergola
Late Afternoon

I suppose one could conclude that the lush, beautiful gardens we are passing through right now are meant to replicate a heavenly paradise. I mean, we *are* at a monastery. And the religious who live here pray to hopefully enjoy their eternal reward in, perhaps, a place like this.

Maybe if I come to grips with my wandering, sinful ways, and see what eternal life may be like, should I be cleansed by a willing but skeptical priest, this could be my life as well.

Right?

Not.

The path we're presently on leads away from the monastery to an area that looks quite a bit like an outdoor chapel. Considering these guys don't bathe all that often, conducting daily prayers in the clean, fresh air would certainly be a plus.

There's a large cross strategically placed near a marble table that is likely the alter.

Alongside the perimeter are statues of Saints. I should be able to recognize some. But, of course, as you would expect, I don't.

The large one on the left has a striking resemblance to that infamous former Congressman, Anthony "the package" Weiner.

My eyes, for some uncontrolled reason, shift to his groin area.

No bulge.

Marble benches make up the available seating area.

The ground looks as if the weeds have won the battle against the hard blue stone pavers in front of the benches where the priests and brothers kneel.

I guess the protocol is BYOK.

Or, bring your own kneeler!

Malcolm has stopped, looking off into the distance at the surrounding mountain tops and valleys that make up the Shenandoah National Park here in the Blue Ridge Mountains.

Bonnie walks up next to him and takes in the view.

I watch from a distance. I'm doing visual 360's, looking for strangers.

With the exception of the chirping birds, you could hear a monk fart up at the monastery.

"I find peace with myself here, Commander Biersack."

He looks sadly at Bonnie.

"It's the lord's way of comforting me. My reckless youth. My sinful, undesirable ways during those long, sleepless nights at The Abbey."

He seems to have suddenly gathered an inner strength. A level of confidence. And has become less threatening.

"My old and very dear friend, Noah David, is running for the office of Israeli Prime Minister."

He shakes his head, developing a thin smile.

"Who would have thought such an individual could get that far?"

Bonnie adds, "he could win."

Malcolm takes in the spectacular view.

A moment passes.

"The wise man has eyes in his head. The fool walks in darkness."

Pause.

"Do you recognize that short passage, Commander?"

Bonnie shakes her head.

I recognize it from a Bob Dylan recording. I'd raise my hand to answer, but I think twice about that.

"Ecclesiastes, Commander."

Bonnie gets it.

Malcolm walks off a short distance. Then turns at Bonnie.

"Archbishop Mendoza taught us that the Church, our Church, the Church of Rome, has always had a responsibility to reclaim its heritage. From the time it was pushed to Rome, with Saint Peter, followed by Saint Paul, in the first century.

The writings are there. The mission has never changed."

"Brother Malcolm, hasn't the Church reclaimed its heritage over the century's? Look at it today. Over a billion faithful. And growing."

"Commander, you must understand that the Archbishop sees this mission as unequivocally unfinished. The land of Jesus, the Christ, His footsteps in the dirt and sand of the desert, are over-run with those who reject Christianity. Who look to wipe its teachings from the planet. No, it has not yet been reclaimed. And the Iranians? They want control. But, if Mendoza succeeds..."

Malcolm's voice trails off.

Bonnie gets closer to him.

"Succeeds at what?"

Malcolm gazes, deep in spiritual thought as Bonnie gathers her thoughts.

"Did you expect me, Brother?"

Malcolm looks knowingly at her, taking a moment to reflect on her question.

"You're the messenger... the Lord has guided you to this place."

Now Bonnie takes a moment to reflect on that revelation, looking almost relived. Then, with a knowing, controlled voice, she informs Malcolm with what is now, her understanding.

"Mendoza's resignation as Headmaster set the plan in motion."

Shifting, he nods at Bonnie.

"Mr. Gonzmart, the President's father, made a fortune off the fortunes of others."

Pause.

"One of them, Noah's mother."

And Bonnie gets it. The sub-text, hard to follow, but crystal clear to Bonnie.

"It was the affair, wasn't it, Brother?"

Malcolm nods ever so slightly, once again. But with an apprehensive look, almost afraid to confirm the facts.

"Noah's father, a wealthy Jew, left him and his mother. Emigrated to the newest Middle Eastern State at the time...Israel...when Noah was a young child. A woman would suffer untold embarrassment at that time should the event become wildly known.

She was a devout Catholic. Attended Mass daily. Volunteered at a local soup kitchen. You know, the usual penance practiced by Catholic women, those who quietly hide their secretive guilt.

In the process, she spoiled the boy...Noah. Father Mendoza... raised a son."

Bonnie says softly.

"Her affair with the President's father would've destroyed her then if it were exposed."

Folding his hands as if to pray, and gazing off, lost in the spectacular view of the Blue Ridge Mountains, Brother Malcolm Lamb preaches.

"The covetous man is never satisfied with money...so it is written, Commander.

Pause.

"She was then chosen. For fear of exposure. And the fear of being an outcast from the social society she so happily embraced.

Pause

"An acceptable, useful conduit for hefty political contributions...and the destructive, evil purchasing power that accompanies each of every dollar."

Listening not far behind them, I feel compelled to add my own two cents. Not that anyone asked. But this matter is taking on a larger cast of bad actors than we initially thought. And my primo role here is to protect Bonnie, no matter what the outcome. The guy who put me here somehow determined that the more she learns, the more likely she is in danger of something bad happening to her.

I chime into the conversation with my unparalleled expertise.

"More like Mendoza held the Sodality matter over her head."

And I'm surprised that the good Brother here has confirmed my suspicion. It's the body language that gives him away. I am pretty good at this crap.

Bonnie adds.

"What then was his plan?"

"We were young boys. On the cusp of maturity. But, not yet there, I'm afraid. The beginning of his words, his words at the time, of course, was pure folly. As it is said in the scriptures.

Pause.

"The end of his little, soft spoken, humbling talk was utter madness."

Okay.

I think it's safe to say, after a quick, sideways glance at Bonnie, we're both clueless.

And Malcolm gets it.

That is, our dumbness.

"Archbishop Mendoza wants so badly to be a Cardinal. A Prince of the Catholic Church. As his boys, he had us refer to him as The Prince.

Pause.

I'm sure you're aware, Commander, such a role comes only to the most revered. One is selected by a messenger from our Lord, Jesus, the Christ...The Holy Spirit."

Bonnie is awe-struck. Captivated by the words spoken with reverence and feeling by Brother Lamb.

I, on the other hand, have a different take on this revelation.

"A Machiavellian syndrome...impossible without connections."

Bonnie shoots me a frown.

"In Rome, Mister Connolly, there is a Cardinal with enormous power. Antonio Cardinal Pulgar. A childhood friend from Venezuela. He and Mendoza are closer than brothers."

And my little brain thinks two young boys playing banjos together on a cabin porch in the woods, barefoot, Ross Perot ears, eyes close together... I really need some serious therapy.

Bonnie interrupts my mind journey...

"But, does he if –"

"– if Noah is elected, Commander? Noah's been paid for. The crafty plotter..."

He drills me a look.

"...yes, Mister Connolly, yes...you are correct. Machiavelli...The Prince."

Bonnie adds.

"And with that, a carefully, well financed political campaign for Noah David paid for over time."

Malcolm ties up a loose end.

"And actually not that much less than what has gone to the political careers of the President and Senator Hennessy."

Joining in the fun, I add.

"The good Bishop cannot simply deliver suitcases full of cash. The FEC, and others, notably Congressional watch dogs and staffers as well as Eric Holder's Middle East terrorists clients will be at his door looking for a handout."

Uh oh!

I don't think Bonnie liked my point of view.

Maybe Malcolm didn't hear me.

He comments.

"Opus Dei...and his rather shady cousin in Venezuela, Alfredo. He manages the Mendoza family fortune. But the Prince calls all the shots."

"Opus day?"

Bonnie sighs.

"Opus *Dei*, Jack. A worldwide Catholic organization based in Madrid, Spain. Think of it as a larger Sodality....more or less."

"Close enough, Commander."

Malcolm continues.

"Local Bishops make the decisions. The Prince decides for all of North America."

My law enforcement instincts and that honest to the core training I got at the Naval Academy raises that large, controlling part of my brain I call the B S meter. Or is it matter?

"Brother Malcolm. Excuse my direct approach."

Bonnie spins quickly at me.

"But you appear to be too well informed for someone whose whereabouts is unknown. From our extensive research, I mean the research conducted by our pal, Tommy, you don't really exist.

Unless you find someone, like, say, a nerd named Tommy Trumble, who can hack into IRS files."

Malcolm glares at me.

I'm not looking at Bonnie.

I kinda know where she probably stands at this moment.

Malcolm explains.

"It was the Sodality that was and still is, well informed, Mister Connolly. All information flows from the source. Remember. We were...we were his sons. And we were embraced by his genuine love.

Pause.

"At least we were led to believe that love truly existed, sir."

I'm going to presume here that there was nothing for his "boys" in the envelop at graduation.

Instead, I ask.

"So it's Noah David that must deliver?"

"The Gulf of Aqaba agreement, engineered by Archbishop Mendoza behind the scenes, will give Noah the flexibility he needs. And the Prince will feed him instructions once he is sworn into office.

Pause.

"There *is* a hidden agenda, Commander Biersack.

"I can only assume it's the madness you speak of, Brother."

"Jerusalem...The Holy City...surrounding holy sites that one can easily trace the steps of our Lord, Jesus, the Christ."

Now I'm getting a little crazy.

"That's not an agenda. That's treason."

"Mister Connolly, at one time Christians represented 25% of the region. Today...2%! The Prince intends to change that dynamic. He'll flood the Holy Land with pilgrams. Perhaps, his close friend, King Abdulla of Jordan, would welcome the kind of financial assistance he needs to handle the Syrian refugees. Many of whom are Christian, not Muslim."

"Not possible! The cost would be prohibitive."

"I'm talking about an oil rich family in Venezuela that's closer to the leaders of that troubled country than the leaders of our own country realize. And the Venezuelans are a deeply religious people who want to see The Holy Land returned to its Christian roots."

Malcolm glares at me for a moment.

"Your family, Mister Connolly, has a stake here as well. The cross. And the Bishop will eventually pull those strings. "

Oh. Maybe I need to talk with Grandma again.

Brother Malcolm strolls away from us, but not far. He grabs a long, thoughtful look at the Blue Ridge.

"Our prayers are being answered. I've been praying for you, Commander, ever since I learned you were to be the, shall we say, spear head."

He spins at us.

"Expose this evil plan."

"Told about me by whom, Brother?"

Malcolm gives her a pleasant look. Then checks his watch.

"I'm expected at Vespers. I must leave you now. I hope you understand. I will continue to pray for you, Commander Biersack...Bonnie, if I may.

Pause.

"Follow your heart, Bonnie. The Lord will show you the way."

He starts to leave, taking several steps away from us before he stops and turns.

A long moment.

"God bless you...both."

He turns back, heading for the Monastery, disappearing in the gardens as Bonnie and I are speechless.

Well, score one for yours truly, Jack Connolly.

He's gonna pray for me.

I grab a stare at the heavens above, thinking, maybe he knows something.

Taking a look over at Bonnie, it appears that steam is pouring from her ears.

It's the body language.

She's definitely not a happy camper...or rather a down to earth, honest, Ohio bred Naval Officer.

Opportunist, phony and liar are not what you find in a woman from Ohio.

Check out Hilary Clinton.

She's from Pennsylvania...forced to move to Chicago, then exiled to Arkansas after an appalling performance during the Watergate hearings in 1973 as a legal staffer. The late Senator Sam Ervin is still spinning in his grave.

Then, with her teeth clenched.

"The Bishop! He took a vow of poverty."

"He had his fingers crossed."

But now Bonnie is studying her watch.

"I gotta see Hennessy. We'll go to my place first. Grab my notes from the talk I had with President Gonzmart."

"Right."

"Then off to see Hennessy. He's expecting opposition? I intend to deliver it."

"Right."

She's already bolted away from me.

I need to get an extra Kevlar vest for her to wear.

And check my ammo supply.

Chapter 39

United States Senate
Majority Leader's Office
5:42:02 PM

MAJORITY LEADER FRANKLIN HENNESSY paces
nervously across the width of his massive office. His suit
jacket thrown haphazardly across a leather arm chair. Sweat
has formed quite noticeably under his armpits. His tie is
loosened.

He speaks with anger and forcefulness at the speaker
phone located on his ornate desk.

"For chrissakes, Howard, she has damaging
information. And she's quite pissed. Your idea of damage
control is an utter failure."

The stutter and hesitation is noticeable in Howard
Hall's voice.

"It's unraveling, Franklin? Is that what you're trying to
tell me?

"Somehow I knew I should have taken control of her.
Been more involved with her assignment. Letting you jackass
staffers make the rules at the White House has been a constant
problem since the Obama days and his ideological bird-brain

assistants re-shaping the course of government with executive orders."

"Franklin, don't lump me in with that failed administration. I've been trying my god dammed best. It's the Prince who's been giving the instructions.

Pause.

"I'm at my whit's-end, Franklin."

"Calm down, Howard...I'll take care of her. She'll be here sometime after six pm."

Silence.

Then...

"No...no...I need to be there, Franklin. I need to be part of the solution. The Prince will expect me to be there."

Hennessy thinks about this. He knows well enough that if this goes south, the Prince will look for a scapegoat.

And what better moron to get put into the Prince's vise than Howard "the Hump" Hall.

It's time for the strong to survive.

And the weak to vanish.

"Fine, Howard. She'll be here by six thirty. Don't be late."

Hennessy jams the disconnect button on the speaker phone.

A furious, but silent moment.

Then...

"Jackass."

Chapter 40

Suburban Street
Alexandria, Virginia
Early Evening

About Halfway Down the Street

A rusty old Buick clanks its way down the one-way street. It's now at a location roughly ¾ of a mile from the North end of this very quiet residential street.

In the heart of Alexandria, Virginia.

Just several miles from downtown Washington, DC.

Inside of this train wreck of an automobile sit two very tough looking car thieves.

The driver, Harvey, someone clearly with a criminal look to his features, peers to his left.

He's checking the interior of each parked automobile as they slowly coast down this suburban street.

The other guy, Leo, riding shotgun, looks carefully for passers-by. This is one nasty dude. Someone who has perhaps spent more than half of his twenty something years in the lock-up.

The sunny, pleasant afternoon has brought the neighbors out. Neighbors who may be watching these two thugs.

From the North End of the Street

I turn onto Bonnie's street here in Alexandria. I quickly note that both sides of the street are packed with parked cars.

And I can see an old Buick coasting down the street about ¼ mile away, probably looking for a prime spot. He'll likely grab the last spot. There's no point going any further.

"You're up ahead about ¼ mile, right, Bonnie?"

She sighs.

"I think I'll grab a spot up here. We can walk to your place."

I pull into a tight spot. I shut down the engine.

"Time for a short stroll, babe. Let's hold hands."

Bonnie sighs, again.

We exit the car, and I fiddle with my annoying fob to lock the Beemer. I bet it's the battery.

'Beep. Beep.'

Okay. There we go.

I look up at Bonnie who's intently focused on something down the street.

"What's up?

Halfway Down the Street

The old Buick has stopped alongside Bonnie's Honda. Leo carefully checks the Honda for a moment or two then turns. He nods to Harvey sitting next to him. Leo takes a long pull on the cigarette dangling from his lips, then flings the butt out the window. He opens his door, quickly exiting the Buick.

Leo is a young thug who has perhaps spent the previous evening sleeping in a dumpster by the looks of his wardrobe. He stands alongside the driver side of Bonnie's Honda.

Jack & Bonnie on the Sidewalk

"That man down there, he's standing next to my car looking inside."

I zero in that dude. But my law enforcement instinct kicks in. I try to eye the tag on what appears to be an older sedan.

"Let's get a little closer. Stay behind me. And don't stare at your car."

We casually walk down the sidewalk, both looking at the classic homes along the way.

At Bonnie's Honda

Leo takes a moment to quickly scan the sidewalk area, and up and down the street. He holds for a nano second on Jack and Bonnie. In his little brain he concludes they're too far away to be a problem. He removes what looks like a metal credit card from his pocket. He inserts it into the tight space between the driver side window and the door frame. Pulling hard on this card, he separates the window from the door frame. He inserts a wooden wedge into the space. With his fist he slams down on the wedge creating about a 1 inch opening between the window and the door frame.

Jack & Bonnie Now 75 yards Away

"He's breaking into your car. Except, without the electronic key, he's going nowhere."

Bonnie stops, and quarter turns to face a small brownstone style home. She thinks for a moment.

Then she quietly says.

"I think I left the key in the ignition this morning. I was blocked by the Fed Ex guy. I took my motorcycle."

If I did that she'd say something like 'idiot.' But, I hold my tongue. I keep an eye on our carjacker.

At Bonnie's Honda

Leo turns and reaches back into the old Buick, pulling out a shim. He places the shim into the opening of Bonnie's car that he has created with the wedge. Moving the one end of the shim still in his hand he catches onto the locking device inside of Bonnie's door. Jerking it up quickly the door is unlocked. He removes the shim, throwing it back into the old Buick, hitting Harvey in the nuts.

"Hey! Watch what you're doing, you jackass!"

"Yeah. Yeah. Cool your jets, Harvey!"

Leo slips into the driver seat and closes the door.

He has already noticed the key in the ignition, obviously left there by Bonnie before locking the car earlier that morning.

Jack & Bonnie 50 Yards Away

I focus sharply on the Virginia tag. At this distance, I'm not sure. We move closer.

"Bonnie. Write this down."

She grabs a pen from her shoulder bag, and a small note book.

"Okay."

"Virginia Wine Country tag ECR 0843."

"Got it. Now what?"

"We'll stay here. Wait for them to leave."

"Why not arrest them?"

"It's safer to call the Alexandria PD."

Bonnie grabs her iPhone from the shoulder bag as I keep an eye on the situation.

Bonnie lifts her iPhone up, and snaps a photo of the situation.

"Good move. But get the PD on the line, Bonnie."

At Bonnie's Honda

Turning towards Harvey in the old Buick, Leo smiles and gives him a nod. The old Buick then creeps ahead, rolling slowly down the suburban Street.

Leo, in Bonnie's Honda, has engaged the starter. He shifts the gear in the center console into drive.

A moment passes before a LOUD EXPLOSION takes place, engulfing Bonnie's Honda in flames.

The old Buick stops down the street. Harvey turns looking through the rear window. He notices what has happened to Leo in the Honda.

He quickly floors the gas pedal, leaving some serious rubber on the suburban Street.

Harvey is gone in 60 seconds.

Jack & Bonnie 50 Yards Away

I'm certain Bonnie's conversation with the 911 operator has been suddenly cut short. Given the fact that the force and sound of the explosion, we've been sent reeling backwards. Her iPhone has taken flight into someone's front yard.

I role to my right to check on her.

"You okay?"

"Holy fuckin' shit!"

I guess she's okay.

"Now you see why law enforcement guys always tell folks near a scene of possible trouble to keep back."

Sitting on the sidewalk, she says.

"We need to see if anyone nearby was hurt. And check on the guy that got into my car."

I give her a long, frowning stare.

"Whatdaya think, Jack?"

Does she really wanna know what I think?

Okay.

But, it's not gonna be pretty.

"If you wanna check on that dude who got into your car, and chose, incorrectly I might add, to start your car, than be prepared to start collecting pieces of his former self."

"Huh?"

"I would suggest we wait for the Alexandria PD, and their forensics team to arrive. You know, those guys with latex gloves and little plastic bags."

She's on her feet. She's holding a stare on the crime scene.

In a frightening, nervous voice, she says.

"That was supposed to be me, Jack."

Hopefully, she now gets the point of my assignment.

Chapter 41

In Jack's Car
Crossing the 14th Street Bridge
6:23:06 PM

We answered a few questions with the Alexandria PD. Bonnie admitting she, perhaps, had left her ignition key in the Honda. The Detective on the scene indicated that may or may not be an insurance issue.

We're both more concerned, including the PD, why there was a bomb placed under her car sometime between last evening and this afternoon.

I informed the Alexandria Detectives that the Secret Service will assist in this investigation. They now know Bonnie could be the target of some nasty behavior by certain individuals not on board with a Federal investigation.

Such a revelation, in the absence of specific details, makes local law enforcement more suspicious than they should be.

Then I cleverly suggested that the FBI will likely jump into the investigation. This downright pisses off those local guys.

It's a school yard territorial thing.

Kinda like '...hey, I didn't know she was your girlfriend before she said to poke her. No? Well take this, you bastard. Bang!'

Why can't law enforcement just get along like grownups?

With the FBI involved?

Not!

Anyway, she still wants to get in Senator Hennessy's face. And right now!

"Drop me in front of the Senate, Jack. I'll be down as soon as I finish with Hennessy."

I'm not sure I feel comfortable with me hanging away from her. But, inside the Senate Majority Leader's office it is less likely there will be any bad actors around to cause a problem. Just to be sure, I'll give her a "plan B."

"If he gets threatening, in any way, Bonnie...or if you see those two morons that work at the White House for Hall...you know who...Henning and Pelicane, right?"

"Yeah."

"Leave the building. Get out into the open where there are people. Lots of people. Make your way to Union Station. Across the street. Plenty of folks there. "

I check my watch.

"I'll get you there. At the Google kiosk. 7:15 sharp."

"Okay."

"Remember, I'm very punctual. If I'm not there, something's wrong.

"As a matter of fact, get over to Union Station, regardless what happens with Hennessy."

She places her hand on my arm.

"Thanks, Jack. Thanks for being there."

She smiles.

I return the smile, thinking her smile means she owes me, well, you know...okay, I'll skip that thought pinging around my sex starved brain.

At the United States Senate
6:31:17 PM

Showing my creds, I get passed the intense security that surrounds the Capital Building. And pull in front of the underground entrance, on the Senate side.

"Good. Drop me here."

She leans over, and kisses me.

"Remember, Bonnie. Anything. Anything at all. Run. Don't look back."

She kisses me again.

"I do love you, Jack."

She bolts from my Beemer.

I watch as she heads into the street level, lower entrance to the Senate side of the Capital. She slings her purse around her neck to her right shoulder, so it rests on her left hip.

And I get a very bad feeling.

On my iPhone, I send another text to Monsignor Roger Schneider, giving him an update on our exciting day. I ask him to take appropriate measures regarding our pal, The Prince. This one should complete the scope of our mission.

After a moment, I pull away and make the forced circuitous security route to Union Station. It would be faster just to walk over. But, I'll need my car after getting Bonnie for her next stop.

East Front of the Capital

The plain dark blue Ford Econoline van creeps slowly away from the Capital. The driver has Jack's BMW in his sights. All falls in behind him, about 50 feet away.

On the driver side door panel a magnetic sign ID's the blue van as Capital Police.

However, the dude driving is anything but a Capital Police Officer.

He's dressed in a uniform, but from the outside it looks way too small for this guy. As a matter of fact, this could be Jaws, from the James Bond flick, "The Spy Who Loved Me."

And the expression on his face is not the look of an Officer on patrol. But someone whose mission is perhaps evil in nature.

In Jack Connolly's BMW

I presume Bonnie's next stop will be the White House. She'll probably want to drop in on President Gonzmart for a small chat. You know, filling him in on our interesting visit with his old bud from boarding school, the non-existent Brother Malcolm Lamb.

Maybe I'll grab a Pizza to take into the Oval Office.

The Beemer Passing Stanton Park
6:36:14 PM

Now that's weird. I think Pizza, and parked over there in Stanton Park is a Pizza delivery van. On the side it reads, "My Cousin Guido's Pizza," "Cheap Delivery."

Kinda looks familiar. Seems like I've seen that van before. Perhaps it's a popular Pizza delivery service.

In the old days, working late at the White House, when I was an active Naval Officer, and aide to the now very dead President Giordan, we would order Pizza for the staff.

Ah, the good old days.

That was before the Obama administration took over in 2009. And changed the honest, hardworking and productive culture that existed between the White House and Congress.

What's on the horizon next?

I need to get to Union Station, and hold out for Bonnie.

No more of this wishful thinking crap.

Chapter 42

Apartment Building
New Jersey Avenue
6:41:07 PM

SILAS, an elderly resident of the apartment building on New Jersey Avenue, exits the elevator in the building.

On a leash is his dog, FANNY, a cute Jack Russell terrier with high octane energy.

Fanny goes down, lying on the tile floor, her eyes fixed on that front door.

The doorman, Ralph, greets the gentleman, and his pet.

"Good afternoon, sir. Taking Fanny for a 'w- a- l- k'?"

Now Ralph knows very well that *saying* the word, 'walk' will usually turn Fanny into a rocket propelled dog, dragging her master, Silas, all over town.

That's why he spells out the word 'walk' in Fanny's presence.

However, Fanny starts to get a little hyper.

And is up on all fours.

Silas, looking down at Fanny for a moment, looks at Ralph.

"She's learning how to spell. We need to be careful, Ralph."

With that, Silas walks off with Fanny, leaving Ralph somewhat bewildered.

He stares at the old guy and his dog for a long moment. Then…

"Old people and their pets. Jesus H Christ. Is that what I have to look forward too someday?"

"Maybe I'll get shot someday by a jealous husband before I get old and senile. Yeah. Now that's the way to go."

Chapter 43

Senate Majority Leader's Office
Senator Franklin Hennessy (R-CT)
6:42:05 PM

Bonnie is standing facing the rather grumpy old Senator, who's seated at his desk.

She's mad.

He's morphed to being defenseless. But he's confident.

Being the Senate Majority Leader comes with the false perception that you are above it all. You have the right and obligation to speak your mind as you see fit.

Truth and fairness play no role in your pronouncements.

Especially if they're made on the Senate floor.

And if you want to change the rules, then, so be it. What you want to do is all that matters.

Yes, it is a change from the way things used to get done in the Senate.

But, with the arrival of Hop-a-long Harry Reid, that mentally deficient cowboy from nowhere Nevada, and Obama's personal water boy, the rules changed.

But Hennessy may feel a moment of weakness when Bonnie places her hands firmly on his nutmeg desk. She is leaning in towards him, getting in his face.

"Your secret pact with the devil won't work, Senator. I have all the information on your little scheme hatched 40 years ago at The Abby Prep School in Connecticut.

"You and your fellow gay boyfriends, and that two faced leader of yours, Mendoza, have reached your waterloo.

Hennessy, at first looking quite distressed, leans back in his chair. He studies her with an intensity reserved for only members of the opposite party.

"Next stop for me, Senator…the main stream media."

A movement from the shadows startles Bonnie.

She straightens, and starts to turn.

"Is that so, Miss Biersack?"

Howard Hall steps closer to her.

A wicked, evil smile crosses his face.

"And what are you going to do, Mister Hall? Kill me?"

He chuckles.

And as he glances over at Hennessy, through a concealed door from the far side of the office, Henning walks in, flashing the smile of a psycho.

Bonnie backs away from both Hall and Henning, getting closer to the main door.

She quickly checks her watch.

Henning removes a weapon from his jacket pocket.

"Got a pressing appointment, Bonnie…my love?"

Hall eyes Henning sharply.

"Put that away, Henning!"

Bonnie pulls a large chair in front of the door, and bolts from Hennessy's office.

Hall says to Henning.

"Get Pelicane! Now!"

Hennessy stands. "You've gone too far, Howard."

"Not yet, Franklin! Not… just…yet."

Chapter 44

Capital Building
United States Senate Side
Public Corridors
6:44:38 PM

Bonnie stands for a heartbeat in close proximity to the Senate Majority Leader's office suite.

She's tense, and on edge as she scans the corridors in both directions. And past several school groups on tour.

Fortunately, there are lots of people in the corridors, mostly school children on "special" VIP tours to the restricted side of the Capital.

A bright, young guide, Monica, speaks to a group.

"Folks, we're still in the main open area.

Members will need to get thru this area quickly, without delay.

So, please stay close to the walls.

Now, follow me."

Bonnie loses herself in the group.

She is checking her wrist watch.

And walking.

Union Station, Washington, DC
6:44:58

I'm beginning to see why visitors say it's impossible to park in DC. Of course, I'm not sure why there is a parking problem. Such as the one I'm having now driving around the Union Station garage. It seems like all the cars in DC are on the roads, not in parking garages. I've arrived in the garage at Union Station, which took less than 15 minutes. But it appears it's going to take longer to find a spot.

I should have walked over from the Capital.

More exercise examples I can tell my PCP.

Wait! I have Obama care.

I lost my PCP.

He quit medicine.

Owns a Bed and Breakfast in Charlottesville, Virginia.

And is having trouble paying off his medical school tuition.

I think he's in need of therapy.

U.S. Capital Corridors
6:45:27 PM

While walking with the tour group, Bonnie spots Henning about 50 feet away. He sees her, and quickly turns, heading right for the group, determined to get her.

Bonnie bolts in the opposite direction.

Henning is stopped by the group. It crowds the corridor.

Bonnie turns a corner across the corridor from the Senate Appropriations Committee Room door.

Stepping from the unlocked door is Mister Ford, an ancient Black maintenance man. He's having a conversation…with himself.

"I gotta get me more good light bulbs. Well, why didn't you bring dem in with you, ya ole black fool. Youse just like the rest of dem fools in the place."

Ford vanishes around a far corner.

Bonnie checks the time. Then rushes into the Committee Conference Room.

Senate Appropriations Committee Room
6:46:27 PM

It has a large conference table that takes up most of the room. Portraits of former Senators line the walls.

Bonnie looks to lock the door. But, it's old and she determines it needs a key.

There is another door on a wall to her right. An inner door that perhaps leads to offices with people.

She runs over to the inner door. Grabs the door knob. "Shit."

It's locked.

At which point, Henning bursts in from the corridor door, startling her. She freezes, her back against the inner door.

Henning slams the outer door, hard.

"The lovely and very talented Miss Biersack. Missed you yesterday in Connecticut, sweetheart."

And now she can only conclude this guy is a psycho. She remembers Jack telling her that Henning is a psycho. Something about he and his sidekick, Pelicane, chasing him from Texas to South Carolina.

She panics.

He's about 15 feet from her, across the conference table. He moves to his right.

She moves to her right.

He stops.

She stops, and notices that he's wearing a 'green' lapel pin. The kind only issued by the Secret Service. It must be "green" week.

But how did he get one?

Those pins are very carefully distributed. And no one knows which one to wear, except the higher-ups at the Service.

She looks to her left, noticing a portrait of Senator Harry Reid.

The pose frightens her.

She wants to say something to Henning, but is speechless.

Sheer fright, from Henning's presence, and perhaps the Reid portrait, has paralyzed her.

"Is this our very first date, Bonnie? I sure hope there will be plenty more in the future. If you behave, of course."

Henning just stares.

Mustering an inner strength, she gives him the finger.

He chuckles. But says nothing. Just reaches into his jacket and pulls a Beretta hand gun from a shoulder holster. Then reaches into a pocket on his suit coat, and removes an illegal silencer.

He slowly fixes it to the weapon.

The twisting of metal clearly visible.

Bonnie panics.

"No...please..."

Henning takes aim as Bonnie sees something in her right peripheral vision. No more than an arm's length away.

"It *is* personal, Bonnie."

Union Station Parking Garage
6:47:52

Standing behind my Beemer, I think I've left enough room on both sides in this parking space.

Not to mention, the dope who owns the Honda on my right needs a parking lesson.

Thump…"…huh?…hey…oh."

"Jaws" stands over the now unconscious Jack Connolly.

Senate Appropriations Committee Room
6:48:09 PM

Bonnie grabs the Spectra Wasp Spray can, reaching to her right. Her ducking motion throws Henning off. His shot goes wild.

With Henning re-grouping his stance, Bonnie fires the Wasp Spray aimed at his face. The burning white spray gets Henning in the eyes.

His weapon has fired as his hands go to his eyes, now burning both.

The shot goes wild, hitting the portrait of Hop-along Harry Reid in the likeness of his forehead.

The portrait crashes to floor.

It breaks into several pieces.

Henning's weapon hits the Conference Room table with a loud thud.

It slides halfway across.

Henning is now screaming quite loudly, holding his hands at his eyes.

Bonnie drops the Spray can, and bolts around the Conference Room table, heading for Henning.

She gets within 4 feet of this guy.

Her right foot cocked back, she lets him have it with a "field goal" kick to the family jewels.

He hits the deck in excruciating pain.

He screams with whatever breath he has left in his body.

Bonnie hits the outer door. She pulls it open hard where it hits the portrait of Senator Chuck Schumer. The portrait crashes to the floor.

Senate Corridor H
6:48:59 PM

Bonnie takes off in a full sprint down the H Corridor, and past Monica's tour group.

"That's not someone heading for a floor vote, folks."

Bonnie stops to shelter in a doorway. She catches her breath. She looks up and down the corridor.

Out of the doorway, she heads for the Rotunda. The huge space that separates the Senate side from the House of Representatives side.

She freezes in place.

She has spotted Pelicane, who appears to be looking for someone, but not in her direction.

She reverses course.

The Capitol Rotunda
6:49:16 PM

Pelicane is dumbfounded. Where is she? He turns, looking in several directions.

Bingo!

There she goes. Away from the Rotunda area.

He's off and fast walking in her direction.

Chapter 45

**Union Station
Parking Garage
6:51:00 PM**

"Jaws" has lifted Jack Connolly and now carries him in a traditional fireman's rescue position.

Because of his size and strength, the effort involved here is of little consequence to "Jaws."

He takes Jack to the blue van marked "Capitol Police."

Opening the rear door, he flips Jack into the rear of the van. Jack's body hits with a thud, making an unusually loud sound inside the windowless van.

"Jaws" searches each of Jack's pockets, finding his iPhone. He examines it as if it's a foreign mechanism, unknown to his little brain.

He pockets the iPhone, checks the other pockets, finding nothing of interest. However, not turning Jack's unconscious body over onto his belly, he fails to find Jack's Glock 357.

Now finished, he moves to the passenger side door, opens it, and tosses in Jack's iPhone onto the front seat.

"Did you restrain him with the duct tape, Albert?"

Howard Hall has slipped quietly into the spot behind "Jaws" and startled the big guy.

Turning, and giving Hall tough look, he goes to grab him, but then backs off, noticing the suddenly fearful Hall.

"Sorry...Albert. Didn't mean to surprise you."

"Jaws" a/k/a Albert can only grunt.

"The duct tape, Albert?"

He nods at Hall. Then moves to the rear of the van with the duct tape in hand.

Hall watches, shaking his head and whispering, "dumb ass freak."

Stanton Park, Washington, DC
6:51:47 PM

Two young boys are bouncing a basketball down the sidewalk alongside Stanton Park. They stop to check out a van parked up ahead. They see it's a Pizza delivery truck. They scheme, curious if they could score a couple of slices. They sneak up to the trucks rear door.

Seated in the driver's seat is Guido.

Pizza guy extraordinaire, so he believes.

He sees the two boys. And knows they're about to open the rear door.

He smiles broadly as they approach.

One boy nods to the other.

They shorter boy grabs the handle, and yanks open the door.

At that moment a loud, ear splitting siren goes off.

And the boys bolt the area.

In the van, Guido laughs, then flips a switch on the dash. The siren is silenced.

At that moment, his cell phone chimes the tune Voltaire.

Glancing down Maryland Avenue from the van, he can see the Capitol, Northeast. He checks the caller ID, letting the caller, his Mama, go to voice mail.

Capitol Police Visitor Reception Booth
6:52:14 PM

Standing next to the booth, Bonnie sees that the post is empty. Looking up the steps towards the Senate entrance, she spots Pelicane at the top of the stairs. He's making his way down.

She heads for the open driveway entrance area that runs towards the Senate Russell Office Building. She's muttering to herself.

"Union Station...Union Station."

She takes a sharp left turn and fast walks to Delaware Avenue. A moment before she checks the time, then a look back.

Pelicane is hot on her tail.

She stops to slip out of her Ferragamo half heels.

Off she goes, sprinting in bear feet.

Pelicane sees this change of pace, running up Delaware Avenue.

He stops. Yanks his cell from a pocket, and, smiling, punches in seven numbers.

Pizza van at Stanton Park
6:53:47 PM

Guido answers.

"Yo."

"She's running up Delaware, towards Union Station."

"Yeah? No shit, man."

"Take her down."

"Done."

With that, Guido throws his cell on the floor.

The pizza van tears away at break-neck speed. It leaves some very serious rubber capturing the attention of the two young pizza thieves. They stop and watch the van disappear.

"Man, he must've been really pissed at us, Lee Boy."

"Yeah, bro. Ya think he knows what we look like?"

The van cuts off a car trying to make a left turn.

Guido leans on the car horn.

The other guy, with Congressional tags on his car, gives him the finger. Nice.

Delaware Avenue, NE, Towards Union Station
6:54:12 PM

Bonnie is now sprinting up Delaware towards Union Station, roughly 700 yards away. She's running against the traffic. Cars use their horns to make sure she sees what's ahead of her. Her purse, still hanging off her shoulder, flops.

Terror grips her expression with every car blast.

About halfway up Delaware she tosses her expensive Ferragamo shoes to the curb. Now, in her hands is her iPhone. She doesn't want to stop to check the time. But is confident that Jack will be on time, and waiting for her.

She pours on some speed.

D Street & Delaware Avenue, NE
6:54:21 PM

The pizza van approaches the intersection from D Street where it intersects with Delaware.

About 200 yards from Bonnie's current position.

Two tourists stop to have a look at the speeding van.

"Those Congressional aides make a big deal about having their pizzas delivered on time."

"No. I think it's their bosses, who think they're God."

"Yeah. It's why the hookers are close by."

Chapter 46

Delaware Avenue at D Street, NE
6:54:37 PM

The elderly gentleman, SILAS, and his alleged, highly intelligent Jack Russell Terrier, FANNY, stop on the corner of Delaware and D.

"Okay, Fanny. Now let's look both ways."

Fanny wags her tail, and turns her head to the left, watching a squirrel dart in and out of the under carriage of a parked car.

Silas looks to the right, scanning the area, stopping to watch a shapely blonde cross Delaware. She catches his eye, and gives the old dude a little smile, and a wink.

Fanny now shifts, moving his look to the right, eyeing an elderly woman who has now stopped on the opposite corner. She holds a dog leash attached to Mexican Chi-wa-wa.

Fanny must be thinking "...hum, a dinner snack."

Silas looks left.

They both look straight ahead.

"Okay, Fanny. All clear."
They step off the curb, and onto Delaware.

Delaware Avenue, NE
6:55:07 PM

Bonnie is terrorized sprinting up Delaware. She presses
to run faster. Tries to catch her breath. The sweat rolls down
her forehead, into her eyes. The saline fluid burns her eyes.
She's pushing herself to the limit. Union Station looms large
just up ahead. Then, a screeching sound comes from not that
far from her. She tries to focus, despite the moisture in her
eyes. She snaps quickly to her right, where she has
determined the location of the screeching sound comes from.
Her expression contorts to fear.
"Oh my God!"
She falls to her left. She hits the pavement.

325 Block of Delaware Avenue, NE
6:55:21 PM

Tires screeching. Thud. Thud. Bump. Bump. Crash.
Glass breaks. A radiator hisses. A hub cap rolls.

Delaware Avenue, NE
6:55:40 PM

The area is perfectly quiet. Pedestrians have stopped,
speechless, with horrific expressions. Some look down
Delaware Avenue, towards the U. S. Capitol. An extra cheese
and tomato sauce pizza is airborne for a moment before goes
splat onto the driver side window of a Mercedes 500 SEL. It
has Congressional tags, and is parked at the curb. It oozes
down to the street.
An 8 sided pizza box rolls, then falls over.

Chapter 47

Active Crime Scene
Delaware Avenue, NE
7:09:45 PM

LT C. EASTON, Metro Washington, DC Police
Department, and SGT B. Miller stand, fixed on something on
the ground. Their reluctance to go from here to the next step
in the investigation is apparent on their faces.

Easton takes the lead, as usual.

"Let's have a look."

They both crouch down. In front of them is a body
sheet that covers an accident victim. Easton takes a corner of
the sheet, and lifts it so both can see what's underneath.

Miller grimaces, and looks away.

"Whoa! Man, that had to hurt."

Easton thinks for a nano second, then adds.

"We'll have to check for ID. Can't tell much from just a
quick look."

Easton takes a closer look at the covered area.

"What's this thing stickin' out?"

He eyes a heavy duty blue strap of some kind coming out from under the body sheet, and stretching about 8 to 10 feet to behind a parked car.

He gets up and follows the straps path to another, yet smaller body sheet covering another accident victim.

"Oh, shit! I hope it ain't a kid."

Miller looks as if he may barf after thinking about what he just said.

Easton eyes him with suspicion, pointing at the blue strap. He says nothing. But, moves down to remove the sheet. Sticks his hand in to read something that he has found.

"Fanny."

"Say what, Boss?"

"Fanny...the dog's name is Fanny."

Easton and Miller stand and survey the accident area.

"I don't like the looks of this mess, Miller."

Officer Root, a young, uniformed officer and recent graduate of the Police Academy, approaches.

L T...found this cell phone next to the dead driver in the pizza van."

Easton takes the cell phone and examines it carefully.

"You're not gonna believe this, Miller."

Miller shrugs.

"A label on the back...Property of Homeland Security...PPD 44."

Officer Root needlessly has to say.

"I think that means Presidential Protective Detail."

Easton and Miller look at Root as if he's a moron.

"Miller. Find out who was issued this particular piece of official government equipment. And by whom."

"Right, Boss."

Easton sighs heavily, eyes closed. Then...at Miller.

"PPD 44? That was Obama, right? 44?"

"Yeah. We're still dealing' with those incompetent jackasses he brought to town."

Chapter 48

Avondale Campus
Office Complex of the Archbishop
7:12:41 PM

ARCHBISHOP MENDOZA burst from the doorway that leads into his office out into the semi-darkened and quiet hallway.

Hands on his hips, he looks with some level of anger up and down the hallway as if for someone who is supposed to be nearby. And at his beck and call.

Which, by the way, is practically everyone.

A moment passes, and with no live body in sight, Mendoza steams down the hallway about 30 feet. He barges into a private office.

The name on the door reads Monsignor R. Schneider.

He startles a Nun, Sister Mary Redemptor, who is hovering over Monsignor's desk, adjusting papers.

She's momentarily frightened. But being of an advanced age, she recovers quickly knowing the ins and outs of this nasty prelate.

"Where is he, Sister?"

"You mean Monsignor Schneider, your excellency?"

"Yes. Of course that's who I mean. Now, where is he...please?"

"Well, I would presume in the restroom. He's been fighting a nasty stomach bug all day, your excellency. You did not know?"

The condescending tone of her question is not lost on Mendoza.

He just glares for a long moment.

Then...

"Go find him!"

She moves slowly from around Schneider's large executive desk. She goes to leave, softly saying.

"As you wish, your excellency."

He does not see the playful smirk on her face, her head lowered out of respect for his position.

She closes the door with a louder than usual thud.

Mendoza takes a moment to survey Schneider's private office, a room he does not frequent very often.

Standing now at the desk, he moves several documents around. Papers he recognizes from the discussions he has had with his right hand man earlier.

Then, from under a magazine, Sports Illustrated, a vibration is heard. Mendoza, moving the sports magazine, sees Schneider's iPhone.

And the Message App lit up indicating an unread message in the message cue.

Lifting the iPhone, he notes the message is from Jack Connolly.

"Hum...Connolly?"

He reads the message.

And his blood begins to boil.

He swipes down, reading all of the correspondence between Schneider and Connolly.

He takes the iPhone and bolts back to his office.

Furious would not fully describe his current state.

Chapter 49

Union Station
Washington, DC
7:15:32 PM

BONNIE does a 360 degree turn. Not once but twice inside the massive, ornate popular DC landmark. She checks both inside and out.

The taxi cab stand.

No Jack.

Cars waiting beyond the taxi stand.

No Jack.

The Google kiosk.

No Jack.

Faces of people.

No Jack.

People standing. People sitting. People walking.

No Jack.

But also, no bad guys.

She now locates and finds the large clock that supposedly keeps perfect time.

It's just past 7:15, when Jack said he would be waiting. And if he's not here, then…she can't think about that.

Bonnie talks to no one in particular.

"Oh, God. Where are you Jack Connolly?"

She ducks behind a pillar, in the shadows as she yanks out her iPhone. It's in her purse still slung around her neck and on her right shoulder, resting on her left hip. She punches in seven numbers.

And for a moment, she looks down at her very dirty, bare feet.

"Shit."

Fortunately she remembers that she carries a pair of soft, flat, fold-up slippers in her purse. Ones she wears in the office, hiding her feet under the desk while working.

Union Station Parking Garage
7:16:09 PM

Howard Hall has finally gone off the reservation. His evil stare at the unconscious Jack Connolly, now tied and taped in the back of the infamous blue van, speaks volumes.

He smirks, as Jaws waits alongside Hall for further instructions.

Thy both hear the sounds of Jack's iPhone ringing from the front passenger seat.

Hall retrieves the iPhone.

"Yes?"

Bonnie, partially hidden in the Union Station main lobby, just two levels up from where Hall is located, frowns.

"Jack?"

"Bonnie, why don't you just tell us where you are."

"Hall? Where's Jack? Let me speak to him...now."

"He's with us...now, you tell us where you are. We need to clear up this mess."

Bonnie paces away from her concealed spot, enraged.

"Let me speak to him now!"

"He's fine, Bonnie. Comfortable, waiting for tour call."

Bonnie looks frantic at the LED screen. A moment before she slams a finger on the red disconnect symbol.

On his end, Hall smirks at the disconnect. Turns to Jaws.

"Go back to the Capitol. Find her."

He tosses Jack's iPhone onto the passenger seat of the blue van.

Union Station Main Lobby
7:16:57 PM

Bonnie looks around the huge main lobby. Through an open space to the outside she sees the Taxi stand.

She makes a bee line for the Taxi first in line.

She jumps in. slams the door.

The Driver, Mohammed, swings around, facing her.

"Where to, Miss?"

Bonnie thinks for a moment.

"The State Department."

The taxi takes off as Bonnie gazes with a distant expression out the window. He mind pings the same question over and over again.

"What the hell happened to you, Jack?"

She knows he said to her that if he was not there to meet her, something has gone wrong. She knows Jack well enough that, for a Secret Service Agent, it's not a minor issue like not finding a parking space, or being held up getting a traffic ticket.

It means something serious.

She's worried sick.

She's sweaty and scared.

She tries to calm herself, employing mental gymnastics Naval Officers are taught to employ when faced with danger.

She mastered the task at the Naval Academy.

Right now, it's not working.

Now thinking along another vein, she comes to a desperate conclusion about those folks who are chasing her.

She bolts forward, whacking the taxi driver on his shoulder.

"No, not the State Department. Drop me at 19th Street and Virginia. The corner. Go behind the Interior Department."

The Driver, Mohammed, waves after a moment of high anxiety being whacked on the shoulder by Bonnie.

Union Station Parking Garage
7:17:29 PM

Howard Hall watches as Jaws maneuvers the blue van, backwards, into a different parking spot in a far corner. He backs up until the rear doors hit the concrete wall.

Jaws now looks to exit the van from the driver's side door, but it will not open far enough for the big guy to get out.

He strains to move over to the passenger side door.

Hall watches.

"Moron."

Standing in the exit lane, Hall's cell phone rings.

"What?"

Appropriations Committee Room
7:17:45 PM

Pelicane stands, but leaning against the ornate, large conference table. He takes in the many portraits of former Senators, some already dead, some to be soon, most likely sooner rather than later.

He eyes a portrait of Senator Durbin (D-IL). His little brain has to think for an extended moment.

Then, he gives the likeness the finger.

On the floor, below Pelicane, Henning groans, his hands grabbing the family jewels.

He speaks into his cell phone.

"She's gone."

Hall starts to pace in a tight circle, thinking of a plan.

A plan to capture Bonnie Biersack before it's too late. Hall knows that the Israeli Knesset will likely certify the elections tomorrow morning, giving the victory officially to Noah David.

At which point, The Prince implements the final phase of his plan. A plan Howard Hall, Noah David, and Franklin Hennessy helped stich together starting over 40 years earlier.

The Prince, holding their alternative sexual inclinations over their collective heads, set down the rules of engagement.

Not following those rules would result in untold recriminations against each personally.

A fate, the wimpy, spineless, two-faced Howard Hall has feared all these years.

"Stake out her home." He says to Pelicane.

Pelicane stands upright, trying to make sense of another problem at the moment.

"Okay. Got it. But – "

"But what, Pelicane?"

"What do I do with Henning? His in pretty bad shape here. Looks like he's gonna pass out anytime now."

Hall lowers the cell phone to his leg, and slaps hard.

"Where did I find this jackass?"

He replaces the cell phone to his ear.

"Drag his sorry ass out of there. Get help from someone in maintenance. Get him in the elevator and down to the portico.

Pause

"Where you left your freakin' car, Pelicane."

"Okay. Got it."

"Then call me at the White House."

Hall slams the disconnect icon.

"Jackass."

Hall takes a moment as he continues to watch Jaws exit the blue van.

He punches in 7 numbers on his cell.

And waits for an answer.

Then…

"You still outside at State?"

He listens.

"I suspect she's gonna go there. For her it's a safe harbor from us. She is a Naval Officer, you know."

He disconnects.

Punches in 7 new numbers.

Waits.

Then…

"I think you need to call the Prince.

Hall breaths deeply.

"It's time for full press damage control."

On the other end is Senator Franklin Hennessy.

"How bad?"

Hall stutters slightly.

"She's gone…if she does get to the media…someone with connections to Israeli Diplomats…we're screwed, Franklin."

"The Prince is gonna be really pissed at you, Howard."

Hall goes white as a ghost. The failure has been dropped in his lap. And he's probably a dead man.

"I'll be in my office."

He disconnects from Hennessy.

And he thinks hard to himself as his life passes before his closed eyes.. The mis-steps and mistakes he's made over the years.

Maybe not taking that admin job years ago with that pharmacutical guy in Virginia was a huge mistake. How stressful could it have been working for the village idiot.

Someone with more money than sense.

Interior Department at Virginia Avenue
7:23:21 PM

Bonnie exits the taxi, and casually mingles with a small group of people leaving the Interior Department complex. Those employees who take advantage of the flex time schedule help to relieve the massive traffic congestion that plagues the city.

She walks up Virginia Avenue, heading northwest towards the State Department, two blocks away. Now, under the cover of darkness, as the sun has set, she feels some sense of security.

State Department
7:27:00 PM

Bonnie has stopped at the entrance to the underground garage. After giving this some thought, she decides to enter the building through a rarely used public entrance.

State Department
Public Entrance
7:27:49 PM

Inside the building, she heads for the security check point and the guard that is posted. Another guard stands about 10 feet away, and inside the secure area, watches closely as Bonnie flashes her credentials packet.

The guard eyes the creds, then asks.

"Ma'am, your ID card, please."

She hand it over. He runs the card through the electronic reader.

After a moment, and reviewing the information on his screen, the guard hands Bonnie her ID.

"Have a nice evening, ma'am."

She smiles, while passing through the body scan detector. She heads for the bank of elevators.

While standing at the elevator bank, she has another thought. Her eyes shift to her right. She zeros in on the stairwell door.

A moment.

And she makes her way to the stairwell door, bursting through it with some force.

At the security station, the head security guard, who was observing Bonnie check in, casually walks to the guards computer. Looking at it for a moment, he reaches over, and keystrokes and a brief code.

On the screen, he reads "Biersack, Bonnie, Commander, USN, Level 1A, 7:28:00 PM."

To no one in particular.

"Level 1A. That's not military clearance."

The younger, junior guard leans in.

"Level 1A...that's the President's clearance, right Louie?"

State Department
Underground Garage
7:31:04 PM

Bonnie is now in the garage and walks slowly up and down the aisles. She's checking names on the wall, indicating reserved parking spaces.

After about five minutes, she stops at one spot. The name of the wall reads "T Trumble."

In the parking spot, a beat up, ancient Volvo. In this environment, it looks out of place. She checks the area around the Volvo, three or four cars away in both directions.

No one can be seen or heard.

She now moves to a tight space between the Volvo and the wall, under Tommy Trumble's name, sits down, and now begins to softly sob.

Union Station Parking Garage
7:53:27 PM

A Metro Transit Police Officer makes his rounds in the parking garage. He's slow, and meticulous, if not careful. Even touching the wrong car, such as one of the more expensive rides, those preferred by the rich and famous of this town, i.e., the Lobbyists, would set off the alarm.

He notes the Capitol Police Van parked in backwards, and very close to a wall on its driver side.

As the magnetic placard on the van is somewhat unusual, he decides to look through the windshield. He uses his flashlight to get a better look.

Nothing seems unusual to him other than the van being in the garage without an Officer in the vicinity.

Rather than attempt to inspect the van further, nor record the tag number and vehicle ID on his remote MDT, the Officer moves on, forgetting a basic function from his training.

State Department
Underground Garage
8:20:09 PM

Tommy Trumble comes through the garage door from the stairwell. Pushing hard, the door bangs against the wall, sending an echo through the area.

He quickly grabs the door handle, slowly closing the door realizing he, perhaps, created a stir.

He moves down the aisle whistling, and swinging his briefcase at his side.

He gets to the driver side of his Volvo, searching for the key.

"Tommy?"

At the sound of Bonnie's voice, he reels back, bouncing off the car next to his. Then bounces forward where he, again, bounces back to the other car. Then slides to the floor.

He gets a grip, turning towards the voice, eyes now shut hard.

Arms flung into the air.

Briefcase has already crashed to the ground.

"Don't shoot! Don't Shoot!"

"Tommy! Tommy! Shut up, will you. Please, shut up. It's me. Bonnie."

He's breathing very hard now, about to hyperventilate.

He lowers his arms, looking for his glasses on the floor.

Actually, they're hanging off one of his ears.

Bonnie moves over to him, squatting down.

She fixes his glasses. And he now can see it's her, and not some crazed lunatic wanting to rob and kill him.

"Bonnie! What the heck?"

"Tommy. I need you to help me."

Tommy squirms in place, shifting his eyes from her.

A moment.

"I think I...ah...oh, shaw...I didn't, did I?"

"Tommy. It's okay. It's okay."

She grabs his arm.

"I'm sorry. I didn't mean to frighten you. But, I need you to take me home."

"Huh?"

"I need you to help me hack into a computer."

"Huh?"

Tommy settles down. Wipes the sweat from his forehead.

"Whose computer, Bonnie?"

"The President of the United States."

Chapter 50

Union Station Parking Garage
Blue Van
8:26:13 PM

"What the hell!"
Okay. It's dark. But not that dark.
And I'm closed in.
Lucky I'm an experienced submariner.
Or else I'd be suffering from claustrophobia.
And my head hurts like a bitch.
My mouth is taped shut. And my arms are tied behind my back. But they seem to be fastened to something on the deck of this...where the hell am I?
A small truck, maybe.
A panel van.
The front of the truck is behind me. And I'm likely behind the front seats. Except, we're not moving. I don't hear the sound of an engine. So, we're stopped. Somewhere.
Last thing I remember was being in the Union Station garage.
Maybe we're still there.

Maybe the driver went up to the main lobby for a hot dog and a drink.

I need to get loose of this restraint on my hands.

Then swing my legs around, and kick the crap out of the inside panel.

Someone will surely hear the noise.

Someone like, maybe, a Transit Cop whose job it is to check the vehicles in the garage for extended stays. Like those cars in here for more than two hours.

This is not an over-night parking facility.

It's short term.

Park.

Pick up your best friend, or mother-in-law, if you're so lucky, who just got off the train and is staying at your place...indefinitely.

Then leave the garage.

Of course, that's assuming I'm tied up in a truck that's in the Union Station parking garage.

I could be in a parking lot in Southeast DC, next to a 7 Eleven, like the one that gets robbed every 30 minutes by some bad ass "brothers" with guns and knives.

"Shit. I'm screwed."

State Department
Underground Garage
8:29:37 PM

Tommy stands, shaking a little, as he looks over Bonnie's motorcycle.

"Tommy. We can't take your car. We need to make good time over to Alexandria. So, hop on!"

"Well...I don't know, Bonnie."

"And we need to take one way streets...the wrong way...in case we're followed."

"Huh?"

Tommy straddles the bike, holding onto Bonnie.
"Bonnie. Shouldn't I have a helmet?"
She ignores him, gunning the bike.
It takes off, up the garage ramp, taking a sharp left hand turn onto 21st, then left onto Virginia Avenue.
Tommy is not liking this excursion.
"Ahhhhhhhhhh."
Bonnie shoots up Virginia towards the Watergate Complex, knowing that it's likely she'll be followed. Which explains the plan to use one way streets.
The wrong way!

State Department
At 21st Street
8:30:54 PM

The Black Buick, two men in the front, strap on seat belts. They observe the Suzuki Motorcycle tear from the State garage, and fly down Virginia.
They take Virginia on two wheels, and rocket up the wide street towards the Watergate.

At 24th Street
8:31:17 PM

From Virginia, Bonnie takes a right onto 24th Street, then a quick right onto G Street…going the wrong way! A planned diversion. Tommy, noticing the one way sign going the other way, panics.
"Ahhhhhhhhhh."

At 24th Street & G
8:31:55 PM

The Black Buick slams on its brakes.
"Sonofabitch!"

It continues up 24th Street towards K street, entering Foggy Bottom at the edge of George Washington University, and crosses over New Hampshire Avenue.

At 21st Street and G
8:32:09 PM

Bonnie hangs a left onto 21st Street and throttles up, going the wrong way thru the George Washington University Campus towards K street.

"Ahhhhhhhhhh."

"Tommy! Will you please shut the hell up! You're alarming the pedestrians. And drawing attention to us."

They have reached K Street, and Bonnie hangs a left hand turn. Again, at better than a 45 degree angle.

They head west to the Washington Circle, a block and a half away.

At K & 24th Street
8:34:29 PM

The Black Buick is now ½ block from the Washington Circle. And the traffic slows them down to a much safer speed. They must merge into the circle, at the same time keep a look out for that Suzuki Motorcycle carrying their target. And some fat guy who they don't know.

Washington Circle
8:35:51 PM

Bonnie and Tommy hit the Washington Circle at the Northeast point the same moment the Black Buick hits the Circle at the Southwest point.

The Black Buick is unable to see the Motorcycle.

It is fully concealed by the huge statue that sits in the middle of the Circle.

The Black Buick continues, in traffic, out of the circle and east bound on K street.

Bonnie and Tommy exit the circle onto K street. They continue west bound.

At Rock Creek Bonnie exits K Street and merges onto the Potomac Parkway. She heads for the Arlington Memorial Bridge in the distance behind the Lincoln Memorial.

For the moment, she determines they are in the clear.

Union Station Parking Garage
8:36:47 PM

I've been able to get some of the restraint on my hands loosened. Although, not enough to move my legs closer to the side panel inside this truck and kick like shit.

The good news is I can hear cars going by as if entering and exiting the parking garage.

The squeal that tires make in here only happens on a painted concrete or non-asphalt surface. That is what would be normally found on a parking garage surface. This would confirm that we're not parked at some burned out 7 Eleven in the 'hood, presently surrounded by gun wielding youngsters who have dropped out of school.

Of course, you do know they carry a gun in one hand and a basketball in the other. See an urban kid with a basketball, panic!

The basketball was likely stolen from the Dick's Sporting Goods store in Bethesda.

It's where Obama used to buy his basketballs before he decided that golf was more genteel.

Anyway, I need to keep my spirits up as Bonnie is perhaps in more danger than she possibly realizes. If they got to me, and were able to put me in a position where I am not able to help, then God help her. Trust me on that point.

I'm still working on getting free...pronto.

Alexandria, Virginia
Vernon Street
8:49:19 PM

Bonnie pulls over and stops on the small side street that's just off Henry Street, a main street in Alexandria.

"Tommy. We can't go to my place on the bike. Where do you live?"

"Mother and I live on Queen, at Henry Street. It's small, but we both fit."

Bonnie conjures up an image, but quickly erases it from her brain.

"Good. Just two blocks or so from my place. We'll go to your house. Leave the bike in your driveway. Walk over to my place."

She kick starts the bike. And they're off.

Henry Street at Queen
8:53:06 PM

They park the bike. They move thru several private yards, ending up in Bonnie's back yard.

"Quiet."

"Why are you whispering? You live here."

"We need to break in."

Tommy breaks into a serious sweat.

"What?"

"Shut up and follow me."

Using a garden tool, they break into Bonnie's flat on the second level in the rear.

"This *is* your home, right Bonnie?"

"I think so. But I'm not sure. Let's go in and find out."

"Huh?"

Chapter 51

Alexandria, Virginia
Commander Bonnie Biersack's Home
8:56:36 PM

Bonnie and Tommy move slowly thru the kitchen and into the living room, using the moonlight to navigate the rooms.

Whack!

"Don't hold me there, Tommy. My jacket!"

Tommy holds onto Bonnie's waist jacket.

"Why don't we just turn on a few lights, Bonnie?"

"No! I think those guys that tried to follow us may be out on the street waiting for us to get here."

"Oh."

Bonnie pulls the drapes and yanks at the venetian blind cord making the room even darker.

Turning on her laptop, the LED screen now provides light.

"Where's Jack?"

"I don't know…I'm worried."

"He'll be okay, Bonnie. I have a good feeling. Anyway, I know all about him."

Bonnie stops.

And grills Tommy a long stare.

"Meaning?"

"Ah…well, I hacked into this file. You know, the OMB data base over at the OEOB. That's next door to the White House, Bonnie."

Tommy smiles broadly.

Bonnie frowns.

And she's a little ticked off.

"I know where the OEOB is, Tommy. I had an office in that building."

"Oh…so, anyway, Jack has had an interesting career. You know, the Navy and everything. He's very bright and competent. Able to solve most any problem."

"I see, Tommy. And how is it that you know this?"

"Oh, Lieutenant Corey Fanning."

"Fanning? She's a Naval Officer?"

"Oh, more than that, Bonnie. She's a lawyer. You know, defended Jack at that hearing in Pearl Harbor a number of years ago. The submarine crash or something. But her real role is very top secret."

"Really."

"Yeah. She role plays for the top brass. Giving them a "heads up" on senior officers. You know, guys up for Flag Officer promotions."

Pause. He thinks.

"Should I be telling you this?"

"Just guys? And you were exposed to the report she submitted?"

"Well…okay, but I didn't read the whole thing."

"Why? Not complimentary?"

"Well...there's a section where Jack had to provide a review of his experience with her, as an attorney."

"And?"

"It was rather...kinda like an expose."

"You mean of his personal experience with her?"

"Ah...well...it read like a letter to Penthouse. You know the creepy and dirty sex stuff."

Bonnie folds her arms.

"You read Penthouse, Tommy?"

"Oh, no...no...never. Not me."

"Really."

She has a thin smile.

"Well, I hope she was, at least, pretty."

"Oh, she's very sexy, and cute, Bonnie."

Bonnie takes a step closer to him.

And how do you know that, Tommy?"

"The Pentagon. She works at the Pentagon. Been there about a year. I see her all the time."

"Really!"

Tommy senses, perhaps, a problem with this revelation.

"Well, maybe it's not her. Someone that looks like her. You know, hard to tell theses. Can't be sure."

Bonnie paces in a slow circle.

"So, Lieutenant Corey Fanning. Maybe Jack will introduce me."

Pause.

"I'm sure he's thought about that."

Union Station Parking Garage
9:04:47 PM

Okay. Finally I can slide around and reach the side panel with my feet.

Hopefully, I'll be heard by someone once I start banging.

Of course, this sort of reminds of my quarters at Pearl Harbor during the hearing about that "incident" on the submarine.

The reprimand that got me re-assigned to the White House and a cushy job as Naval Attaché to the President.

Of course, Dad and Grandpa, both being retired Admirals, maybe have had something to do with that new assignment.

I'm not so sure.

Taking me off a submarine, where the entire crew is all male, and dropping me into the White House where the staff is 61% female, most of whom are under 30, has had its, shall we say, unintended consequences.

Translation: lucky me.

However, out at Pearl Harbor, most of my evenings involved a lot of banging.

What I mean is the head board of my bed banging against the wall. I knew you'd understand, right?

A wall that separated my quarters from a young Navy prosecutor, some nerd with both Columbia and Harvard degrees, who got lucky when the Navy said they'd pay for his education.

He was at Pearl on a short time assignment.

An assignment to prosecute me for dereliction of duty on board a U.S. Naval vessel. Poppy cock!

Yet, every time he stood to speak in the court room, with the very cute and sexy Lieutenant Fanning giving him her full attention with a lustful, sultry stare, he came apart.

Interesting.

Which reminds me.

I need to take her number at the Pentagon off my contact list.

And commit it to memory, of course.

Anyway, we'll see how the banging goes inside this truck.

Alexandria, Virginia
Bonnie's Home
9:07:19 PM

Bonnie is seated at her laptop. She's typing an e-mail message.

It's addressed to the President of the United States.

Tommy peers over her shoulder.

"Why can't you just send it to his private e-mail address, Bonnie?"

"It's blocked. No one can get in unless it goes through some sort of protocol set up by some secret , mysterious White House IT crew. Also, I need the message to be flagged so he sees it as soon as it gets to his private laptop."

"Yeah. The one in his small sitting room next to the Oval Office."

Bonnie continues to type.

Then, suddenly stops.

Turns at Tommy.

"The one in his small sitting room next to the Oval?"

"Ah...yeah. It's a Dell."

She just stares at this nerd.

Then...

"Who knows about that private laptop, Tommy?"

"Besides the secret IT crew?"

She nods.

"No one."

"And how do you know?"

"Well, I'm the secret IT crew. But, you can't tell anyone, right, Bonnie?"

She sighs.

"Can you get my message on his screen at a specific time."

Tommy postures.

"Of course."

"Good. But you seemed worried about hacking into the Presidents computer."

"I know. That's what the Secret Service told me to do if anyone asks."

Pause.

"Fooled ya, huh?"

She's gonna smack him.

But restrains herself.

"When I get it finished I'll have you send it. It must be done at a specific time. When he's in that small sitting room."

"Well, I don't know that piece of secret stuff, Bonnie."

"But I do."

"Oh? Well that's odd, Bonnie."

"He told me, in a rather strange way, yesterday."

She leans back, having to think about the peculiar item she has just mentioned to Tommy.

The President was somewhat vague in nature, but the point was clear.

She knows she was given a way to contact him, if the need arose.

Odd? Certainly.

Now the questions that ping around her highly gifted brain have risen to a level of unparalleled mystery.

Am I really the messenger?

Or am I just one of Archbishop Mendoza's pawns in a strange game involving both a political and diplomatic ruse?

Chapter 52

Home of Senator Franklin Hennessy (R-CT)
9:08:41 PM

SENATOR FRANKLIN HENNESSY holds his cell phone close to his left ear. He listens to the voice on the other end with a degree of angst and disgust on his face. His eyes dart around the luxurious condo he owns. Thanks to the generosity of his longtime benefactor, Archbishop Joseph Mendoza.

Who just happens to be the voice on the other end of this difficult call.

"I understand, your excellency."

He focuses on the LED screen of his computer. A few more clicks. And he's at the spot he needs to be.

He inserts a thumb drive into a USB port, and clicks several times again.

"Yes. I did confirm with State that the Israeli Knesset will certify Noah's election tomorrow morning in a full session. It's scheduled for five hours from now...roughly 2am Washington, DC time."

A moment before the line disconnects.

Hennessy just stares with anger at the now dead cell phone call. The cell gets stowed in his jacket pocket. He quickly gathers some papers from his desk along with a thumb drive that was inserted into a USB port moments ago.

The items are placed in a leather brief case that carries the initials FH.

He throws on a coat. He leaves his home in somewhat of a hurry.

Hennessy walks down his short driveway, hastily. He jumps into a Black Lincoln Town car. It sports blue Connecticut tags, "FH – 1." He fires up the engine, and wastes no time backing onto the street. He leaves the neighborhood.

Mike & Daisy's Neighborhood Tavern
9:10:26 PM

Jerry Mulderick, a middle-aged man in an expensively tailored blue pin striped suit, the kind worn by the pricey lobbyist attorneys over on K Street, walks unsteadily from the tavern. His tie is loosened and askew.

He mumbles to himself about some young skirt he left at the bar. Someone that would not accompany him to the room at the Ritz Carlton he reserved earlier in the evening.

Clearly the rejection has pissed off this married mover and shaker in the world of Washington, DC influence peddlers.

Mulderick stops on the sidewalk in front of the Tavern, facing the street. He's apparently in some sort of confused state judging by the way he looks around.

A moment.

He decides to go left. He has come up on about seven or eight parked cars in the small lot.

Mulderick is obviously unsure which one of the cars belongs to him. He removes his keys from his suit jacket pocket. Presses the fob. He notices the lights of a silver SUV Lincoln Navigator blink several times.

That's the one.

He's in the SUV. Fires up the engine. Throws the car into drive. He peels out of the gravel parking lot. He leaves some serious dust and loose gravel on several other cars.

A pink Mini Cooper traveling on the street screeches to stop, barely missing the SUV.

Alexandria, Virginia
Outside Bonnie's Home
9:11:53 PM

Two men sit in a Black Buick about ½ block from Bonnie's apartment. They know it's a two story private home in this quiet neighborhood.

And they know she occupies the second level.

In the Buick, a cell phone chimes in Henning's hand.

Pelicane grabs a look at the uncomfortable Henning riding shotgun. Henning's other hand holds his crotch.

He grabs the cell phone from Henning. He answers. "Yeah. Your dime."

From a darkened room at the White House, Howard Hall grits his teeth, momentarily wanting to strangle the moron on the end of the cell call.

"Any sign of her?"

Pelicane looks to the outside, and up to the second level of the house where Bonnie lives.

"Nada. Zip. Nyet."

Hall turns red faced.

"Now look carefully, Pelicane. Anyone in the apartment? Lights would be on. Maybe shadows."

"Can't really tell'…it's a crime scene. Ya know? Someone's car was torched."

"Yeah. Let me make this clear, Pelicane. If you see her, fix my problem. Or I will fix your problem."

Click

The call has ended.

Pelicane looks over at Henning, who is breathlessly waiting for a report on the call.

"Well, he wants her dead. Or us dead. Or both of us dead."

Henning can only just stare.

Pelicane looks back towards Bonnie's home.

"That Nancy, Mister Hall, really needs a boyfriend."

Alexandria, Virginia
Bonnie's Home
9:13:09 PM

Bonnie reviews her e-mail message to the President one last time. She sighs as she reads through the key points of the plan that could have worldwide ramifications.

Her disappointment is evident.

Perhaps it's the bizarre and foolish consequence of what happens when personal ideology and political agendas end up on a collision course. Agendas that should be designed for the common good.

She knows the window for reversing this fiasco is closing rapidly.

And the President's actions to stop implementation of the first stages will require time. It will not take a phone call. But decisive action by several people around the globe.

While the President had to have had knowledge of certain elements of the plan, he was clearly mislead and misinformed by two of his closest friends and advisors, Franklin Hennessy and Howard Hall.

She has accepted her role now. She has learned the President was in a box, not able to directly stop the plan. And perhaps used her to locate and contact his "spiritual" advisor, Brother Malcolm Lamb.

Bonnie thought that he himself, as President, could have used Malcolm Lamb. But would Lamb have filled in some of the holes for his former classmate?

Unlikely. His role is strictly prayer.

So, Bonne was chosen. As so carefully stated by Brother Malcolm Lamb. Who was given her e-mail address by the President.

She looks over at Tommy.

"Time to put it up on his screen, Tommy."

Tommy has finished reading his copy. One printed out for him by Bonnie.

"Gosh. This sure is serious stuff, Bonnie."

"I never want another e-mail again from someone I don't even know. Only friends, Tommy."

No sooner said then her e-mail "dings." A new message. She take a moment to digest it contents, making mental notes of the distressful information.

"I can do that for you, Bonnie. Ya know? Fix your e-mail."

Huh? Oh, she gives him a big smile.

"Okay. Time to hack into the President's computer."

"Cool. Kinda like hacking into that private server Hilary Clinton had in her home up in Chappaqua, New York."

Bonnie drills him a serious look.

Then...

"You didn't, right, Tommy?"

Tommy turns bright red. Then, meekly...

"Someone at the White House asked me to do it."

Bonnie gives this some intense brain power.

Then...

"I don't wanna hear anymore, Tommy."

He hits the keyboard, fast typing a variety of unintelligible codes.

Massachusetts Avenue
Washington, DC
9:14:47 PM

The Black Lincoln Town car – Connecticut tag "FH 1" - rolls down Massachusetts Avenue. But not at an excessive speed. The driver, Senate Majority Leader Franklin Hennessy (R-CT), appears to be deliberately staying under or at least close to the speed limit. The last thing he needs now is to be stopped by a Metro cop.

The several martini's at the office and at home would certainly result in a DUI arrest.

He has been one to eschew the special DC tags provided to Members of Congress and the Senate in the interest of maintaining some degree of anonymity.

Unlike his Democratic colleagues, who prefer the "higher than all others" image as professed by Congresswoman Nancy Pelosi, he takes his position as the servant of his constituency rather seriously.

Traffic is light and absent of those disgusting cowboys. Members of foreign delegations driving themselves to and from local watering holes. Who live and work on this Avenue. Who enjoy the luxury of "diplomatic immunity."

The White House, West Wing
Howard Hall's Office
9:15:13 PM

Howard Hall sits at his desk. Head in his hands, he mumbles incoherently to himself.

He's beat. Worn out.

A bottle of Johnny Walker Black label at his elbow, almost empty.

He's reached the end of his rope.

Fed up with the whole mess.

From being known as "The Hump," to the continual put downs by those he once thought to be his closest and only friends, he's now an empty suit.

He started out with nothing. And has amounted to nothing.

Hanging on to those with money, power, and superior intellects got him very little other than a tiny office in the West Wing.

Breaking the silence of his small world, the telephone console rings.

He lets it ring several times, giving it a fearful stare.

He answers, and listens.

Then…

"Yes…yes, I'm on my way. The staff door near the rear. Pause.

"She's being dealt with now, at her place in Alexandria. Pause.

"I understand, your excellency. Yes. I know. But –"

Hall stares at the handset, the call being abruptly terminated.

He replaces the handset on the console, then drops his head forward, eyes closed, his chin hitting his chest.

SUV Navigator
9:15:59 PM

The K Street lobbyist/attorney, Mulderick, drives slowly through a quiet residential neighborhood.

He flips the satellite radio on. He punches the number 2. The only number he can make out. He's tuned into a favorite Blue Grass station. The other numbers are a blur.

He taps the steering wheel to the beat of the music.

Mulderick now approaches an intersection.

The traffic signal has turned red.

He continues. And runs the red light.

No one sees him.

Alexandria, Virginia
Bonnie's Home
9:16:20 PM

Bonnie has finished reading the frightening e-mail. This one ID'd as coming from Brother Malcolm Lamb.

"Ready, Tommy?"

"Okay. You're sure this is okay, Bonnie?"

"He told me he would be in his study at this time. I guess he figured I'd find a way to get a message to him."

"Like finding me, huh, Bonnie? It's destiny, right?"

Bonnie just gives him a look.

She resets.

"Pull my message from the Word file. Put it on his screen."

"Okay."

He's punching in some more codes.

She's frowning.

"What are you doing?"

"Re-setting a protocol, so I can bypass his security firewall."

Bonnie observes, but thinking about this process.

"So, this won't leave a finger print that leads back to me, right? Like, if the Secret Service or FBI wanna know if someone got into his computer, they'd see who's been there?"

"Oh, sure, Bonnie. They'd be at your front door before you could blink. Just like Hilary Clinton's server."

She leans back and starts to tremble, thinking.

This whole issue is starting to take on a new, yet perhaps criminal chapter to my selection as the messenger.

I hope the President is not totally taken by surprise when he reads my message.

Chapter 53

The White House
The President's Private Study
9:17:32 PM

In the President's small study, just off the Oval Office, is William. He's a White House butler, a long time African American employee of the White House. He has cleared the square table of dishes and flatware President Gonzmart used for his light supper.

William is alone in the study.

He wipes down the table with a clean cloth. Then moves to the President's working desk and collects a tea cup and saucer.

He turns, and walks away from the desk when he realizes that the napkin is missing. He stops to check the chairs at the table. He then walks back to the desk for a look on that chair and the floor.

He spots the missing linen on the floor, under the desk.

William gets down on his knees and retrieves the linen napkin. He bumps his head, when he hears an odd ding.

His bruised head pops up, wondering "huh?"

Straightening on his knees, he notices the President's laptop computer is flashing a red "alert" icon in the upper right corner of the screen.

Immediately, William stands, his eyes fixed on the LED screen. It takes him a long heartbeat to develop a sense of panic. His eyes shift in several directions almost simultaneously. He steps closer to the screen attempting to figure it all out.

What he's faced with is surely a mystery to his aged mind.

He wipes a bead of sweat from his forehead when, from behind him, a door opens and closes.

"William. You about done in here?"

William turns.

Panic has enveloped his features.

"Oh, my goodness, Mister President. I was there under your desk, sir. And hit my head so bad it done made your computer here make a funny noise.

"And then this red thing comes on it."

William wipes more sweat away.

"I'm sorry sir, but I think I did something real bad to your computer."

The President eyes his computer.

Then, chuckles briefly.

He gives William a little pat on the back.

"No, William. That little red icon means there's an important message waiting for me to read."

"Oh. You're sure, Mister President? 'Cause I think I did something real bad, like I said, sir."

Gonzmart smiles.

"Thank you, William."

The butler leaves as President Gonzmart sits at his desk, keying in a series of passwords in order to retrieve the message.

Union Station Parking Garage
9:18:51 PM

My legs are killing me. I can't kick any more.

Huh?

What was that that?

I think someone just knocked on the windshield. I better start kicking some more.

"Hey! Someone in there?"

Having my mouth taped makes answering that guy a bit difficult.

I hear the passenger side door open.

And I grunt like a pregnant pig.

Looking up and behind me, I see this dude looking down from over the passenger seat at me.

"Hey, man. Why ya'all tied up?"

Okay. So I didn't pray for a Noble Prize winner to find me. But I'll take the genius that just found me.

He climbs over the seat, and into the back of the van. And rips the tape off my face.

I breath clean air through my mouth like I've never breathed before. At the same time giving him the once over.

He asks. "What the hell, man?"

"It's a long story, dude. But the guys that did this work in the White House." Thought I'd throw out that tidbit.

"No shit, man. The White House?"

"Untie the dude, Stretch."

That was the voice of a young lady who is now in the passenger seat.

Stretch says. "That's my bitch, man. Leslie."

And the odor of marijuana over-takes me.

"What are you two doing in this garage?"

As Stretch is working on the rope that's been holding me in place, he fills me in.

"This place is where we meet. Ya know. With them dudes from the Capitol building."

I have to ask for a clarification, hoping it's not what I'm thinking.

"Dudes from the Capitol? The House? The Senate? "

"Yeah, man. Like Congress people and their ladies."

"Congresswomen?"

"This is where they buy my shit. They're awesome customers, man. The best. Got one dude from Michigan…I think…maybe Missouri. Shit, I don't know, man…one of them M states. Keeps getting elected. He's always stoned, man."

"Anyone I may know?"

Leslie jumps in.

"Like the big guy with the zipper problem said a long time ago, don't ask, don't tell."

Okay.

Got it.

I'll take that "Clintonesk" as none of my business.

Stretch is finished cutting me loose.

"Hey! I can't thank you enough…Stretch, is it?"

"Yo, man. I'm cool. Say, you wanna buy some shit?"

"No! But, thanks.

Leslie senses a potential problem.

"So, what kinda work you in, man?"

I better be careful here. I think they may want to tie me up if they knew I was a Federal Law Enforcement Officer.

"Look, I'm late. You know. Been tied up for a few hours. But, I appreciate the help."

"Cool. If you need any shit, man, we're here every night. As long as them dudes over there are in town throwin' around their bullshit like they know everything."

This guy's not all that dumb.

They both climb out of the van, and walk away.

Climbing over the seats, I spot my iPhone on the floor.

Checking it, there's still a charge, but no service in this place. I gotta get to Bonnie.

First, I need to find my Beemer.

Alexandria, Virginia
Bonnie's Home
9:21:05 PM

Bonnie is lying on her bed. She holds a tee shirt that carries the inscription, in large letters, "USNA." She misses him and wonders what has happened.

She frightened.

"He's got it, Bonnie. Just opened the message."

Bonnie bounds from her bed to just behind Tommy.

"You're sure, Tommy?"

"Oh, yes. I'm always sure, Bonnie."

Bonnie paces around the tight space.

"Tommy! Does your mother have a car?"

"Oh, yes. It's a brand new Lincoln Town car. Silver. A real hum dinger, Bonnie."

"Where are the keys?"

"Huh?"

"I need to get to that guy."

"What guy?"

"Please, Tommy. The car keys."

He studies her for a long moment, nervous, and skeptical.

But, he'll do anything for her. His fantasy lover.

Slowly, Tommy reaches into his jacket pocket. Pulls out a set of about a dozen keys.

He removes one large key, one with the Ford symbol on the fob. Hands it to Bonnie.

"Thanks, Tommy. You're the best."

She gives him a hug, then a smile.

He's in fantasy heaven.

"Now! Where is it?"

"Oh, yeah. In front of your motorcycle. In our driveway. With a Virginia tag...PORKY 2."

Bonnie frowns hard...huh?

Alexandria, Virginia
Henry Street
9:22:17 PM

Bonnie jumps off the bottom of the steps that go up to her apartment on the second level of this old, yet historic house.

Taking a few steps, hugging the rear of the house, she slides to the corner where she can take a look at the street.

Her heart skips a beat as she takes in the remnants of her Honda Accord, marked off with crime scene tape.

The odor of burning leather and rubber permeates the area. And she shuts her eyes, giving thought to the fact that the explosive was meant for her.

One or two very bad actors come to mind as to who may be responsible. But, that's an issue that will be resolved by law enforcement.

Whomever, their fate has been sealed in the death of some young criminal whose remains were found in the burned out wreckage.

She turns and bolts through the back yard, over to Henry Street, finding the Trumble residence.

She finds the Silver Lincoln Town car. She jumps in, and moves slowly from the driveway.

Bonnie has now found her way to the George Washington Parkway. She zooms past Reagan National Airport.

A moment or two before she vanishes under the Memorial Bridge.

Chapter 54

The White House
President Gonzmart's Private Study
9:23:23 PM

PRESIDENT GONZMART can only just stare at his computer LED screen.

It takes him a long moment to snap back to the situation at hand. He now turns his focus on a portrait of Thomas Jefferson, the 3rd President of the United States, and one of Gonzmart's Presidential heroes.

The most striking example of Jefferson's mind set as a politician, a career he disliked, was his view of difficult situations that he faced daily.

He would remark to those around him discussing alternatives to what action to take to resolve a perhaps sticky issue by commenting "...what is the *common sense* of the issue, gentlemen?"

The machinations of the political process always frustrated Jefferson. As well as Gonzmart.

And that is precisely what further complicates this bizarre plan hatched by Mendoza.

A plan so farfetched and unworkable, was further distorted by the "political process." A process that put up a smoke screen to conceal what was the hidden agenda.

A smoke screen of lies that both Hall and Hennessy fostered all these years.

And related to their personal relationship, and "sexual experiences," with Noah David.

Much at the expense of their former classmate, and now President, Gilberto Gonzmart.

The President, aware of the broad plan put forth by Mendoza, adopted a middle ground.

But not before placing an unwitting foil, Commander Bonnie Biersack, into the mix to strengthen his shaky, but safer position.

He knew Mendoza's plan was not workable.

Gonzmart realized much of the time truth does indeed sit between two extremes.

But, this view can bias ones thinking. Sometimes a plan is simply unworkable. And a compromise of it is also unworkable. Halfway between the truth and a lie...is still a lie.

So, Gonzmart concluded that the middle ground position, the only position left to him to choose, was best captured by forcing a middle ground concept.

But, still a lie.

Ergo, a "framework agreement" to be signed by the parties prior to the Israeli elections.

President Gonzmart still believed that certain key elements of the Gulf of Aqaba agreement were being "fleshed out" via secret "arrangements," not unlike Obama's nuclear agreement with Iranians.

He didn't trust Noah David.

Keeping Bonnie Biersack at arm's length kept his view at a safe distance.

The President moves his hand quickly to the speed dial feature button of his telephone set. As if routine, his finger goes to push the button associated with Howard Hall.

He hesitates. Grits his teeth. Hard.

The finger moves to the dial pad.

He punches "0," then "speakerphone.

From the other end.

"Good evening, Mister President. This is Theresa. May I help you, sir?"

"Yes, Theresa. Find Secret Service Director, Tony Crutchfield. Have him get to my office immediately, or on the telephone. Whichever is the fastest."

"Yes, sir. Is there anything else?"

"Get Ambassador James Walsh on the phone at our Embassy in Madrid.

Pause.

"I know it's the middle of the night over there, but have him awakened. It's urgent."

"Yes, sir. Right away."

The line is disconnected.

The President is up, walking over to the window. It is a view of the South Lawn.

At first, he looks down.

Thinking. Then, a thin smile crosses his features. He looks out into the darkness of the South Lawn.

The Washington Monument barely visible ½ mile away.

Then, the telephone rings.

He moves quickly to his desk, grabbing the receiver while sitting down hard in his chair.

"Gonzmart!"

"Mister Director! Find Assistant Director Connolly. Make sure he's fully aware that Operation Aqaba is now active. And get him what he needs."

Union Station Parking Garage
9:25: 49 PM

I certainly hope no one is coming into the garage right now because a head on collision would not be pretty. Time to test the advertised maneuverability of my new Beemer.

Still no signal on my iPhone. And no messages received, but unread. My brilliant conclusion: Parking garages are only good for buying weed.

Chapter 55

Washington, D C
City Streets
9:26:18 PM

Bonnie has come to a stop light that has just turned red. She checks her iPhone, noticing that the charge is getting low. She searches her purse for a charge cord.

Finds it and plugs the phone into a 12 volt socket in the Trumble Town car.

It drops on the floor board in front of the passenger seat. She reaches for it, but it's beyond her reach, and now driving, she determines it's okay where it is.

She forgets that before going into Senator Hennessy's office at the United States Senate she had switched the alerts to vibrate only.

The light turns green, and she peels out. She's aware that time is critical in her quest to get to the one man responsible before the final financial arrangements can be made. The ones she learned from Brother Malcolm Lamb who sent her an e-mail about an hour ago.

Arrangements that will be codified by Opus Dei.

The West Wing
Howard Hall's Office
9:26:41 PM

Howard Hall stands at his small desk in his small office. He wears a black trench coat. His hands in his pockets. He stares, transfixed on his computer LED screen that now displays the message Bonnie Biersack has sent to the President about three minutes ago.

Unknown to the President, Hall had established a relationship with young Will Burton, Jr. Someone, shall we say, had a "hankering" for Hall. Will is a low level IT guy in the White House. Being a "legacy" employee left over from the Obama administration, was usually called upon to handle minor IT issues. Howard found him approachable, and a friendship resulted. A friendship that included dinners out on the town, sleep-overs, and vacation trips to Sandy Lane in Barbados.

Will Burton was able to quietly link the President's laptop in the private study to Hall's laptop in his private office.

Should the Secret Service ever learn of this, it shall only be Will Burton, Jr. interviewing potential bunk bunnies in Federal prison. Hall managed to keep his name off the file.

After re-reading Bonnie's message, Hall opens the right hand desk drawer of his simple desk.

He removes a 9mm Glock hand gun.

It gets shoved into his trench coat pocket.

He walks to his door. Stops, and takes a long look at the interior.

Then , flipping a wall switch, the office goes dark.

The DuPont Circle
9:27:13 PM

Franklin Hennessy, in his Lincoln Town car, drives around the circle, stopping suddenly. He's stuck in typical Washington, DC traffic. He pounds the steering wheel.

Then, leaning on his horn, he veers to his left, cutting off several cars who return the gesture of their own, an "Italian" salute. One that uses the middle finger. He zooms onto Rhode Island Avenue, heading east.

At Logan Circle, he stays on Rhode Island, now heading more Northeast.

Outside the West Wing
Main Entrance Apron
9:27:22 PM

Howard Hall leaves the West Wing on foot, walking towards the pedestrian gate behind the OEOB. He continues off the "Executive" campus on foot, grunting at the uniformed Secret Service Agents at the gate. He heads for the General Services Building at E Street and New York Avenue.

His collar is now pulled up. Head down. His mind lost in the past.

SUV Navigator
9:27:29 PM

The drunk driver, Jerry Mulderick, takes Georgia Avenue south bound on two wheels from New Hampshire Avenue.

He attracts the attention of a Metro DC Police Officer. The Officer is now in hot pursuit of the drunk driver.

The Streets of Washington, DC
9:27:38 PM

Bonnie turns onto Rhode Island Avenue, at Connecticut Avenue. She rounds Logan Circle, and heads northeast, continuing on Rhode Island, also known as U.S. 1.

Madrid, Spain
Offices of Opus Dei
3:27:59 AM
Local Madrid Time

On a deserted street in a rather plush neighborhood in Central Madrid known as the "Rincon," it's peaceful. In the distance the faint sounds of sanitation vehicles raising and lowering their hydraulic loading gear barely permeates the quiet, serene setting as they get closer.

Street lights illuminate the narrow "calles" and the side allies.

In one alleyway, a fearless junk yard dog, underweight and under nourished, scrounges for food scraps, perhaps for dinner or a late night snack. Knocking over a trash can, he has found a tempting gourmet delight. Getting his sharp, vicious teeth around the bone and its leftover meat, he trots quickly deep into the shadows of the alley.

Directly across the street, in an ancient brown-stone style building are the international offices of Opus Dei where a dim light can be seen in a third floor bay window.

Bishop Federico Jesus-Ruiz has placed the telephone receiver back into its cradle on a small table within easy reach of where the Bishop sits in a comfortable leather recliner. A recliner that, because of his powerful and worldwide influence within the Roman Catholic Church, he frequently must spend many nights sleeping in what has become his favorite chair.

A long moment of prayer and reflection has passed before the elderly prelate makes his way to his large, antique desk. A gift from the Spanish King, Juan Carlos. The desk is no more than 6 feet away.

Now sitting at the desk he retrieves a piece of stationary from a short stack to his left. An ink pen in hand, his shaking hand begins to write.

Avondale
Residence of the Archbishop
9:31:06 PM

The darkened hallway is quiet, as is to be expected this time of the evening. The dim lighting adds to the mysterious, almost ghostly figures whose portraits adorn the walls on both sides of the hallway.

Portraits of the former, now deceased, prelates who held the title, Archbishop of Washington, DC.

A title now held by the esteemed, yet both widely feared and admired, Archbishop Joseph Mendoza. A man who views these portraits each and every day with a superior, condescending mind journey. None of the men that have preceded Mendoza could ever live up to his rule of order for the Roman Catholic Church. Not just in the Nation's Capital, but in the country as a whole.

His leadership shall be the subject of volumes once he has passed.

It *will* happen, as he firmly believes.

That attitude is clearly present as he quietly opens, then closes the door, leaving Monsignor Roger Schneider's private office.

He stops to scan the hallway in both directions.

Seeing no one, he moves swiftly, but with light, unnoticed footsteps to his private sanctum.

Streets of Foggy Bottom
Washington, DC
9:33:41 PM

Howard Hall, hands in his trench coat, head down, makes his way to the corner of 21st Street and Constitution Avenue. He waits for the traffic to change so he can safely cross towards the Vietnam Memorial.

The Lincoln Memorial is less than 300 yards in the distance just beyond the Vietnam Memorial.

Traffic clears and he crosses Constitution Avenue, walking past the Vietnam Memorial.

He stops. And looks back, sadly at the polished black granite, dropped several feet below ground level. And can only think of the more than 50,000 men and women who lost their lives during that non-war so many years ago.

And for a moment, his mind drifts to his former roommate at The Abby, Richard Cerzanski, who lost his life as a Marine in Beirut, Lebanon. The nights when they would crawl into bed together brought peace and calmness to Hall. Why not a memorial to Richard?

He continues in the direction of the Lincoln Memorial.

Franklin Hennessy's Lincoln Town Car
9:34:58 PM

The black Lincoln Town car turns from Rhode Island Avenue onto North Capital Street, and, though the light green, stops before the Michigan Avenue intersection to give way to an ambulance coming from the right on its way to the Washington Hospital Medical Center just off to his left.

While waiting, the traffic signal has turned red.

SUV Navigator
9:35:13 PM

Metro Police are still in pursuit of the drunk driver in the SUV Navigator.

The drunk runs a traffic signal at Columbia Avenue by turning left. He flies around the Washington Hospital Medical Center, and onto Michigan Avenue.

He floors the SUV, leaving rubber on the wide street heading eastbound on Michigan.

Hennessy's Lincoln Town Car
At Michigan & North Capital Streets
9:35:28 PM

The black Lincoln gets a green signal as the traffic light changes. Proceeding into the wide intersection, on his left, Senator Franklin Hennessy does not notice an SUV Navigator has run the red light traveling at better than 60 miles per hour.

The SUV T-bones Hennessy's Lincoln.

In a time lapse of less than 5 seconds, the sounds of glass breaking, metal twisting and tires screeching envelops the entire intersection.

Those sounds are followed by the sound of a thud as the Lincoln is pushed 35 feet over a curb and into a CVS store front near Girard Street, and not far from the entrance to Glenwood Cemetery.

After several more seconds, the sound of hissing radiators is apparent, along with the siren of a Metro Police vehicle that now stops short of the deadly carnage.

As the Officer exits his patrol car he cannot help but notice the clanging of a Connecticut tag hitting the street as it falls from one of the vehicles.

He studies its ID.

FH – 1.

Madrid, Spain
Offices of Opus Dei
3:35:57 AM
Local Madrid Time

The elderly Bishop depresses a button to his right. After several moments, the door creaks open.

Father Tomas Lorenzo enters. He stands before his boss in night clothes quickly working to tie his robe.

Bishop Jesus-Ruiz has finished applying a wax seal.

He hands the envelop to the young priest.

"Tomas. Take this note to the residence of Ambassador Don Javier Ybarra...to him personally."

"Yes, your excellency."

"He must take it to Jerusalem immediately. To the Israeli Prime Minister. By tomorrow night, without fail, my young friend."

"I understand, your excellency. It shall be done."

"Now you must go. There is no time, Tomas."

"Yes, your excellency."

The Bishop takes a long breath, as if needing to catch his breath.

"God be with you, my son."

Tomas leaves, closing the Bishops door with a soft thud.

It takes the Bishop several moments to get up and walk to the bay window over-looking the dark street below.

He strains to look, and sees Father Tomas Lorenzo moving quickly from the front door, and down the street, in his pastoral cassock.

The Bishop finds his favorite chair, and sits. From a pocket he pulls out a small leather pouch. Pulling up a flap held by a small button, he takes out a pair of rosary beads.

Bishop Federico Jesus-Ruiz slowly crosses himself with the rosary cross, kissing it when he's finished.

He begins to work the decades of the well-worn beads in silence.

Westbound on Massachusetts Avenue
9:36:27 PM

At least she's got the iPhone charged and on. That's a significant accomplishment right there. I guess she got tired of me complaining.

The question is why is she not answering?

I need to know where she is.

Is she okay?

I certainly hope so.

I see she has tried to call me many times since about 7 PM. Her last message sounded like that pow wow with Hennessy was not exactly all kissy face.

Oaky. I need to focus on my driving and head for her apartment in Alexandria.

If she's laying low, that would be the place.

No!

Wait!

I put "Find my Friends" on her iPhone.

Right. I did…not long ago!

…open the app… find out for sure where she is.

Let's see. Okay…it's locating.

Huh?

She's not home, but heading up Michigan Avenue. Now, why would she –

Shit!

Of course.

She's heading for Avondale!

Archbishop Mendoza's residence.

Double shit!

Memorial Bridge
Washington, DC
9:42:14 PM

Howard Hall stands at the mid-point of the ornate Memorial Bridge, above the Potomac River. He's on the north side looking up river at the Kennedy Center. To his right, the Lincoln Memorial. A MD-88 roars overhead, leaving Reagan National Airport. Hall climbs over the railing. Stands erect.

Then, let's himself fall, head first, to the concrete supports below. His body bounces, then slides into the river.

A car on the bridge screeches to a halt.

The Avondale Campus
Residence of the Archbishop of Washington, DC
9:49:12 PM

Bonnie parks the Trumble car in a space that is provided to visitors. It appears to be a long walk to the Diocese offices, a place she's hasn't been to in several years.

She visited here when re-assigned to the Washington DC area, specifically the Pentagon, to secure a Mass card directly from the Bishop. A rather unique and special blessing for her Grandmother who had passed away several months before her re-assignment.

Bonnie had always felt guilty about not spending enough time with her Grandmother. A woman who took care of her when both of Bonnie's parents were working.

Those "apron strings" were broken when Bonnie went off to the Naval Academy at Annapolis.

But not the weekly letters from the elderly woman.

And it's been a guilt trip ever since.

And those memories flood back now in waves of "coo coo," her nickname for her Grandmother that Bonnie had invented as a very young child. A nickname that associated her Grandmother with a Swiss coo coo clock in her home.

Walking towards the Diocese offices building she notices that most all the lights, inside and out, are off.

She stops to ponder her next move.

Jack's Beemer
Somewhere in Northeast Washington, DC
9:52:26 PM

Well, that's strange!

Monsignor Schneider is not answering his phone.

He said he would be available 24 -7, if needed.

I need to get to Roger, and alert him to that "special visitor," who's on her way.

Avondale
Diocese Office Building
9:52:49 PM

Sister Mary Anunciata, older than dirt, walks ever so slowly down the dark hallway. It's entirely possible she's lost, and hoping someone will find her, and guide her back to her private living quarters. They all think she's a little loopy.

Actually, she likes to think that's what the others around here think about her.

Frankly, she's sharp as a tack.

Something only Monsignor Schneider knows.

But afraid to let on to that fact for fear of being transferred down the road to Catholic University where they would make her teach some arcane class on some boring subject to a bunch of spoiled rich kids.

No, she'd rather play the "dementia" card, and enjoy her final days here, high on the hog.

Hugging the wall, she passes in front of Monsignor Roger Schneider's office door, her very close friend. They share a similar background: both raised in rural Indiana.

His phone is chiming.

She stops, wondering why he hasn't answered, as that iPhone is part of him.

She knocks quietly.

No answer, so she carefully opens the door.

The iPhone is still chiming as she walks around the desk.

Gasp!

And she keels over backwards, onto the floor, dead of a heart attack.

The sight of Monsignor Schneider's body on the floor, and the blood that has pooled around his head, the result of a gunshot, has literally frightened her to death.

The Avondale Campus
Visitor Walkway
9:55:26 PM

Bonnie decides to take the path leading to the visitor reception lobby, hoping the door will be open. If not, maybe a door bell will be available. Perhaps for someone who has an emergency and needs to see a Priest.

At the door, the lights are out, both inside and out. She locates a door bell button. And depresses it…several times while looking through the glass window alongside the huge oak door.

No answer. No one in sight.

She checks the door to find it won't budge.

To her left, she spots a narrow flagstone walkway that leads into a dark area around the building.

She takes the path, almost feeling her way along the path using the shrubs as a guide.

She finds a small door. A dim bulb above barely lights the entrance. Trying it in both directions, Bonnie finds it as well to be locked. Thinking that security must be paramount to the folks who work and live here.

Bonnie sees that the flagstone path continues, although over-grown with grass and weeds, around to the far side of the building.

After a few moments, she's in front of what could be described as perhaps a service entrance.

She pushes hard at the door, while turning the knob, and, much to her delight, it swings open.

Peering inside and beyond the door, it's very dark.

So dark, Bonnie cannot tell in what part of the building she's has landed. But, she moves in, feeling her way along a wall to her right.

Up ahead, maybe 8 to 10 feet, she sees a dim glow from underneath a doorway.

She turns a knob, and the door opens to a hallway.

Bonnie has stepped several paces into the hallway, noticing almost immediately large portraits of deceased Cardinals and Bishops on both sides of the hallway.

As she slowly makes her way down the hallway, choosing a direction to her right. The eyes of those portrayed in paintings, framed on the wall, follow her.

It's an eerie feeling, and it creeps her out.

But, she continues.

About 15 feet in, she stops.

And thinks.

Then...

"Hello...Hello?...Your excellency?"

She waits, and listens.

Nothing.

She continues down the dimly lit hallway, passing doors marked with names unfamiliar to her.

Except for a closed door on her right that is labeled "Monsignor Roger Schneider."

Bonnie knocks.

She waits.

Nothing.

She continues down the hallway.

When ahead of her she hears a large, custom carved door on the right, up ahead, gently close.

She moves to the door, labeled "Archbishop Joseph Mendoza."

She knocks.

Twice.

Then...from inside.

"Enter!"

Chapter 56

The Avondale Campus
Residence of the Archbishop
10:03:24 PM

According to my iPhone app, Bonnie's iPhone is within 10 feet of where I am presently standing.

Looking around, I don't see her iPhone, nor her, nor her car.

But, obviously not her car, since that blew up into tiny little pieces earlier today. With some small time burglar inside. I presume the Alexandria PD is still picking up pieces of that very unlucky guy.

The only vehicle here is a new Lincoln Town car. Silver. With Virginia tags that read "Porky 2."

Hum...

If I'm that clever, which, as you already know, I am, I would say that car perhaps belongs to someone I may know.

Let's have a look.

Hum…

There it is.

On the floor in front of the passenger seat.

So, where the hell is she?

Office of Archbishop Mendoza
10:04:09 PM

The fireplace is lit.

Flames roar as if fueled with a high octane accelerant.
But the large office is otherwise very dark.

Bonnie enters.

She walks slowly to a large desk on the far side as she
searches for a figure that may be sitting behind the desk.

The size of the office, although dark, is intimidating.
Bonnie can only sense that something is not right.

Her gut tells her to proceed with caution.

She breaks a sweat.

The thought of turning and leaving, forever, hammers
at her brain.

And suddenly, her life flashes before her eyes.

For some unexplained reason, those years of intense,
faith filled devotion give her the inner strength to face
whatever she may encounter at this moment.

Bonnies feels the hand of the Holy Spirit guiding her
moves.

It's a strange feeling that she cannot explain to herself.

But it is pushing her to settle this potentially horrific
problem to an acceptable conclusion.

She's very nervous, her hand shaking as reaches into
her purse slung over her shoulder, and grabs a small note
book, with a pen fixed to the cover.

A notebook in which she has used to transcribe notes
that she intends to discuss with the Archbishop.

But the pen suddenly falls from the notebook cover, and onto the wood floor in front of an expensive oriental rug that lies under the Bishop's desk.

It rolls.

But Bonnie cannot see where it has gone.

She prays for a glimmer of light.

A short "God help me" kind of prayer.

She closes her eyes, as she prays, sensing an evil "karma" present all around her.

A sense of imminent danger.

She bends over to a spot where she thinks it has stopped rolling.

At the same moment she hears a chair scratch along the floor.

A hard, disturbing scratch.

A noise that confirms she is not alone.

And it scares the crap out of her.

Her adrenaline starts to pump, when...

She screams!

A loud, blood curdling scream!

And is thrown against a wall, under a portrait of Cardinal Pulgar.

Large, massive hands are around her neck closing off her windpipe.

She grabs at the hands that are squeezing life form her body.

She opens her eyes.

She pleads with the angry, horrifying eyes of Bishop Mendoza.

His eyes burn a hole in her soul.

She cannot break free of the powerful hands.

Then, her eyes begin to roll upward.

She starts to go limp.

Mendoza, seething with anger, "you despicable bitch."

BANG!

Blood splatters on Bonnie.

Mendoza is thrown into a chair.

Blood flows from his head, down his arm, to the ring of his high office.

Jack Connolly lowers the Glock .357.

Chapter 57

Sts Peter & Paul Cemetery
Mackey, Indiana
Late Morning

The small cemetery in rural southwest Indiana is littered with headstones that date back about 150 years. While the condition of many of the head stones is somewhat disturbing, the grounds appear to have been kept in near pristine condition.

Local conventional wisdom says the farmers in this small, largely farming community take turns cutting the grass, fertilizing and weeding, and general "clean up" tasks. All according to some sort of undocumented, unspoken rule book.

The cemetery itself shares a large track of land with the principal Church that is anchored at the southeastern corner of the cemetery.

Sts Peter & Paul Roman Catholic Church has been a fixture here for those 150 years. Settled by the Franciscans in the 1870's, the priests solicited the help of all able bodied German and Irish immigrants to construct the small Church.

And to build a Christian community for the purpose of propagating the faith. Over the decades the community has come together to expand its Church. And with it, an elementary school.

Thanks to the hard working members of the community, they were able to build a High School known, not surprisingly as, Sts Peter & Paul Academy.

A school that attracts students from all over southwestern Indiana whose families scrape together funds to pay the hefty tuition. A tuition program that has generated enough funds for those extras parents look for in secondary education: a competent, well-educated, experienced teaching staff, AP programs, and, for some, an extraordinary athletic program.

Such a school was the only choice for Louis and Susan Schneider, and their son, Roger.

Both parents worked two jobs to cover the tuition in the hopes that Roger, their only child, would be able to attend a leading University someday, and reward the family with the riches of a successful career.

When his success as an All American football player at Notre Dame looked as if their prayers had been answered, with a pending offer to play football for the NFL Oakland Raiders, there came another offer.

This one from the Holy Spirit. Local lore has it that Mrs. Schneider had always liked to brag that "many are called, but only a few are chosen."

An offer that made both of Roger Schneider's parents aware that their prayers had truly been answered.

A son's vocation, a calling to the priesthood.

Which perhaps explains why both Louis and Susan Schneider are not weeping uncontrollably as they stand, looking at the coffin that holds the remains of their son.

I was touched by the one and only comment made to me by Mrs. Schneider when I had offered my condolences after Father Luke Clarke's funeral Mass.

Watching the coffin being carried over to the family burial plot, I said to her that I had not known him very long. But developed a quick liking for him.

She said, "Director Connolly, he's not over there in that box. You should be aware that I'm relieved to know, in my heart, that Roger is now in a much better place. He's with the Lord."

She walked away towards the burial plot, and I thought she may have been smiling.

Thinking about that moment, my Mom would quickly bond with Mrs. Schneider. Soliciting her support to help in any way possible to "fix" her son.

Namely, me.

Standing here in the cemetery, as Father Clarke finishes the service at the burial site, I can't help but notice this service is anything but a small family service.

There must be a hundred people here.

I don't recognize many, but can point out current and past members of the Notre Dame football coaching staff. And with them a number of well know current and former NFL players. Some who played with and against Roger Schneider at the College level.

But holding Mrs. Schneider's hand is another luminary.

The President of the United States.

He looks as if he lost a brother, and he needs to comfort the mother.

There's something peculiar there.

Father Luke Clarke has finished, and well-wishers are streaming towards the Schneider's, or back to their cars.

Commander Bonnie Biersack streams towards me. And she looks absolutely wonderful in that Navy uniform.

And it looks like she has cast off those expensive Ferragamo shoes for standard Navy issue.

But, I can tell she's not happy at the moment. Nor has she been happy after finding out more about my involvement with this Gulf of Aqaba fiasco.

I need to work on her brain a little.

And also clear up this outrageous misconception she has about my "involvement" with a Naval Officer, who is also a Navy attorney who goes by the name Lieutenant Corey Fanning.

Rumor has it, she's moved to Washington, DC.

Not good.

That scene could get a little dicey.

But first, I need to figure out a way to hitch a ride back to Washington, DC on Air Force One.

Somehow, I don't think it's in the cards right now.

Bonnie stops next to me, turning back towards the family.

"What a beautiful service, Jack."

"Right. It took my breath away. The whole thing. Just simply…wonderful."

Bonnie gives me that look. The one that has sent the BS meter off the chart.

"So, Bonnie. I'm thinking about asking the President for a ride back to the death star. Shall I include you in my request?"

"No."

Well, that was quick.

As I'm wondering about a new approach, the President approaches.

"Commander Biersack."

"…yes, sir?"

"Thank you."

"Sir?"

As the President steps closer to Bonnie, behind him a gentleman in a black suit, with an open white Roman collar fills the space just behind him. The Roman collar is not covered partially by a black undergarment as is normal with ordained priests. But the white collar has a thin black line running top to bottom at the front of the collar.

He wears a large hat that conceals his identity from us.

The President's eyes and head move slightly to his right. An indication for the gentleman to step forward and remove his hat.

Stepping next to the President, the hat comes off.

Brother Malcolm Lamb is clean shaven, and has been given a decent haircut.

"I needed another trusted messenger, Bonnie."

"And me, sir? You're the President. You could have prevented the whole thing."

"Commander, the power of the President is often compromised by the people who surround him. Sometimes, fortunately not often, wrong decisions are made by very bright people. Recent history at the White House has taught us that painful lesson."

"If you knew even most of his plan, you're as much to blame for the results."

"And I will take my share of the responsibility."

The President shifts his gaze over to the Schneider family still lingering around the burial site.

"Roger and I were the best of friends. Roommates at Notre Dame all four years. He a football star. Me...well, a member of the debate team."

I suddenly realize my instinct to not believe in coincidences, so I ask.

"So, Mister President. You brought Monsignor Schneider to Washington, DC?"

"It was my decision, of course, Director Connolly. I poached Roger from a comfortable teaching position at Notre Dame, and a valuable assistant football coach who helped re-shape the defensive back field."

Bonnie's anger jumps up a notch or two.

"He was murdered...sir. On your watch."

"Mendoza had Howard Hall provide him with a weapon, thinking there was a mole at the Diocese. Roger was aware of that. Then, something, very, very briefly, went wrong. We don't know exactly what happened. But the FBI determined Roger was murdered with a zip gun. The remnants of such found in the ashes of Mendoza's fireplace."

There's a long moment of silence, broken by Brother Malcolm reciting a brief prayer.

The President removes an envelope from his pocket, handing it to Bonnie.

"Came in the diplomatic pouch earlier today."

Opening the envelope, she sees it's a personal letter from the Prime Minister of Israel.

"He's very grateful, Bonnie."

She reads some of the note.

"He says that Noah David has been indicted."

The President takes another step closer to Bonnie.

"I anticipated the potential for danger, Bonnie."

His eyes shift quickly to me, then back to Bonnie.

"I provided you with the very best protection. Director Connolly here. Plus other individuals you didn't know about."

Bonnie gives me a hard, anguished stare.

And holds it.

"I trusted Director Connolly with my life, Bonnie. I trusted him with yours."

Another moment of silence.

Then, the President looks over at his Secret Service detail. Then, back to Bonnie.

"Again…I'm sorry. Can I give you a ride back to Washington?"

"No…thank you sir. I'm driving over to Dayton. Plan to spend a few days with my family."

"Very good, Commander. Take as much time as you need. I'll clear it personally with your Commanding Officer."

The President turns, and starts to walk away.

Brother Malcolm nods at the both of us, and leaves.

The President gets about 15 feet away.

He stops.

Turns back at Bonnie.

"When you get back to Washington, send me an e-mail, Commander. We'll have lunch."

Bonnie takes a heartbeat to think.

"Thank you, sir, But…

Long pause.

"I don't think so."

The President's features harden, but only for a nano second. They then soften. With a thin smile.

"I understand, Bonnie."

The President and Malcolm fast walk to the Beast, his armored vehicle.

Bonnie watches the big guy and his pal from boarding school, Malcolm, jump into the limo. A split second before it takes off.

Looks like I'm gonna miss my ride back to D C.

"So, we're driving to Dayton? What's that, about 2 – 3 hours from here?"

She gives me a long, hard stare.

"I'm driving over to Dayton. You're…well, maybe if you run you can jump onto Air Force One as its rolls down the runway, Jack."

I guess I had that coming.. perhaps, there's more to come in the next few weeks, or months, or maybe forever.

I give her one of my sad dog looks.

It doesn't work as she fumbles through her purse, slung over her shoulder. She takes out her iPhone. The one I slipped into her purse several days ago.

"Here, you can have it back. I believe it's Secret Service issue. Make sure you get mine back to me soon. It's U S Navy issue."

Interesting.

Besides the beauty, knock out body, and great personality, she *is* that smart.

She's up on her toes, and plants a long kiss on my cheek.

She smiles, but doesn't say a word.

I take a moment to return the stare. Then…

"Lunch…someday…soon?"

She grips my hand, and tightens for just a second.

Then, turns and walks away.

And here I am, in a cemetery in nowhere, Indiana.

Now what?

If memory serves me well, I think that "secret" number at the Pentagon is 202-555-6303.

Coming Soon!

Sign of the Cross

A New Jack Connolly Novel
and
Episodic Television Series
in 55 One Hour Episodes

We go back in time to Jack Connolly's childhood, and his first introduction to the family's parish priest. An old parish located on the North Shore of Long Island, New York. And a Roman Catholic Church, St. Mary's, built in the 1870's. Built by Jack's Great Great Grandfather, Jeremiah Connolly, and his brother, John. Two young teenagers who emigrated from Ireland, landing on Long Island in 1875.

On Jack's mother's side, the Segui Family has its roots in both Spain and Venezuela.

And it was the Venezuelan connection that brought the family into contact with a young new parish priest who moved from Caracas in 1961 to assume the role of Pastor.

Father Joseph Antonio Mendoza.

It was not coincidence that brought Father Mendoza to Long Island. But a family feud. A feud that the Segui family offered to the Mendoza family in Venezuela. An offering of an olive branch...of sorts. Provide their youngest son a place in the United States. Far from the impoverished parishes of

Venezuela. A place to use his family's influence and wealth freely. In the open and free community of the United States.

It's widely known that both the Segui and Mendoza families are the wealthiest in Venezuela.

Wealthy as in oil.

Between the two families they control over 80% of the oil production in that South American country.

Or, at least did so 60 years ago.

The ownership was evenly split. Until about 1962 when Elbano Spinetti, a nephew in the Segui family made a deal with a very high Venezuelan official.

El Presidenti!

The "pay-off" was huge. And in return, the Segui family took control of almost 55% of all Venezuelan oil. production.

And the Mendoza family has never forgiven this treachery.

Made in the USA
Charleston, SC
26 May 2016